Sword of Damocles

Some things are scarier than dead bodies

Andrew Barrett

The Ink Foundry

Contents

Praise for Sword of Damocles

~ Once again Andrew Barrett has knocked me for six.
~ My mouth was hanging open on the last page!
~ Hard-hitting and imaginative, this book is an absolute cracker.
~ An emotion packed Eddie Collins with surprises peeking around every page.
~ Marvelous plotting and beautifully defined characters.
~ The final chapter moved me to tears - not something I can recall ever happening to me with a book before.
~ Easily compares with Jeffrey Deaver, Lee Child, James Patterson, Patricia Cornwell.
~ Another gem with a gripping storyline and surprises popping up with Eddie's work methods and exceptionally brave storyline.
~ VINE VOICE – I was sorry to finish it and can't wait for the next offering from this author...highly recommended.
~ Andrew Barrett at his very, very best.
~ This is my favourite in the series so far with just the right mix of suspense, humour and bittersweet moments.
~ I am still stunned by the ending I didn't see coming!
~ This is a must read book and you are certainly in for a treat. The ending - WOW.

Preface

Proud to swear in British English

Chapter One

The Flutters

Early April

EDDIE PULLED HIS SHIRT back down and sat there with his foot tapping on the floor, fingers never still, nervously drumming some unheard rhythm on his leg. "It feels like it's tripping over itself, like it's fluttering and not getting a full charge of blood." Eddie stopped talking and watched him. Alex was studying the computer screen, clicking the mouse, and reading. "You're looking it up on Google, aren't you?"

"What?"

"You haven't a clue what I'm talking about."

Alex turned and said, "I'm looking into your history, Eddie. And for your information, I'm nowhere near Google just yet."

"So what it is, then? It thuds like hell at night when I'm trying to sleep—"

"How much do you drink?"

Eddie just stared at him.

"I have to ask. I'm your doctor."

"Look, it sends me light-headed."

"No booze?"

"No booze! None worth mentioning, anyway. Couple of cans a week, maybe."

"Caffeine?"

Eddie nodded. "I like coffee. I tried that caffeine-free shite once. Gave me a headache and sent me batshit crazy."

"Still smoking?"

Eddie shrugged, "Gotta die sometime, doc."

"This might be that sometime."

"What?"

Alex crossed his legs and propped his face up on a lazy fist. He sighed, "It will kill you, Eddie. Aside from all the other dangers associated with smoking, it's a stimulant. It makes your heart work hard; makes it erratic, too." He went back to the computer.

"Will you leave that bastard thing alone and pay attention to me for a change? Are you checking your lottery results or something?"

"Oi, cut it out." Alex faced Eddie again and asked, "Are you uptight about anything?"

"Nope."

Alex glared at him. Sat back and folded his arms.

"Okay, I'm uptight about everything. I just want to sleep, Alex."

"I can remedy that," he said. "That's easy. But you need to get to the bottom of it; you need to understand why you're having these panic attacks."

Eddie laughed. "Panic attacks? Me? If I were any more chilled, I'd have frostbite."

Alex nodded at Eddie's twitching foot. "It's a message. It's your body telling you that something needs attention."

"Ah I see. So my body, realising that I'm worried about something, decides the best way of helping me is to make me think I'm having a fucking heart attack at three in the morning, and give me something else to worry about?"

"Well it can't send you an email!"

Resigned, Eddie sighed. "What do I have to do then?"

"Think. What's troubling you? What dreams do you have, what nightmares?"

"I don't dream."

Alex cocked an eyebrow.

"What? I don't. None that I can remember, anyway."

Eddie had walked from the doctor's surgery with a prescription for zopiclone to help him sleep, and another for propranolol for the dodgy ticker, and a vague understanding of what was wrong with him. He also had a desire to redesign the human body and eradicate a few serious design flaws.

He had driven to work on full autopilot, the Discovery seemingly knowing where to go all by itself, and Eddie concerned himself with the lie he'd told Alex, the one about the dreams. But the dreams were so abstract that they couldn't possibly have any meaning let alone any relevance to the panic attacks.

In full-blown daylight he could almost laughed at them, the palpitations. But what made him analyse his dreams in a little more depth right now was the steady approach of yet another night where he couldn't hear the wind in the trees outside because of the racket his lumpy old ticker made, and the hollow cataclysmic feeling of doom in his chest. It was not at all funny at two in the morning. Not one bit.

It was the quilt.

It was girlie; another thing Ros had chosen, along with the bright green throws for the sofa, the welcome mat by the door (how he'd laughed at that!), the funky new telephone – pink – and the countless other adornments she'd filled the place with. As well as being pink, the quilt cover had various shades of violet interlaced over it in a kind of wavy pattern. It wasn't unkind on the eye – far from it, but it… it was cloying.

When he did fall asleep, it was luxuriously comforting being snuggled up in it, protected from the cold and cosseted. But it quickly became claustrophobic, and he felt trapped, and no matter how hard he struggled to breathe and break free, that pink quilt with its violet intricacies smothered him and held him so tightly that he couldn't move. But worse, if he concentrated closely, as you're apt to do in a dream, he could feel its softness decreasing, could feel it becoming quite hard and unforgiving, unwilling to mould itself to his shape. He knew for certain that it was growing spikes; it was like trying to sleep inside an iron maiden.

There were several versions of that dream, but they always ended up with him being smothered and impaled, and he always woke after an hour fighting for air and desperate to get free. And dreams were, supposedly, a reflection of whatever was current in the dreamer's life, the fears he held, the hopes he felt, the desires he nurtured. But he had no idea what this one meant.

Eddie sat in the car park, suddenly realising that he'd made it all the way to work without even being aware he was driving. He angled the rear-view mirror, stared at the reflection of a face he barely recognised, and made himself smile.

Chapter Two

A Tight Squeeze

Mid-April

THE NOISE WAS APPALLING. Up on the stage, his equipment illuminated by red and green spotlights, a DJ spoke unintelligibly into a face mic positioned so close to his mouth that he might as well have been shouting through a pillow. And Terry would've volunteered to be the one holding it there.

Why couldn't they be more dignified? Why couldn't they play some Vivaldi, or if they insisted on a band, something melodic perhaps like Creedence Clearwater Revival?

He grimaced at the music – correction, he thought – at the noise filling the room from a pair of huge loud speakers, mounted on poles either side of the stage. When the light was right, you could actually see the speaker buzzing behind its protective wire mesh.

Around him, the crowd had taken its first steps towards merry. Of course, there were always the ones who had been merry two hours ago, and were now blitzed; either sitting rigidly still on chairs while holding tightly onto the table as the room spun around them, or those who had suddenly been reincarnated as John Travolta but living in Bernard Manning's body, bopping and rocking to a tune wholly different from the one inflicted on everyone else.

And then there were the other members of the crowd; those who, like Terry, were obviously here enduring this assault on humanity out of a sense of decency to the newly married couple. Or more specifically, those who were frog-marched to this charade because of an RSVP handed over in person and a rash promise made eight months ago at a civilised dinner party.

"Are you enjoying yourself?" Liz was standing next to him, smiling, and all Terry could hear were vowels and all he could see was the reflection of red and green lights twinkling in her earrings as he brought his face closer to her mouth.

"What?"

"I said are you enjoying yourself?"

His face replied, 'Don't ask silly questions.'

Liz laughed at him, and then she pointed and shouted, "Oh, they're here."

Terry's shoulders slumped as the bride and groom, obligatory smiles stapled in place, and no doubt already making their cheeks ache, shuffled into the room to a warm ripple of unheard applause, accepting claps on the back, handshakes galore.

"Shit," Terry muttered. "Go do the 'congratulations' bit," he shouted. "I'm off to the bar." And then he walked away, miming to her, one hour.

"Terry? Terry!"

Thirty-five minutes later, Terry was at the receptionist's desk, enjoying the relative absence of noise and the clearer, cooler air out here. "Book me a taxi, please."

"Terry?"

Terry closed his eyes, and turned towards Liz who walked his way with a confused look on her face.

"I know I said an hour, dear, but this place is killing me. It's for the young ones."

"Not the old farts, eh?"

He had to nod his agreement. "Look, we've toasted their marriage, given them the obligatory Kenwood Chef, and now I'm sorry, I just can't…"

"Alan?" Liz hurried to a tall, slender man who was halfway through removing his outdoor coat, eyes scanning the reception area, trying to gauge the atmosphere like dipping his toes before diving in.

"Well, well, look who the cat dragged in," Terry joined them. "The years haven't been kind to you, have they?"

"Liz!" Alan stooped and kissed her cheek, "Great to see you," and then he stood back and admired Terry. "I may have wrinkles, but at least I can still see my feet." He clapped him on the arm, smiling.

"I can still see your feet too." Each man looked sternly at the other before cracking into laughter and hugging the other. "What the hell brings you to a craphole like this?"

"Terry!" Liz said.

"Well… it is."

"I'm family now. The bride is my wife's niece."

"Wife?"

"She's a diamond, mate."

Just then the automatic doors opened, and a cold breeze pulled Terry's gaze away from Alan. A woman strode into the foyer and Terry's friendly smile evaporated. Recognition turned to consternation turned to apprehension, and all the joy fell out of his face as though someone had opened a trap door. They were all staring at him.

Liz reached out, "Terry." She looked at the woman, then back at Terry.

He yanked his arm free, ignoring Liz completely, and stared at the woman. "Scuse me," he muttered and headed quickly for the toilets.

"Terry?"

Terry crashed through the toilet door with enough force to knock an old man struggling with his zipper to the floor. He rushed to the sink and splashed cold water on his face.

The old man got to his feet, grunting, and checked for damage. He asked, "Are you okay?"

Terry splashed more water.

"Want me to call someone?"

"No."

"You sure—"

"I said I'm fine!"

"Well if you're fine, might I suggest you apologise for being so bloody rude the next time you hurl a pensioner to the floor. Ignorant bastard." The man tutted and, more cautiously this time, reached for the door.

Water dripped; Terry looked into the mirror. Had a stranger been looking too, he would have seen a man who appeared petrified.

Standing in the doorway between the wedding hall and the foyer was a woman in her mid-thirties. She saw it all happen, the small gathering by the reception desk, the exchange of pleasantries as new people entered from outside. She saw the look on the old man's face change in an instant; how all the colour drained away, how he staggered backwards a step, and then how he practically fell through the toilet door in his haste to get away as though he were running from something.

She knew how he felt.

Her glass had paused on its way to her mouth, and then, when he turned around and she'd caught a full unobscured look at him, the glass fell. And she didn't even notice. She went ice cold from the heart outwards and for a moment she thought she was going to throw up. Instead, she wet herself and then collapsed.

Terry recovered enough to leave the toilet, helped by Alan. His face was pale, hands shaking, and for some unknown reason, he couldn't string a sentence together. All he kept saying was, "I'm fine, I'm fine." When it was obvious to Liz at least that he wasn't.

She wondered if he'd had a mild coronary, or was displaying the first signs of an impending stroke. It frightened her to see him supported so heavily by Alan as they'd emerged from the toilet.

"He's legless, Liz, that's all," Alan said. "He'll be okay in the morning, don't worry."

"But I do worry." The symptoms looked like shock.

"Brings back memories, eh," he laughed, "like being back at uni."

Liz didn't laugh. Liz wasn't listening; she was staring at Louise Walker, wondering why the sight of her would cause Terry to explode like this.

Terry knew where Louise was standing, and averted his gaze. On their shuffling way to the exit, his attention fell upon a small crowd of people that had gathered to assist a woman who, seemingly, had collapsed by the wedding hall doorway. He craned his neck to see past Alan's supporting arm, so much so that Alan had to stop and reassert his grip. He was obsessed, almost fighting to get a better look. Liz stood back, her hand to her mouth as she saw the fear in Terry's eyes.

The journey was a blur. He stared out of the window, his face brightening and darkening as the streetlights sped past, and all he could hear was the thrum of the tyres and the hum of the news channel that the taxi driver had chosen. The quiet, almost lullaby-quality of the newscaster's voice was such a contrast to the vulgar music they'd left behind, but its story held a weight over him so powerful that it felt crushing.

"...raped a teenage girl on Wimbledon Common in 1997. DNA was recovered from the scene and checked against police databases without success.

"Twenty years later, Barry Hope was stopped by police for dangerous driving. His fingerprints and DNA were taken routinely..."

'Crushing' was a good description. Terry laid his head against the cold and misty window and felt a stranger's hand encircle his heart and squeeze, slowly, deliberately; occupying his entire mind with consequence and reason until he thought he was taking his last few breaths. There was a brief moment when Terry couldn't decide if that was good news or bad; it was scary of course, but it wouldn't last long, the pain would soon—

"Terry, will you pay him!"

He blinked and came round like someone had slapped him. "What? Sorry, how much?"

In the lounge, Terry poured himself a long fat measure of Bacardi and slugged it back in one fluid movement. The liquor twisted his face but went some way towards loosening the hand that clamped around his heart. For a second he felt better; it distracted his mind from its concerns, and he sighed out a little gratitude for the nuance of peace he'd found. He poured another and ambled into the kitchen.

"You think that's wise?"

The peace dissolved. "I'm alright."

Liz came to him, placed a gentle hand on his arm. "What's going on?"

"I'm fine."

"What is it? Tell me?"

"For Christ's sake!" He slammed the glass onto the granite worktop hard enough to smash it and fast enough for his hand to slide along the newly formed edge, where it sliced open the skin quicker than he could gasp. Soon there was blood splashing across the sink.

"Quick, put it under the tap."

"Leave it, it's okay."

Liz turned on the tap and reached for Terry's hand.

"I said leave it!"

───

Liz rubbed her tired face, and from her bedside cabinet took a bottle and shook out a small white tablet. She threw it into her mouth and gulped water. Her eyes drifted to the bathroom door, the strip of light coming from beneath it and the sound of running water.

She had no idea what the hell had become of him. She knew he'd hate the damned reception, the music they played made him bad-tempered, gave him a headache, but this was more than that, much more. Liz didn't believe in letting things fester. Liz believed in research – Liz believed in getting to the bottom of problems, and quickly.

She found that if she held her breath, she could hear him in there. It sounded very much like he was crying.

Chapter Three

Two Bars and Almost a Doctor

Mid-April

MONDAY AFTERNOON AND MICHAEL Tailor was almost a failure.

But not quite.

He was a doctor, had graduated with honours from Leeds University in 1982 and his future was, it appeared, secure. He'd done it; he'd taken himself from no-hoper to would-be high-flier in five smooth years. And then all he had to do was join a practice and rake in the cash.

Easy.

Bad decisions had eaten away at those plans like termites drilling through a foundation post, and eventually they'd destroyed that promising future. It had been like taking a prime beef joint and forcing it through a mincing machine. All that came out of the other side were fat maggots, thousands of them.

Women were his downfall; two of them actually. And both had divorced him, milked him dry and waltzed off into the sunset with his money, his trust, and his motivation. Laughing at him.

Somewhere around thirty years later, Michael Tailor stared at the dregs in the glass, and reached a decision. He grabbed himself by his shirt collar and gave himself a shake-down, gave himself a mighty talking to: he still had what it took to be a successful doctor, he didn't need a woman in his life anyhow; self-reliance would make it all happen. He put down the glass and, filled with renewed optimism for a future that should have been rotting in the maggoty waste bin, he stood and walked to the exit, nodding at the barman on his way.

Michael felt the motivation grow with each new step he took. To begin with, his eyes looked straight ahead along the muddy path, the graffiti-daubed pub wall to his right and the overgrown, weed-infested, litter-choked hedge to his left. But contemplating his plan soon made them turn earthwards, until he avoided each puddle as it entered his shaky field of vision. He concentrated hard; the plan would succeed.

All it needed was hard work, something he'd never been afraid of; and a good word in the right ear from his old colleagues wouldn't go amiss, either. Wallowing in maggoty self-pity was fine for a while, he decided, but if the chance was there, if there was something he could do to rescue his future and sink new foundation posts, to resurrect it and hoist it into the realms of optimism, then no one could stop him.

The path opened out into a wider alleyway, the hedge still to his left, but the pub wall to his right ended, and wet, shiny grass took its place, stretching off into the near distance where the main road through Holbeck assaulted his ears and disrupted his thoughts. The glare of orange streetlights and the flare of car headlights made it difficult to see.

He landed in a puddle. Dirty cold water splashed up onto his face and saturated his hair. He could feel his body twitching yet had no control over it. He was vaguely aware that he wasn't breathing, and could do nothing about it. He was equally aware that his heart had stopped. He saw the man, iron bar swinging from his hand as though he were Charlie Chaplin at the end of a movie. The man, small with a big nose, climbed into a red car and was careful enough to indicate and look in his mirror before pulling out into traffic.

There was no panic. Michael Tailor just gave in. No danger of failing any more.

Chapter Four

An Unwanted Gift

THOUGH ONLY HALF WAY into the office, Eddie could smell the aftershave. Too much of it. Brut or something equally cloying. Deodorant too. The glare from the overhead lights made it difficult to be sure, but Eddie thought there were dark patches beneath Jeffery's pits.

"We're being relocated to G34. I'm putting you in charge of the—"

"Why? What's wrong with where we are?"

"Personnel changes out there; they're recruiting more detectives, bringing in more—"

"Just a minute, G34? The dead end along the corridor?"

Jeffery smiled meekly.

"That place is like a cross between a phone booth and a... and another phone booth."

"It has its own kitchenette. Anyway, we don't have a say." And then Jeffery beckoned him all the way in. "Close the door, Eddie."

Eddie watched Jeffery slide behind his desk and sink into his seat. "Why?"

Jeffery tutted. "Are you menopausal again?"

"Nervous," he said. "You never invite me in here unless you want to demean me."

Jeffery cracked his knuckles and glared.

"I'm not closing the damned door, okay. I might need a quick getaway."

"Close it and sit down!"

Eddie peered over his shoulder out into the main office. No one took any notice of him curling around the doorframe, clinging onto it like a pre-schooler clinging on to his mother's leg. There was just the usual banter out there; people typed, others watched egg-timers, read logs, or checked exhibit labels. Across the far side of the office, where the little brew-kitchen was, Duffy was shouting again, something about putting a padlock on his jar of Nescafé.

Eddie closed the door quickly and sat. "My coffee's going cold."

Jeffery cleared his throat and smiled. "I just got back from seeing the ACC Crime."

It explained the dark patches and the smell of deodorant. He tried to see if Jeffery's tongue was brown.

"Not curious?"

"I assume you got us a better slice of budget. Which is good because it's still cold out there and the heater in my van doesn't work."

"Not even warm," Jeffery smiled confidently.

"I know, that's what I've told the sodding mechanic every week—"

"I mean your guess is way off."

Eddie thought. "He's letting you take early retirement on account of your mental instability. Look, I'm tired. I don't know, I hate guessing games, now can I go finish my coffee?"

Jeffery leaned forward. "He's promoted me."

"Ah," Eddie grinned, and Jeffery leaned back, satisfied at last, fingers laced behind his balding head. "To what?"

"You're hard work, Collins."

"What do you expect; I'm dying of thirst here!"

"I'm head of MCU, Eddie."

Eddie punched the air, "Woo hoo!" And then he stood and headed for the door.

"Wait. Is that it, just a fake show of surprise? I thought—"

"I thought you'd reached your ceiling. I mean look, it's rubbed all the hair off the top of your head."

"Everyone out there knew changes were coming. And now they've happened."

"Hold on, I thought the head of MCU had to be a copper?"

"He's putting Cooper—"

There was a quiet knock at the door, which opened into Eddie's face, and then Melanie appeared with a slim wad of paper. "Murder—"

"Melanie. I'm in a meeting!"

"Murder?" Eddie took the paper from her and began reading.

"It's a male, beaten in Holbeck."

"Sounds painful," Eddie sidestepped Melanie, "I've got this one," and was out of the office before Jeffery could even stand.

"Eddie? Eddie!"

Eddie trudged back in.

"Sit down."

Eddie sat and slid the paper into Jeffery's outstretched hand.

Jeffery glanced at it. "Is it a domestic?" he asked Melanie.

"Nope," she said. "Stranger. An old man just phoned it in."

"Get James in here."

"Oh come on, Jeffery, I want—"

Jeffery silenced Eddie with a stare, and they both waited for Melanie to show James in.

"Jeffery?" James stood in the doorway like a timid kid ready for beating up.

"Stranger murder in Holbeck," he handed the paperwork over. "Want to be lead examiner on it?"

James's face shone, "Me?"

Jeffery nodded, "You take Ros as your number two, okay?"

"But I'm lead, right?"

"Chance to redeem yourself." There was no friendly smile on Jeffery's face.

And it killed the smile on James's too. "Never going to live that down, am I?"

"You will. Do a good job for me on this one, okay?"

James nodded and was about to close the door when Jeffery spoke up again.

"And don't miss anything. Right?"

The door closed gently and Eddie stared at Jeffery. "You're such a heartless wanker."

"I beg your pardon!"

"You built him up and then tore him down. And you expect him to perform at his best at a murder scene?"

"It was a gentle gee-up, that's all."

"It was a kick in the knackers, Jeffery. Whatever happened to protecting his ego? He's never going to gain confidence if you keep fucking him over—"

"He needs reminding of how important this job is."

"Do you seriously think he's ever going to forget it? Really? And if you knew how important this job was, you'd be encouraging him." He stood, "Now if there's nothing else."

"Sit down, I haven't finished yet."

Reluctantly, Eddie sat. He glared.

Jeffery cleared his throat and grew a smile on his face. "I've been promoted—"

"You already said that. And your first task is to get your head out of your arse and apologise to that kid."

"Will you shut the fuck up and let me speak?"

Eddie blinked. "No need to swear."

"Detective Chief Superintendent Cooper has overall responsibility for crime division and now major crime as well. But I'm its department head. I'm filling Lisa Westmoreland's shoes."

"With dog shit, I hope."

"That leaves me with a hefty workload. Far too much. I need someone to do my old role, I need someone—"

"You could try The Yorkshire Echo, they do job adverts on a Thursday."

"Are you being obtuse on purpose?"

Eddie thought about it. "Erm, I'm not sure; I don't think so."

"I'm offering you my position." Jeffery smiled wide, caressed his tie, and almost winked in friendship.

"Why?"

The caressing stopped. "That it: why?"

"I could never get my head up my arse the way you can with yours."

"Eddie," Jeffery warned.

Eddie stared. "I let my coffee go cold for this?"

"I'm offering you promotion!"

"No thanks."

"What do you mean, 'no thanks'? It's a hefty wage increase, increased status, a chance to make real decisions—"

"Aside from the human resources scandal that would break out—"

"It's cleared. I wanted you, and the ACC—"

"I don't want it!" Eddie stood. "But thank you," he whispered.

"Sit down. Please."

"You hate me, remember? When I started here you said they were stupid to take me on."

"You've proved your worth."

"As a crime scene investigator. I belong in a crime scene, not in an office. I'm useless on the phone; I'm shit at dealing with people – not as shit as you, granted, but still shit."

"You're disappointing me, Eddie."

"Like I give a fuck." He sat back down and leaned forward, "I walked from SOCO. I can live without this job too. I learned that I'm better all ways round if I do what I enjoy, not if I try to be something I'm not." He stared at Jeffery but got the feeling that the message went right over his head. "I'm good at what I do. I'd like to carry on doing it. Besides, am I really the best candidate for the job?"

Jeffery squinted. "You couldn't walk from this job, Eddie. I know you better now, I've come to understand that swagger in your walk and that arrogance in your voice. It's there as a shield to protect you, to get you through the day without collecting a scratch—"

"You're so full of—"

"Am I?" Jeffery stood and strolled around the desk. Eddie sat back, trying to give himself some space. "You'd shrivel up and die without the purpose that MCU offers you. Life on the outside isn't all about fishing or walking in the countryside, you know. You'd be bored in a week, an alcoholic in two. Dead inside six months."

"You should write scripts."

"And you should grow up. I'm giving you the chance to move up the ladder—"

"I never understood how a government could just swap and change its department heads around."

Jeffery thought about it, then declared, "I'm not with you."

"I mean, you'd think the guy in charge of the Ministry of Defence would have a clue what he was doing, same goes for Minister of Education – have they ever fought in a war, have they ever been a teacher?"

"I still don't follow."

"You need qualifications to do that kind of stuff, some hands-on experience or at least a keen interest. Being a generic manager isn't good enough, and it's the same here too. I can interpret and work crime scenes all day long. Give me a shift rota or a meeting with the ACC and I wouldn't have a clue. Horses for courses, Jeffery."

Jeffery sat back down, hands in his lap, eyes down, cheeks grinding away.

"Congratulations though. Seriously, well done." Eddie held out his hand.

"This is your chance, Eddie, to really make a difference. And with the office move coming up, you can—"

"Arrange the desks? Decide where the bin goes?"

"No one says you can't work crime scenes too; but it'd give you the chance to push your team forward, to select the right staff… Hell, you could even change submissions regulations to suit your style. It needs someone with your dynamism, someone the staff would look up to, and someone the detectives would respect."

Eddie pulled in a breath, folded his arms. "It's good of you to offer—"

"It is, I know."

"But seriously, this job has Ros stamped all over it. She'd be…"

Jeffery was shaking his head.

"What?"

"Let's just say she's not in the running."

"You can't do that—"

"She's not in the running of her own choice."

"What's that supposed to mean?"

"You'll have to ask her. Confidentiality and all that."

Eddie stood, "Confidentiality my arse, you've never—"

"I haven't finished. Sit down."

"This is getting annoying."

"Ros isn't in the running. You've declined. That means your new head is Peter McCain." Jeffery sat back in his chair and watched Eddie's face turn crimson.

"You are kidding me, right?"

Jeffery said nothing.

"He'd ruin this place. You know he would, just like he ruined SOCO! How can you sit there in your stripy fucking suit and appoint a knob like that?"

"He's the only candidate left in the race. He gets it by default."

"You bastard." Eddie reached the door before Jeffery could get out of his chair. He stood in the main office and called for her. "Ros?"

"Eddie," Jeffery said from behind him. The whole office paused to watch the sparks flying off Eddie and the buzz of tension between him and Jeffery.

"Ros!"

"She's left already."

Eddie swivelled to face Duffy, a grey-haired CSI with a bloodhound's face. "Get her back here. Now."

"But she's gone with James. She's his number two."

"Wrong. You're his number two, go bring her back."

"But I've got paperwork—"

"Now, Duffy."

Duffy looked past Eddie towards Jeffery.

"Well?" Jeffery asked.

Eddie paused. "Okay," he said.

Jeffery nodded at Duffy who threw his pen across the room and grabbed his coat.

———————

Eddie grabbed his car keys and jacket and rushed out of the office leaving a row of confused faces. He caught up with Ros as she came back in through the main doors. "Come on," he said, "we're going out."

"What? Where? I have important—"

Eddie grabbed her by the arm and turned her around, pushed her back out through the doors, "Nothing's this important."

Chapter Five

Don't be Sorry

EDDIE NOSED THROUGH THE ever-expanding gap as the gate crunched its lazy way over the rails, and then hit the wing mirror in his haste to get going. Ros smiled, "You know this is kidnapping and false imprisonment, don't you?"

He made no reply. She could see his mood was as foul as the weather.

"What's up?"

"Wait till we're more comfortable."

"I'm comfortable now, Eddie. What the hell's going on?"

"Just wait." His hands gripped the wheel so tightly the tendons in his wrist looked as sharp as razor blades.

Ros folded her arms. "Let me guess, you're taking us to McDonald's."

"I need coffee. My last one went cold."

"Okay, I'll indulge you. Why did your last coffee go cold, Eddie?"

"Don't indulge me. I'm not in the mood to be indulged. I'm so not in the fucking mood to be indulged."

In a brave attempt to at least force some kind of an explanation from him, she ventured on. "Why did your coffee go cold?"

"Because Jeffery wouldn't shut up talking. I should have been on that murder; the one Duffy's now going to mess up. The one that's going to take him so long to misinterpret that James will have reached puberty by the time he sees daylight again."

"Is that it? You're pissed off because—"

"No. That's not it."

———————

And it wasn't it. Well, not exactly; it was the result rather than the cause. Eddie looked over his shoulder at Ros who was sitting in a booth by the window tapping her fingers on the table and staring out into nothingness. "You want a McFlurry?"

Ros shook her head.

He asked the cashier, "What's the free toy?"

"Scooby Doo."

"Again! Two coffees," he said. "And a McPrivacy."

She smiled, but her raised eyebrows said she didn't have a clue what he meant.

"Me and the lady over there are having a serious discussion. Leave us alone. Okay?" He slammed two-fifty on the counter and picked up the coffees, "Keep the change."

Eddie slid the coffee over to Ros, took a seat facing her and said, "Now what the hell's going on?"

"Can you be more specific?"

"Jeffery told me you withdrew your application."

"Ah."

"Yes, bloody 'ah'."

"Don't you think you're over-reacting?"

"You haven't even seen me reach under-reacting yet, kiddo. He's only gone and promoted me! I didn't want the fucking job in the first place – I didn't even apply!"

"Sir?"

Eddie looked at the nervous girl who'd served him the drinks. "Christ," he said, "should I have ordered a large McPrivacy?"

"You didn't pay enough for the coffee."

"What?"

"I need another—"

"Here." Ros gave her a fiver. "Keep the change," she smiled at the girl who almost bowed as she retreated, and then told Eddie, "You're a tight bastard."

"Inflation," he said. "Anyway, stop trying to change the subject. Why did you withdraw your application?"

Ros played with her cup for a moment, sipped and then said. "I have a feeling of déjà vu. Why do we always come here when we have a heart-to-heart?"

Eddie stared, said nothing, and eventually Ros looked away, the embers of her smile became serious and she said, "I don't want the job anymore."

His foot tapped the floor, matching the beat in his tripping heart. "I already worked that one out. Why?"

She looked at him, her face expressionless. And then, after what felt a minute or two, she looked away, licked her lips.

"Come on. Has someone upset you at work? Benson? Jeffery?"

She shook her head, "No, everything's fine."

"Okay then, let me ask you this: why did you join the police?"

"Kind of question is that?"

"Just answer."

She shrugged, "Seemed like a good idea at the time." The smile accompanying that shrug was placating. "There's too much badness in the world." She shuffled in her seat. "I mean, that was the motivational force that made me join up. You either fight evil or turn a blind eye – which is abetting evil, isn't it? And there was too much badness about for me not to join." She looked aside, thinking, "I had no choice but to join up."

"Does it bother you, the work I mean?"

"Bodies?"

He nodded.

"No. Nothing like that. I'm fine with them."

"It doesn't add up, Ros."

She sighed and stared at her fidgeting hands. "There are some things scarier than dead bodies."

"Like what? Come on, tell me."

It seemed like minutes before she spoke again. Eddie let her take her time because he had a feeling it was big news and to rush her now would see her running out of the door or collapsing into a puddle of tears. And part of him felt as though he'd backed himself into a corner somehow; and that part of him wished he'd not asked the question. Only the stiff upper lip part – a very small part indeed – wanted an answer now. He steadied himself as she said, "I'm leaving, Eddie."

Usually his first reaction was to laugh, because that was Eddie's first reaction to all bad news. Laugh first, run away and consider the implications next. Worry third. But he surprised himself by not even feeling the need to laugh. He felt nothing. Fear maybe. But simple thoughts triggered by her words queued up at the serving hatch in the Pain and Anguish Department inside his mind, tapping impatiently on the scratched melamine-faced chipboard with their sharp little knives, just as Ros had tapped on the table a minute ago.

The first one slipped through uninvited, cheating the system, giving no time for implications or worry, causing his mouth to open and say, "You mean me, don't you? You don't mean the police? You're leaving me, Ros?" His heart was all over the place, and for a moment he felt light-headed, and reached into his jacket for the pill bottle.

She watched him throw a pill into his mouth and swallow, then the clouds scooting by tugged at her attention, and a bunch of schoolkids screwed their faces up against the rain. Right now it seemed as though anything was better than talking. "It's all about perfection. Well," she corrected, "not perfection, but close to it."

"Perfection is flawed. Why? Because you can never achieve it. Therefore it doesn't exist."

"Life according to Eddie Collins?"

"Not Confucius, I grant you." He shrugged. "But go on."

"We were great, only now we have nothing to fight for."

"What about fighting the evil, the badness?"

"I..." Ros shuffled again, feeling uncomfortable. "I gave in. I lost the battle."

The restaurant was getting busier with school kids, with executives taking a late lunch, with salesmen grabbing a quick bite between motorway stints.

"That makes no fucking sense whatsoever."

"Think about it—"

"I am thinking about it." He considered for a moment before continuing. "Do you know how many women I went out with between Kelly leaving and your sudden reincarnation?"

"No."

"None. Want to know why?"

She sighed, "Ooh, yes please!"

"Gee, thanks for indulging me." He sipped his coffee. "I took an age to make sure Kelly was right for me, that we were compatible, that I could trust her completely. And then she fucking left me. Took everything I loved. I still miss that stupid dog." He looked up, glared at her. "She broke my trust."

"Eddie—"

"The way I see it, if it took me an age to choose someone who still fucked me over, what chance do I have? Really, how could I ever make the right decision?"

"But—"

"Until you arrived." He rested his chin on fists and stared at her. "Now this might sound ridiculous coming from someone who views romance and issues of the heart as Mills and Boon fodder, but I couldn't believe my luck when you showed up again. And for the first time in years I felt relaxed and comfortable." The foot tapped faster. "I felt like someone was watching my back, that it was me and you against the world."

She swallowed, and whispered, "It was."

"But it turned out to be just me again, against the world and you."

Ros examined the table, a fingernail pushing around a grain of salt. The staff were shouting orders to the kitchen, and the seats nearby were filling up.

Eddie's unease grew: a bad situation in a busy place that was getting busier. "And there's something else, isn't there?"

"No."

"Course there is." He smiled, but it wasn't a smile of happiness, it was a smile of victory – of knowing. "Tell me."

"I have to get away. I just have to go. I feel… claustrophobic here."

"I'll come with you; we can be claustrophobic together."

She was shaking her head. "I have to go."

"No you don't. You have to stay here with me."

The salt grain forgotten, she quickly said, "My mum's dying. I want to go and be with her."

Eddie closed his eyes, sat back and sighed, partly with relief but partly with anger too. "We've been together all this time, and you've never mentioned her, let alone that she was ill." Something inside his mind countered that by saying he'd been in no hurry to introduce her to his father's company either. And why was that? Because such introductions were a stamp of permanence that neither really wanted? "Why the hell didn't you tell me?"

Ros bit her lip and looked away.

And then Eddie got angry. "I said, why didn't you tell me!"

"Because it wouldn't have made any difference."

"To what?"

"To us. I'd still be saying goodbye to you, so why drag it out?"

"What about your job?"

She shrugged. "There'll be others."

"Really? You read the papers recently?" Eddie sighed. "Are you on drugs? We share things, Ros. If your mum's ill go and be with her, fine. But come back again. Use it as a break."

"I am using it as a break."

Eddie stopped, and now it was his turn to watch the sky darkening and the rain hitting the glass. "Okay, I have to understand this. You've decided not to accept the promotion, you've decided you're moving back to Scotland, and you've decided to break up with me. That correct?"

She nodded.

"Why?" He looked into her eyes, as deeply as he could, but he failed to understand her. She was so dismissive about it all, as though the breakup and the resignation had somehow been pre-ordained and so there was no point in fighting it, but not only that, not only no point in fighting it, but no will to fight, no regret, no... just a casual shrug of the shoulders at one of life's inevitabilities. She was so determined to leave, resolute as though she'd come to a decision that she would stick with regardless of what Eddie put her through.

"When you were with Kelly, and I couldn't have you, you were all I wanted. When I didn't see you for those two years, I thought of you all the damned time, and then, when I found you and I was with Brian, and I still couldn't have you, you were still all I wanted."

"And now you've got me—"

"Shut up!"

The counter staff began looking in their direction.

"I'm just saying—"

Ros growled at him. "You wanted to know, didn't you? Didn't you!"

"I'm not sure I do now."

"Well you're going to know because then I can leave with a clear conscience."

"How frigging delightful for you." How blasé, he thought.

The customers nearby had noticeably quietened now, the way people do when they don't wish to appear as though they're trying to catch every word of a developing argument.

"Let's just say I thought I was getting cream and I ended up with semi-skimmed."

Eddie's mouth fell open. "If I wasn't so pissed off that'd be funny."

"It's not meant to be fucking funny, Eddie!"

The restaurant quietened further, so much so that it was easy to hear the sound of the manager walking towards them.

"It's meant to tell you how... how fed up I am."

"Then why the fuck didn't you—"

"Sir? Madam?"

Eddie's head snapped around. "Oh now what? I asked not to be disturbed, can't you see we're having—"

"If I have to come over here again, I shall bar you."

Eddie noticed how quiet the restaurant had become. He looked at the wan little man, and felt like dipping his head in the fryer. "I'm your best customer."

"Last chance," he said, and walked away. Slowly, voices grew again and people slurped and ate, but still they stared.

"Next time we'll go to Starbucks," he called. And then he saw the customers. "What," Eddie shouted at them, "Scooby Doo not entertaining enough for you?"

"Eddie," Ros whispered. "It's okay. Calm down."

"It's not okay. I spend a lot of money in here."

"Now it's time to be funny, eh?" She stood and gathered her bag, checking it to make sure the phone and purse were still there. Eddie reached up and gently took her wrist, which she shook free.

"Is there someone else?"

Ros walked. The light was diminishing still, and Eddie scrambled out of his seat trying to catch up with her. The rain was falling heavily now, not just spitting any more, and Eddie caught her by the car.

"How dare you?"

"I had to ask," he said. "I mean, how weird is this? This morning I woke up," under that pink quilt, he thought, "and everything was normal, hunky dory. And this afternoon I've been promoted into a job you wanted and then found out you're leaving. With no good reason."

"There *is* a good reason," rain seeping into her hair, turning her jacket shiny. "And things haven't been hunky dory for a month or two. Better sorry than safe."

Those eyes still mesmerised him, even now – especially now. They seemed open, naked, yet there was something foreign in them, like a lie hidden among the truth so it was easy to disguise. They were already saying sorry to him, as though there was nothing left to say. "You already tried 'sorry', remember? And it nearly killed you!

Hi," he said, "I'm safe…" He paused, his forehead wrinkled up with a thought that was sour to the taste, "It's as though you've got somewhere else to be, Ros. You're bored. I'm boring?"

"No, you're not boring, Eddie. But yes, I am bored. With the job, with us. I'm sorry. Now will you open the door?" Rain hammered on the Discovery roof, and danced on the surrounding tarmac.

Eddie's heart leapt and fell again as his mind tried to reconcile the calm way in which she was ending their lives together, how matter-of-fact she was. How she'd already accepted everything, and how abnormal it all was to him. "And when were you thinking of telling me?"

"Tonight. I had a table booked."

"A table? So a napkin and clean cutlery would have made me nod politely and wish you well?"

"You still could wish me well."

And that's when he saw she was crying, and he drew her to him and held her.

"What am I going to do without you, Ros?"

"I never wanted to hurt you. But I've got to get out of this city, out of this life. The ghosts…they're killing me." Ros didn't keep eye contact for long.

"Just my luck you get itchy feet now, eh?"

"I'm sorry, Eddie."

After a moment, he slackened his grip and looked into her eyes. "Don't be."

Chapter Six

Nobody Loves the Hero

IT WAS DUSK WHEN James and Duffy pulled up outside the cordon at The Crooked Billet. Orange streetlamps gave the scene a Mediterranean sunset glow but incessant drizzle and the prospect of squelching grass and dog dirt underfoot killed stone dead any further comparison. It was just another chilly English evening in a noisy and neglected part of the city.

Despite that drizzle, despite the chill in the air, and despite it being almost dark, there was a sizeable crowd at the cordon tape. It looked like they'd drafted in a few more PCSOs to help control them; the kids were the rowdiest, especially those who rode around on their bikes and shouted obscenities. Some, though, were there catching the spectacle, perhaps hoping Calendar News might get them in a "Hello Mum" shot.

For some it was work.

Duffy tapped the dashboard as James read the log again. It was sketchy, giving only the barest details: unidentified male lying in a puddle on a muddy path having just left the Billet. No witnesses. It may as well have said: "Dead body. Deal with it."

He looked across at Duffy, at the old guy's quiff that caught the glare of oncoming traffic and gave him a halo. But James knew Duffy wasn't exactly keen to be on this job. Duffy wanted to go home and watch *Coronation Street* or *EastEnders* or whatever crap he chose to relax to, not stick around at yet another murder scene, and certainly not stick around at yet another murder scene being second to him, to James. That was for sure.

It crossed James's mind that Duffy would later be asked questions about his performance.

But James had worked murders before, by himself; he wasn't such a rookie, not as much as Jeffery liked to think. He'd missed some blood at a scene last year and he'd not been allowed to work a murder scene single-handedly since. And considering James was a crime scene investigator, it hurt. A lot.

This was his ticket back to pride. This was his way back into Jeffery's good books, his way to prove himself to everyone else on the team, and he couldn't wait to begin whether Duffy was reluctant to muck in or not.

"Well?"

James's head snapped around.

"What's first, lad?"

"Common approach path, then tent."

"How about having a natter with CID first?"

"Yeah, I meant after that." James smiled and they climbed out of the van just as a DS was walking past. "What have we got then?" James asked him.

The DS gave him a reproachful look and just carried on walking. He got into a car at the edge of the grassed area and drove away as DI Benson approached. Benson looked through James and addressed Duffy. "Right," he said, "we've stolen this job from divisional CID, cleared the pub, got the tape spun out like a fucking web, now get a move on." Rain dripped from his hair, and he didn't wait for a response before turning away.

"Hold on," Duffy took hold of Benson's arm. "He's running this now, so speak to him about it." Benson looked across at James who stood there with hands behind his back, almost hopping from one foot to the other, a benign smile on his face. "He needs a briefing."

"A briefing," muttered James.

"A briefing?"

James nodded, then added, "Please."

Benson closed in, eyed him up and down. "Dead man. Over there. Wet, and getting wetter." He turned away, "Now get on with it."

James looked from Benson back to Duffy.

Benson shouted, "And get me an ID!"

Duffy smiled at James, "See how much clearer the scene exam has become now you've had a briefing?"

"He's a good communicator, I'll give him that."

"Come on, let's get the bleeding tent up."

Half an hour later, the tent was over the wet dead guy. They'd arranged a very bright LED standard lamp at each end of the muddy path and their beams turned the drizzle into a dazzlingly bright snow-storm. A third lamp inside the tent made it glow like an oversized Chinese lantern. They'd dressed in wet overshoes and full scene suit complete with face masks.

Despite the constant drizzle, James's enthusiasm was still going strong. He'd tried to temper it by concentrating on the enormity of the task ahead of him, but somehow, just thinking he was number one on a stranger murder seemed to keep it permanently buoyed. The only negative factor now, as far as he could see, was Duffy. "You don't want to be here, do you?"

"And you drew that conclusion how?"

"Because you've hardly spoken a word since DI Benson left."

"Bring the camera." Duffy disappeared inside the tent.

This was not like being number one at all. This was definitely still like being number two. He was still a fetcher and carrier; he was still acceding to others' orders when it should be him shouting the odds. James's jaw ached from all the grinding his teeth were doing.

Rainwater poured down the flap as James reached for it with a gloved hand, and ran up the sleeve of his scene suit. In anger he pulled the flap back and a mini-waterfall cascaded onto his head, trickled down his back, and sent a shiver up his spine. He stepped inside and stared at Duffy feeling that buoyed enthusiasm diminish a little.

"What?"

The sound of rain on the tent roof turned Duffy's question to a whisper. He raised his voice, "If you'd rather not be here, I can manage."

"Can you, lad?"

James swallowed, here we go.

"I was told to come and assist you, and assist you is what I'll do."

He put particular emphasis on "assist", noted James. "Listen, I'm trying to make up for... I'm trying to do a decent job here. I need you to back me up, I need you to tell Jeffery I did well."

Duffy smirked, "Jeffery's out of the picture, lad."

James stared, confused.

"That meeting they were having when you left? It was Eddie Collins's promotional meeting. He's your gaffer now, lad. It's him you have to impress. And it's him we all have to get along with – might as well shit a golden egg."

James stared into nothing, his jaw dropped open.

Duffy cleared his throat. "So now what?"

It was a shock. Eddie Collins found the blood that James had missed last year. Just one spot of blood. One! And he'd missed it, had been made to suffer for it ever since. And now Eddie was in charge, James felt the pull of insecurity welling in his mind, felt the extra pressure. Eddie Collins was the definitive scene examiner, Eddie Collins never missed evidence, Eddie Collins was a fucking God! Eddie Collins was a nasty bastard, and it explained Duffy's cold mood. James felt insignificant, worthless.

"James?"

James looked up to find Duffy, arms folded, staring at him.

"Now what?"

Now what, he thought. Now, Coronation Street seemed appealing. He sighed, looked down at the body and noted tiny curtains of steam floating from the wet clothing. The dead man lay on his side in something resembling the recovery position. It had obviously failed.

His left eye, the only one James could see from this angle, was open and water from his saturated hair had settled in the little hollow between it and the bridge of his nose. Eyelashes were wet and clumped together. His face was white, and his mouth was open just enough to give a glimpse of his lower teeth, the very tip of his tongue protruding from the lower corner of his mouth as though it were a slug climbing inside out of the weather.

His clothes were shiny under the stark white light from the LED scene lamp, and his fingers and hands were white and wrinkled because of the water. Part-submerged in the water alongside his head were some AED pads and nitrile gloves left behind by the paramedic who'd pronounced life extinct. And indeed, at the puddle's edge, there were slugs, the tiny black ones; supping diluted dead man's blood like this was their very own tap room.

Duffy's arms were still folded.

James shivered. "Photography," he said at last. "I'll crack on with photography in here, if you can go onto the path and begin searching for footwear marks."

Duffy raised his brow.

"Is that wrong?"

"Not wrong as such, but we'll be keeping the scene guard on all night so we could probably do any searching when it's daylight. Get much better results."

"Yep," James said, "fair enough."

"And it's raining out there," Duffy smiled.

James took shots from each corner of the tent, and then closed in for further detailed shots of the body, paying particular attention to the hands and the nails. "No point taping exposed flesh really, is there?"

"You tellin' or askin'?"

James lowered himself still further until his lens was just above the saturated ground. He fired off several shots of the face, bouncing his flash from the ceiling to reduce sharp shadows, and then stood and edged around to the back of the body, Duffy shuffling out of the way. "Telling," he said, not even watching for a reaction this time. The body was wet through; nothing would stick to the tape. They'd have to bag it and hope that any trace evidence wasn't lost.

"Correct."

James knelt again and brought the camera up to the back of the dead man's head, and then stopped. He brought a torch in for a closer look, and saw that blood had swelled the puddle, turned it a deep pink against the lifeless white skin. And that familiar smell, the smell you get when walking past a butcher's shop, wafted through James's mask. "Found the cause of death."

With considerable effort, Duffy got down on his knees too, whistled at the wound that gaped like an open mouth at them. "Not even Tramadol would sort out that headache," he giggled.

It had been washed clean by submersion in the puddle, and then further cleaned by the falling rain after the body had been moved. The edges of the wound were white, frigid-looking skin, probably six or seven millimetres thick with hair curling into the wound like an overgrown moustache. The bone at the base of the skull was shiny too, and at first the cracks and the deformation were not easy to see.

James angled the torch and it became clear to see how the skull had cracked and then recessed, breaking through the meninges and into the brain by well over an inch.

"It'll have been a quick death. Won't have known what hit him."

"And what did hit him?"

Duffy and James looked up to see Benson staring down at them. His head and hand well inside the tent.

"Don't know yet," Duffy started to say, but then James barked, "Get out!"

"What?"

"I said get out until you have the correct PPE on."

Everything went quiet, even the rain on the canvas roof hushed. Benson stared at James, eyes narrowed. And then he was gone. The sound of the rain came back as James heard Benson trudging away through the mud on the approach path. And this was the point he expected Duffy to start laughing at him and to tell him how painful life was going to be for him from now on, but he was surprised.

"Well done, lad. You were quite right. Just because he's a DI doesn't make him immune to the rules." Duffy patted him on the shoulder and stood, arching his back and groaning some more.

"Thanks," James said, "I was just—"

"Best get him a result now, lad, or he'll bounce your head off the fucking pavement." And then he laughed.

"Cheers. Just what I needed to hear."

"Gaffers don't like it when they're reminded they have to follow the rules too."

James carried on and got the wound photographed, and was about to stand when his torchlight picked out something on the upper edge of the wound. He closed right in, focused the light and saw several small flecks of red and a few of brown, tangled into the hair. "Duffy."

"I know, you want me go through his pockets for a wallet."

"Can you bring me some tweezers and a make up a Beechams wrap?"

"You found something?"

He had. James photographed the flecks, only one or two millimetres across, some of them embedded into the skin, others caught in the hair, and one or two had floated on water, down into the wound itself. He left those, but the exposed ones he took, one by one, and placed them into the folded piece of paper that Duffy held in his trembling hands.

"Looks like paint," James said. "Red on one side, and like some kind of rust on the other."

They looked at each other and together said, "Iron bar."

Within sixty minutes of Benson's ejection from the scene tent, James was knocking on the steamed-up window of his car. Fifty yards away, behind the scene tape that flapped like bunting in the wind, photographers captured him resting his hands on the sill, smiling.

Benson put down the Mars bar. "Well?"

"We found his wallet. All cards and cash appear undisturbed. Michael George Tailor."

"I know that. We got his name from people in the pub. Landlord says he leaves at that time every night. What else have you got?"

"There's a massive wound at the base of his skull, big cracks in it, so we think that's how he was killed."

Benson stared. "Pathologist now are you?"

James stood. "Bollocks to this." He began to walk away, stripping off his suit as he went, but before he'd even got his arm out, Benson was at his side. The photographers' flashes intensified.

"What else, James?"

James stopped dead. *James. He called me James. He knows who I am.* And just that one thought triggered off a small but hot feeling of pride. The man who'd been rude to him earlier, who'd marched into the scene tent, actually knew him by name.

Maybe he's rung the office about me. And then the thoughts turned sour. *Maybe he's rung the office about me and complained to Jeffery or to Eddie.* "These." He held up a small tamper-proof bag with a paper wrap inside it. "Flecks of red paint. On the reverse side is rust." He didn't grin as he'd thought he would when presenting Benson with his evidence, but the thought of Benson complaining had skewered the pride, and now all he wanted to do was go home and get as far away from him as possible.

Benson nodded, and without saying a word, turned around and got back into his car.

James pulled out an arm from the wet scene suit and was working on the other when Benson shouted to him.

"James?"

James turned.

"Good find."

Chapter Seven

In for a Penny

— One —

THE FLICKERING LIGHT ATTACKED his eyes, but he didn't see it. He didn't see anything except the bottle on the table next to him. It remained unopened, but he could feel his resistance to it melting like chocolate on a bonfire. Maybe constantly challenging himself to see who was in control – the alcohol or him – was a bad idea, or at least was *becoming* a bad idea.

It was two-thirty in the morning and Eddie felt wiped out, but his mind was in a tailspin again and that, combined with a thudding heart, refused to let him sleep. Tonight, the drugs were as useful as Smarties.

So here he was, torturing himself with the memories of whisky-induced slumber and a repeat of Jeremy Kyle. His nails dug into the arms of his favourite chair and his toes clawed at the carpet until he could stand it no longer. He leapt up and kicked out at the television. It crashed against the wall. The sound died immediately and the picture fuzzed, became a trapped rainbow and then it too died.

Eddie was panting; felt like opening his skin and crawling out, anything to be free.

The hall light to his right came on and Ros stood in the doorway with her hair a tangled mess. He couldn't see her face, but he knew she was crying again. "Baby," she whispered.

— Two —

Jim listened to Slade playing *In for a Penny*. Everyone wore flares with waistbands a yard deep fastened by two-dozen buttons, platform shoes a yard thick, tank tops, and hair a yard long, sideburns and ridiculous shades. But it wasn't just the lack of fashion sense; there was something else wrong with the scene.

The disco was blurred around the edges, as most dreams tended to be. There was a distinct lack of definition, and up there on the stage, Noddy Holder stopped singing as the thud came again. The rest of the band followed suit, and Jim's vision widened to see the whole thing was a bad re-run of *Top of the Pops*, and all he heard from the old TV was the banging, and the mumbling of the crowd, their platforms tapping across the BBC set. Noddy stared at Jim, and asked if he was ashamed of himself. The entire audience turned to look at Jim.

Jim sweated, looked around to make sure Noddy was actually talking to him. He must have been, for Jim was the only person in the cell.

He snapped awake, thankful to be away from a dream that seemed to be turning into a nightmare. The bedsheets clung to him and his hands ached from gripping the mattress. Slowly he came down, and regulated his breathing, blinking in the darkness and reassuring himself that he was back in reality now. He prepared a brave smile as the memory of it wafted away, when he heard it again. The banging noise, the same banging that had interrupted *In for a Penny*.

He turned on the bedside lamp and listened again. And there it was.

In less than a second, Jim was outside his bedroom door, jemmy bar in his hands, descending the stairs quietly, preparing himself for the inevitable confrontation.

At the foot of the stairs, his feet halted outside the lounge door, the cold from the bare floorboards seeping into them as he tightened his grip on the bar with one hand and clutched the lounge doorknob in the other. From inside the lounge a drawer scraped open and Jim burst into the room, bar held high and war-cry killing the silence.

Sam screamed and Jim's war-cry ended abruptly. He saw her there, cowering on the floor next to the open cabinet, one hand over her mouth and the other up in the air as some sort of weak defensive gesture. He dropped the bar and left the room.

"I'm sorry, Jim," she said.

He trudged up the stairs, Noddy singing *In for a Penny* again.

"I said I'm sorry!"

———

He shook the stained quilt out and prepared to climb back in to bed when behind him Sam turned on the light and said, "Hey."

He closed his eyes, dropped the quilt and turned to face her.

"Don't be angry with me," she pleaded, "I need help."

"Really?" he laughed. "You needed help about two years ago. Now you need new kidneys."

Sam moved closer and went to embrace him, but he pushed her away. "Please, I just want—"

"You wanna know what I felt like down there. When I saw you. I was disappointed. Yeah that's right, I was disappointed, 'cos I'd actually convinced myself that you were dead this time, and you wouldn't be coming back here no more to feck me about again, and you were gone this time, and I could—"

"Don't say that!" She edged closer, "Look at me." She reached up and took his head in her hands. "Jim," she whispered, "look at me."

Jim pulled free of her hands, grabbed her wrists and said, "I poured it away. Every last drop."

"Poured what away?"

"You make me feckin sick."

"I wasn't looking for that—"

"Get out," he said. "Get out!"

Chapter Eight

The Wisdom of Youth

— One —

AT LEAST IT HAD stopped raining this morning.

The tent was still standing, the traffic was considerably lighter, and James felt sorry for the PCSOs standing scene guard. The press too had gone, and there were but two or three people staring into the scene now, compared with the thirty or so last night.

Duffy rubbed at his eyes, "I'm too old for this shit."

"Plenty of life left in you yet."

"Really? How the fuck would you know?"

James looked at him to see if he was kidding around, but his face was deadly serious.

"They say youth is wasted on the young, and in your case they're fucking spot on, lad."

"That right? Well sometimes, wisdom is wasted on the old."

That cracked the sour cringe on Duffy's unshaven face, and he smiled at James. "Touché," he said.

They had done well last night, recovering the pieces of rust-covered paint from the victim's head, bagging the head, the hands, and the feet before placing him into a body bag ready for transportation to the mortuary. And now they were back, doing something which on the face of it was nonsensical. They were looking for footwear marks in the path's many muddy parts. It was a long shot that they'd find any worth taking because before the killing it was a well-used path, but also because if they found the killer's footwear marks, he could claim it was a public right of way and he had nothing at all to do with the death of Michael Tailor.

So searching for, photographing, and casting footwear impressions was only to add weight to the prosecution case. There was no way they'd get a conviction through footwear alone. But if they could link the red paint to a person, then the addition of his or her footwear impressions found at the scene would strengthen the evidence against him, and make it more difficult for the suspect to explain away.

The PM was booked with Professor Steele for this afternoon, and it seemed as though Kenny would drop for it. James was glad. He didn't mind PMs, but sometimes they lasted hours and there was never anywhere to sit. By the end, his feet ached like he'd run a marathon, and his neck did because of the camera dangling from it by its strap. Scene work was the way to go; it was definitely the place to be.

Today, James had insisted they need not bother with scene suits and overshoes as there was no trace evidence to contaminate now the body had gone. He hated those suits, hated how constricting they were and how the hoods crinkled each time you moved as though someone were screwing up an empty crisp packet in your ear. No, today was simply a footwear recovery exercise, no need for a suit.

And so it had proved in the end.

Because in the end, as it was again growing dark, they had gridded the entire path, placed markers at each grid square and further markers within each grid indicating footwear marks they thought of as having potential – those having some good detail, not obliterated by other footwear marks, or the weather, or by someone's dog trotting up and down the path all night long.

Twenty-seven footwear casts and countless photographs would see James working well into the night tonight as he processed them all back at the office and then arranged for a special courier to transport the casts to the footwear bureau across the other side of the county.

And then there was the report to write up as well as the photographic titles. The report would include his own interpretation of footwear manufacturers too. You could guarantee that there would be a dozen Nikes, all different, some Rockports, Reeboks, and the like. But there was one type that caught his eye because it was so unusual these days.

"Christ," laughed Duffy, "they were all the rage in my day, lad. Don't see them about at all now, really. They were as common in the seventies and eighties as Nike are today. Big business was Doc Martens."

— Two —

It was almost deserted. The place was vast and full of those mini-mansions that every city has. At least two or three very well-known roads or streets that are packed with houses as big as grammar schools that the elite liked to call home. But there was never anyone about.

One doesn't walk the street in this part of Leeds, you know, he thought. No, one climbed into one's Range Rover on the feckin drive, let the automatic gates trundle open on their runners, and then drove to the golf club, what! No one walked any more. If God had meant us to walk He wouldn't have given us Bentleys, dear.

So the street was rammed with million-pound houses, each driveway was rammed with expensive cars, but the street itself, wide and lined with oak trees, was frequented only by those too poor to live there – the gardeners, the builders, the car valets, that sort of thing. Oh, and of course the tourists gawping at what they could never afford.

It didn't bother Jim.

Actually, that was a feckin lie. It bothered him a lot. And he vowed to rectify it at some point in the very near future.

The house came up on his right, and he slowed ever so slightly. He peered through the black wrought-iron gates at the huge turning circle in front of the it, all lined with conifers. On the drive were a Jaguar and a Mercedes. "Nice," he said, and gently accelerated his red Escort away.

Chapter Nine

Silence and the Old Echo

— One —

ROS HAD BROUGHT ALL the sentimental and "must have" stuff from her own house in Kippax months ago, just after she'd moved in with Eddie. And Eddie had smiled when she'd unpacked it all at his place, remarking how glad he was she didn't play the piano. "It's a small place, Ros, you sure you need that many potted plants?" He was grinning when he said it. *But many a true word spoken in jest,* he thought.

Then she had elected to have the rest of her old house emptied by one of those clearance companies. It wasn't the most profitable, but it was the most efficient. The house itself sold within six weeks, and Ros and Eddie had officially become a couple. And that was when the sleepless nights and the heart palpitations began.

Living is one of life's biggest distractions, he thought. And these days, he was more distracted than ever. He imagined his day split into the hours of a clock face but the minute and hour hands were missing, just a second hand sweeping past the little numbers carefully etched into the face. Work seemed to swallow up fifteen or twenty seconds, travelling and eating, showering, and all the other time-wasters, all the other necessary evils ate another five seconds. The rest, he deduced, were spent thinking of Ros. It wasn't something he planned to do; it wasn't something he could prevent either. It just was.

And then the clock face melded into a tin of paint with the lid missing, staring straight down at the uninterrupted surface of magnolia. But it began to move, to stir, and the carefully structured clock face with its etched numbers, and the meaning it represented, became a colour depiction of life as a black streak appeared. These, he knew, were his thoughts. But no, that wasn't really true, this was the state of his mind; how it went from uninterrupted consistency to a rather frighteningly hostile take-over bid by a dominating theme that meant to destroy his peace and tranquillity; it was irrationality and perplexity.

And now, as he stared across at her, an untouched bacon sandwich growing cold on the table between them, an uncomfortable silence had evolved. The polite nod, the friendly smile, as though their relationship had regressed to a first date status. "Do you come here often?"

"What?"

"Never mind," he said.

"You don't have to wait, Eddie. Go home; I can see myself on to the train."

"I want to wait." The black streak grew in strength.

She laughed, "To make sure I get on, right?"

"Is there nothing I can say to make you change your mind?"

"A little late for that old line, wouldn't you say?"

"Well, is there?" There was a look on her face that he couldn't quite read. Well, that wasn't right – he could read the look, or at least he thought so. It said one word: regret. It said she didn't really want to go, it said she was happy where she was, and it said she still loved him. But her words were resolute – they said, I'm leaving, no turning back.

And that's why he was confused.

"No," she whispered. "We did all that last night."

"Will you at least ring me or send me a text when you get to Edinburgh?"

She nodded and stood. "I have to go." And when Eddie got to his feet too, she said, "No. Please, let me walk to the platform alone."

"Right."

"I hate long goodbyes."

"Yeah," he said, "me too. I love you."

"Me too," she whispered.

"Not too late, you know. To change your mind."

"And I'll miss you." And then she paused, looking directly into his eyes. Her own eyes welled, and she said, "I lied. About my mother."

Eddie grew more confused.

"I'm sorry. I just... I had to say something to make leaving more... more plausible for you."

"But—"

"I have to get away, Eddie. From everything. Right now."

"Plausible? I don't understand. It's not too late."

But it was. Ros hugged him one last time and walked away without looking back.

Eddie watched her for a while with a sense of loss, feeling a hole open up somewhere inside his chest, and wondered how long it would take to get over her, and what kind of mess he'd find inside his head once he had.

He could see her, among the throng of travellers, heading towards platform six.

The train for Edinburgh left from platform twelve.

The magnolia finally turned black.

Eddie slammed the door and dropped his keys on the table.

For a full minute he stood in the centre of the lounge and slowly turned. How bare things looked now that all Ros's ornaments and plants had gone. It was like the twelfth day after Christmas at his folks' home when all the decorations came down and the house became naked and drab once more. "Hello," he said. There was the old echo again, returned like it had found its way home.

But there was one overwhelming sensation that haunted him so soon after he closed the door behind him, something so tangible he thought he could reach out and grab it.

Silence.

I spend too much time inside my own mind.

It was so odd, so foreign now that he could even hear the buzzing inside his ears, something he'd not known for months.

Keep busy, he'd thought to himself. If you keep busy the day will pass quicker, and then you can climb into bed and not worry about it until the morning. Keeping busy, he knew, was just a sure fire way of postponing the inevitable thinking process until bedtime and so pushing away any slight desire he might have had to sleep. But right now wasn't a time for applying rational thought, and so Eddie ripped open the cardboard box containing the TV he'd bought and never got around to fitting. It took him twenty minutes to unpack the bloody thing, and just over eight to set it up and get it working.

And when he had, he turned it off.

Eddie did three things then. First of all he put his old pale blue quilt cover back on. Second, he took the pink house phone, coiled its wire up and dropped the whole thing in the bin.

The third thing he did was to sit in his favourite window seat, stare out into the countryside they'd walked through a thousand times and cry like a kid.

Out there, beyond the budding trees, the sky had turned a strange shade of magnolia.

— Two —

Three o'clock in the morning, the quietest part of the day, and he trod gently over the gravel, and climbed the low gate. Once on the path he walked quickly along the side of the house into the enclosed back garden.

In the lawn, maybe twenty yards away, sunken lamps glowed almost meekly, shining up towards the back of the house. Beyond them was the deepest blue that carried on for a hundred or more yards until the lawn gave way to a summer house, a high fence, and then woodland.

Within a minute, he was standing on the conservatory roof, pulling the forced window wide. He slotted the screwdriver he'd used back inside the shoulder bag, took a last look behind him, and then climbed into the darkness within.

Once inside, he pulled the window closed, even managed to latch it again before the alarm sounded. He fumbled for the tiny switch located in the LED lamp he wore over the balaclava; thick leather gloves hindered the process, but eventually a cold and sterile light illuminated the study sufficiently. In here, the sound of the alarm was muffled, and that was good for he needed no distractions as he slid open the desk drawers and cupboards and searched within.

Across the road, people stared at the red strobe light coming from Terry Shaw's house alarm, unable to see the ground floor because of the conifers growing along the front of the property. They also saw the police car, blue lights flashing, but no sirens sounding, draw to a halt outside.

Two officers alighted. One ran across the gravel driveway, leapt the low gate and was lost from view. The other officer shone his torch at the front windows and doors.

The house alarm fell silent and the intruder heard sharp radio chatter from outside, covered the glow from his LED torch and watched the police officer's own torchlight gliding across the study ceiling. He waited, patiently covering the light, for a minute until he could hear the radio no more, and then he exited the study. He closed the door after him, saw the red LED on a PIR in a corner at the far end of the hall, and paused, waiting for it to blink. It did, and then the alarm sounded again. He headed towards it and the stairs, and turned off the torch.

Both officers arrived back at their car as the alarm sounded again. Across the road, a bedroom window opened and a woman wearing curlers in her hair leaned out and said, "Is everything alright?"

"Are they away?" The officer nodded over his shoulder at the Shaws' house just as the alarm sounded again.

"They're in Cornwall. Has someone broken in?"

"Looks like a faulty alarm," he shouted, "don't worry."

"Don't worry? That bloody thing'll be going on and off all night."

Without disturbing the landing curtains, the intruder peered out of the window, and although he couldn't see the police because of the high hedge, he could make out a woman from the house opposite leaning out of her window. He couldn't hear what she said because of the alarm, but he knew she was talking to the police officers. He saw the police car drive away, saw the woman slam her bedroom window and yank the curtains back across, and then he switched on his LED lamp again and trotted down the stairs into the kitchen.

There were a dozen or more drawers and cupboards, and his shoulders slumped until he spotted a neat row of hooks on the wall next to the fridge. He selected the mortise key and walked along the carpeted hallway to the internal garage door just as the alarm sounded again.

Once inside he headed directly to the consumer unit, his LED light bouncing along the expansive garage floor. He looked to his right and saw the dusty bikes hanging from the ceiling, the cobwebbed fishing tackle in one corner, the two sets of golf clubs and caddies by the far wall, the petrol-engined strimmer and ride-on lawnmower, and two cans of petrol by their side.

The cover of the consumer unit was screwed closed, and so he reached into his bag for the screwdriver he'd used to break in with but its blade was far too big to get any purchase. This hadn't been part of the plan. The torch flicked around the garage quickly as he searched for tools.

There must be some tools in here, it's a feckin garage!

And then the torch became still as he focused on the bench and the cantilever toolbox beneath it. Inside there was a brand new set of screwdrivers, from which he selected one with a smaller blade. The intruder opened the consumer unit door and turned the mains power off using the big red switch. It echoed in the garage as the sunken lamps in the front lawn went out. The alarm however, continued.

The man opened his bag, peered inside and brought out a pair of side-cutters, then approached the consumer unit again. He isolated a slim back wire and carefully brought the cutters up to it. He breathed out, and listened. Then snipped the wire.

The alarm stopped.

Chapter Ten

Suffocated

May

— One —

THERE WAS A TERRIBLE atmosphere in the car. It had begun a long time before they even began their annual trip to the in-laws in Cornwall, but somehow over the weekend it had progressed into something approaching... well, hatred, he thought. But it wasn't quite in that bracket yet. Not from *his* perspective anyway, but it was dense enough and cloying enough to make him feel cold.

He reached across and turned the heating up a little. And while his attention was away from the road, he stole a quick glance at her. Liz's face was stony, and he wondered if she'd shatter if he shouted "boo!".

Instead, he cleared his throat and said, "You okay?" Well of course she wasn't okay. It was a waste of a good question, but he felt the need to break the ice – ice being the operative word. He felt the need to see if her demeanour had mellowed over the few hours they'd been travelling.

"Terry, please."

"What? You can talk to your mother until your throat goes dry, but—"

"I don't want to have this conversation. Just drive, please."

"Just drive. That it?"

She tutted, looked straight ahead.

"What the hell's the matter—"

"You want to know what the matter is?"

"It's why I asked."

She paused before saying, "I'm not sure you're the man I married anymore."

Terry tried to suppress the childish giggle that came out anyway. He immediately felt as though that was another step back from a resolution. "I haven't changed, Liz."

"Are you suggesting I have?"

Exasperation stroked his face, and he shook it away, and tried again. "No, I'm saying I am the same man you married; I'm saying I haven't changed."

"Well you'll forgive me if I spend some time making a re-evaluation of our position."

"Wait, is this me you're talking to or some business partner? Because I have to say, for a wife of twenty-eight years you sound like I bounced an invoice."

"So you think this is funny?"

"Think what is funny? I'm trying to get to the root of the problem, whatever it may be, so I can fix it."

"I'll decide whether it can be fixed or not."

"Well, in your own time, grace me with a response so I don't have to live like a chastened child any more – I'm getting sick of it, Liz, and if you don't start talking to me soon—"

"A threat! You're threatening me now?"

"No, I'm just—"

"Mark my words, Terrence Shaw, you'll know when the time for talking has come."

Terry swallowed his anger. It burned, though, and he gripped the steering wheel until the healing cut on his right hand, the one caused by a broken glass of Bacardi, began to sting again. This could not continue for much longer. He meant to have it out with her in the morning, but for now he'd let the approaching dawn and the loneliness of the motorway soak up the dread that slowly permeated into his heart.

And he let his eyes glaze over as they merely followed the spread of light from the Jaguar across the road's surface. He'd had his suspicions for some time, but her reluctance to speak of it, her reticence even in the face of direct questions confirmed his most cruel fear.

He had an idea the resulting conversation, if it ever came, would hurt both of them. He wondered where it would eventually end.

It was still early, about six o'clock, but the day was wonderfully light, and Terry was looking forward to a good, long sleep to pull him back into reality. And perhaps while he was dreaming, he might come across a way out of this mess he was in with Liz.

He pulled the big Jaguar onto the driveway behind Liz's Mercedes, looked across at her and was about to speak when she slid the seat belt off and climbed out without so much as a sideways glance. "Welcome home," he whispered, and climbed out too, rubbing at the ache in his back and marvelling at the dizziness in his mind, and the buzzing in his ears. "Get the door," he said, "I'll sort the bags out."

Liz unlocked the front door and rushed along the hallway to the alarm pad, and then just stopped.

"What's the matter?" Terry dropped the first two bags in the hall.

"The alarm," she said. "It's not working."

"It must be working, I remember setting it."

Liz said nothing, just pointed to the little pad and all its buttons.

"Strange," he said. "The screen's blank, and the keypad isn't lit up."

And then a cooling through-breeze blew the front door shut, and Liz screamed.

"Wait there." Terry rushed into the kitchen, and shouted, "Fuck!"

Terry cradled the coffee in his cold hands and watched the SOCO making a mess on the windowsill. His name badge said "Roger". The powder from his brush glistened like some strange stardust in the air, and though most of it went on the window, a considerable amount landed on the draining board and in the sink.

He yawned so wide he thought his jaw would snap, and then he put down the cup and rubbed his eyes until they stung.

"Late night?"

"Haven't been to bed yet."

"Well, he's had gloves on, I'm afraid."

Terry looked up at Roger. "Nothing?" Roger shook his head. "Not even a foot print?"

"I have a footwear impression, yes," he said, "but I was hoping for more."

"Like what?"

"Blood would've been nice."

"About eight pints worth."

"I mean look at the mess he's made of the frame. Plenty of sharp edges there."

The plastic window frame had been savaged; it was cracked, warped, deformed and mashed by some large screwdriver or jemmy bar. The glass had fractured and looked like a spider's web painted in silver. "Can you get fibres then?"

"I can and I have. But to be honest, they're not much use without a suspect to link them to."

"They make it look so easy on TV."

"Annoyingly so, yes."

"What about DNA? You hear it on the news all the time about how police got DNA from a crime scene and the next thing, they've arrested someone." He paid close attention.

"If only it was that simple. We don't write the scripts, I'm afraid."

"I know but... is it true? I mean if you had found DNA, you could link it straight back to him, couldn't you?"

"In theory, yes."

"In theory?"

"Well, you have to be on the DNA database for it to provide a match."

"So if he's not on the database, what then?"

Roger shrugged. "It sits there until he is."

"Until he commits a crime?"

"Yeah, one that we've caught him red-handed at."

"Like?"

"Well," Roger put down his brush, "anything really. Any recordable offence."

"Such as drink driving?"

Roger nodded, "Yep, that'd do it."

Terry heard her rushing down the stairs, and moments later she strutted into the kitchen with her arms rigidly by her sides and a stern look on her face.

"They've been into the study. My laptop's missing."

Terry groaned, "We'll get you—"

"It had personal things on it."

"Personal, like what?" he asked.

She squinted at him, and for a moment he thought she was going to yell, but instead, she calmly whispered, "Personal things. And some paperwork is gone too."

"What kind of paperwork?" Terry asked.

"Terry. Paperwork, that's all."

It was the look in her eyes that stopped him probing further, but he had a good idea of what kind of paperwork she was referring to. "Can it be replaced?"

She folded her arms. "No. It doesn't matter."

"Why would they take paperwork?" Roger said. "Was it your passports or bank documents?"

"No," she said, and then stared at them, inviting no further enquiry.

"Study. Right," Roger picked up his jar of powder. "Anywhere else?"

"I'm going in to work on Sunday," Liz said.

"What? Why? You're half way through our holiday."

"I have things to attend to."

"So, anywhere else?"

"Liz, you're a bloody volunteer, Christ's sake. They can manage without you."

"They've been in the garage too," Liz said to Roger, and then walked out of the room.

Terry and Roger stared at each other.

— Two —

Eddie slid the keyboard away and looked at him. "Don't look so scared."

James barely moved. He was standing by the door with his hands behind his back, fingers tapping the wall silently.

Eddie could tell he was bricking himself because he had barely blinked, and he was pretty sure he was holding his breath. "James?"

James blinked, "I'm okay."

"Sure you are, and Miss Moneypenny got her tits out for me this morning."

James's eyes widened, "Did she?"

"No."

"Thought not."

"Now relax."

"What's up, why did you want to see me? Have I done something wrong?"

"No. Now sit down will you, I'm getting a crick in my neck."

James lifted a box file from the stool against the rear wall, and looked around for somewhere to put it. There was another stool but it was obscured by boxes. In the end he just sat down and held onto it.

"I've had a chance to review your work on the Tailor murder a few weeks back."

James leaned dangerously far forward on the stool, "And?"

"I've been through your photos, checked the evidence you found, had a chat with Duffy. And DI Benson too."

James cringed.

"All's good. You found some good evidence, you handled yourself well."

At last a smile, and he breathed out, "Thanks."

"No need for thanks, just telling it how it is. You did well."

And then both paused for a moment, James finally relaxing, allowing himself a blink every now and then, and Eddie pondered his next course of action. "Now, enough with the bollocks, let's get down to it, shall we?"

James took a breath again.

"I know when you worked for Jeffery you were made to feel very self-conscious about some stuff."

"The blood I missed."

Eddie nodded. "The blood you missed."

"Blood you found."

"For starters, you need to know some things about me."

"You have X-ray vision?"

Eddie couldn't tell if that line was a defensive measure, a bare-faced insult, or a compliment. He let it go. "Listen, I've been doing this shit almost three times longer than you have. And during that time I've messed up and missed more things than you can shake a shitty stick at. So I've got more work experience than you, and I've got more mess-up experience than you have too. So don't feel bad about missing one little spot of blood." He stared at James until James noticed the pause and looked back. "But don't hate me for finding it. Okay?"

James said nothing.

"Talk to me."

James shrugged, "Okay."

"Thanks for your input." He leaned back in his chair, wondering why Jeffery had put him in this position. "Jeffery was very unfair to you, I think. You work for me now, and so long as you work the way you did on the Tailor murder, you'll hear no complaints from me; you did well, James."

"Thanks."

Eddie slapped the desk. James jumped. "Look, what I'm trying to say is get the fuck out of my office. You're one of the team, no junior or senior shit, no number one no number two, no lead no follow. Get it? You can call yourself one of the team, one of the shower of shit sitting out there complaining about the weather, about the pay, the job, their boss, whatever. Let the past go."

When Eddie looked up, James was smiling. "Thanks, Eddie." He stood, fumbled with the box file and shook Eddie's hand.

"Go on, get out."

James dropped the file on the stool and opened the door.

"Oh, one last thing," Eddie said. "Don't tell them out there that I missed things. I have a reputation to uphold." Eddie returned to his keyboard as James, grinning, closed the door behind him. It had been closed less than a minute when someone, James no doubt, knocked on it.

"Piss. Off."

The door opened, and Jeffery poked his head in. "Looking a little bit greyer, Eddie."

Eddie put his two index fingers on standby and pushed the keyboard out of the way. "Twenty-six letters in the alphabet and only two fingers – someone seriously fucked up." He stood up as Jeffery came in. "Now I know why you went bald."

He took a lever arch file off the stool by the wall, and then, like James had done, spun around looking for somewhere to put it. In the end he dropped it on the floor.

"If you want to stretch out you'll have to knock a hole in the wall first. Or go into the corridor. No such problems in your office though, eh?" He slumped in the chair. "Don't see much of you round these parts any more. Is it hard work pushing blank sheets of paper around your oak desk? Or maybe you've got carpal tunnel from all the video games you play? Or is golf these days?"

"Very amusing, Eddie." Jeffery perched on the stool, fingered his tie. "So how has your first month been?"

"Do you want me to give you an honest reflection, or would you prefer something from the Human Resources Management Handbook?"

Jeffery laughed, "You've read that? Really?"

Eddie stared at him.

"Thought not."

"It's not all you made it out to be."

"But it's been good for you. You've been stretched, you've had to lead a band of workers against some pretty close calls, and you've excelled—"

"If you shout 'Freedom' next, I'll slap you, okay?"

"No, really, I mean it."

"And stretched? I'd prefer not to mention where I've been stretched or who did the stretching."

"Cooper has to be tough where protocol is concerned."

"Yeah, well all I'm going to say is 'Vaseline', alright?"

"And I'd like you to consider wearing a shirt and tie while on duty. You're a manager now, and it'd create the right image."

Eddie nodded, "Okay, considered."

"Oh, good," he smiled. "Now, how are you finding that lot?"

"That lot? You mean the band of workers?"

"I know Duffy can be a bit cantankerous, James is still learning, and Kenny just frets all the time, but their hearts are in the right place."

"Couple of weeks ago, a pissed-up wife-beater threw his baby against the wall. I can understand it," Eddie said, "the damned thing wouldn't stop screaming and he was trying to watch an episode of QI." He watched Jeffery's reaction, waited a second or two and then continued. "I remember Kenny saying 'At last, some action', and I remember Duffy checking his watch, racking up the potential overtime, and I remember James almost falling off his chair to get out of sight."

"So who went?"

"The old guys went. No point sending James because you'd frightened everything apart from straightforward suicides out of him."

Jeffery swallowed, casually crossed his legs.

"You leaving was the best thing to happen to them."

"Okay, okay. I was too hard on him!"

Eddie stared. It had finally sunk in. Maybe that day when Jeffery offered Eddie the job, and the things Eddie had to say to him, had finally reached home. "You were," Eddie said. "But I'm working on him."

"Anyway, how did the move go?" Jeffery smiled, subject successfully changed.

"They don't like it; they're cramped. But on the plus side, the defectives leave us alone." He sighed, "I'm doing okay with them. I won't say they respect me, but then again, I've never given a toss whether they do or not; they knuckle down if I shout loud enough."

"If you don't mind my asking, how are you getting along without Ros being around?"

"You know I'm short-staffed out there?"

"Can't you manage? It's quiet—"

"Oops, now you you've done it. Shouldn't have said the Q-word."

"And we're still having our budget squeezed."

"And I'm having my balls squeezed. I bet if you were still doing this job, you'd have filled those vacancies by now."

"So how are things now Ros has gone?"

"And I need some admin support too."

"Why?"

"Why? Cos I'm shit at it. And don't look at me like that, I told you I was when you forced me to take this job. So the problem is I'm running around all over the place cos we're down by two, and I still have loads of paperwork to ignore. I need help. And the next time one of them has a go at me for their annual leave requests not being processed, I'll just send them to you. Shall I?"

"What about Melanie?"

"Too busy doing research for the defectives. She can't manage as it is, and it's a ballache going down the corridor every ten minutes to ask her something. I mean it, I'm putting my foot down with this; if you want me to stay, you get me some help."

Jeffery took a breath, "Okay," he said, "I'll look into getting someone for you."

"No, don't look into getting someone. Get someone. You've got till Monday, and then I stop worrying about doing any paperwork at all."

"Monday? It's Thursday now!"

Eddie clapped. "Feeling stretched, are we?"

Chapter Eleven

The Aggravated Burglary

THERE WAS A THUD.

In the darkness, Charles's eyelids flickered and inside his mind, the thud was absorbed into his dream. It was Steph slamming the back door, kicking it shut with her heel like she always did. "Come and get it," she yelled. In his dream, Charles smiled and climbed out of the chair, tossing the newspaper down as he strode into the kitchen. The smell was wonderful; Friday night fish and chips from The Empire was a tradition.

And then, as he'd expected, there was a smash, glass harpooned across the floor, and Steph muttered, "Shit," and her hands flopped to her sides as the smell of vinegar blundered through the kitchen.

Except, that was wrong.

She had never dropped the vinegar bottle before. And she never, ever, swore.

In the darkness, Charles opened his eyes. "Steph?" Instinctively, his hand patted the bed, but the space next to him was empty. As it had been for eight years. Only then did he realise the dream was just that, and the swearing and the sound of broken glass were real. That thought was reinforced as he saw the landing light suddenly shine beneath his door, and heard footfalls on the stairs.

As if trying to bring clarity to his confusion, he turned on the bedside light and sat up, rubbing his eyes. And then the door opened.

There were two of them. Both wearing black woollen gloves and balaclavas with evil-looking holes for the eyes and a slit for the mouth. Charles shrieked and the man at the front came into his room. As he neared, he brought up a pair of pliers, but they were incidental; Charles could not stop looking at the man's eyes through the holes in the black hood. They were slitted up like he was laughing. And his jaw pounded up and down relentlessly as he chewed gum.

Behind him, in the doorway, the other man laughed, and Charles scrabbled back up the bed until he was sitting upright against the coldness of the wall. The man came close and the air was filled with pungent spearmint, the sounds of open-mouthed chomping were lost still as the eyes laughed.

He brought the pliers up to Charles's face, and Charles held his breath, wanted to screw his eyes tight shut but he dare not. He dare not move. Then the man reached by him, snipped the phone wire. He chuckled as the old man's head swivelled around, tracking him across the room where he picked up Steph's wristwatch from the dresser. "Leave that alone!"

The masked man put the watch in his pocket. And then he opened Steph's jewellery box, tipped it out on the dresser and shuffled through it all with a gloved fingertip.

Charles could feel his chest beginning to hurt. He felt the sting of tears in his eyes too. And he was going to shout, but his breath felt laboured.

The man found it, her wedding ring, and her engagement ring too. He held them up to the light and Charles could see the bastard grinning even though he wore a balaclava. They both went into the pocket too.

"Put them back. Now."

Suddenly more light came into the room as the other man disappeared from the doorway, presumably to plunder the rest of the house.

"Keep quiet, granddad." The masked man patted Charles's trousers slung over the back of Steph's pink padded chair. He found the wallet, pocketed that too.

Charles growled, threw back the bedclothes, and yelled, "I said put them back!"

The masked man stopped chewing and spat the gum through the mouth-hole. He advanced on Charles.

Chapter Twelve

No Turning Back

— One —

SHE WAS UPSTAIRS GETTING ready for work.

Terry paced the lounge, his fourth bourbon almost empty and a sick feeling developing in his stomach. He peeled back the curtain and peered out into the night; through the reflection in the glass, he saw the lounge light behind him shimmering against the bodywork of her car. He swallowed the rest of the drink and let the curtain go.

He went into the kitchen and stared at the wooden board they'd screwed over the broken window and then reached into a drawer and took out a packet of cigars. He wasn't sure if tobacco products had a sell-by date, but if they did, these surely were fit for the bin. He lit one from the gas hob anyway and stared at the board.

His hand trembled slightly, and the scab on it itched, and then he heard her coming down the stairs.

"Terry?"

"In here."

She stopped dead, "Since when did you start on those awful things again? I can smell it right through the house."

"Do you have to go?" He threw the cigar in the sink and stepped towards her. "You're a volunteer; it's not as though—"

"They need me?"

"They can manage without you for one more night."

She ignored him and walked away into the lounge, and Terry sighed, shoulders rounded in despair. A moment later, she was back, stuffing her purse into her handbag, moving aside her hairbrush so the leather wouldn't get scratched. She was ever fastidious, he noted. "Liz?"

She looked up at him, no sign of compromise on her face.

"Please," he said. "Stay here. Please."

"Why? What's so important that you don't want me to go out?"

"I just... It's... Please," was all he could muster.

She didn't even smile. She just turned around and walked away from him up the hall towards the front door, "I'll see you tomorrow."

And then she was gone.

Terry looked with some regret at the dead cigar and reached for another. He took the empty bourbon glass back into the lounge; crystal chinked against crystal, and he opened the curtains again just in time to see the tail-lights of her car disappearing slowly off the drive.

He downed the drink in one and then picked up the phone.

— Two —

She travelled in silence, pointing the beams of light into the darkness ahead, able to see only blackness all around, hills and hedges, dry-stone walls and trees silhouetted against the deepest blue of the night sky.

The Mercedes was quiet, just a gentle hum that let her mind drift away from thoughts of work and back towards the black cloud spinning like a maelstrom over her marriage. It wouldn't be long now, she knew, and then there would be no marriage any more. The information...

Wait, what was that up ahead?

The blackness of the next bend glowed orange intermittently, and before she knew it, she could see amber strobe lights, bright and rapid. She slowed and then she could see it was a breakdown truck. Across the back were those reflective chevrons, and standing by the side was a man wearing high visibility clothing, smiling apologetically at her. He was short, a lot shorter than Terry, and he had a big nose.

He waved a hand and approached, bending as she drew up alongside and wound down the window.

Liz put the car in 'park' and looked up as he punched her in the face.

— Three —

The road was empty now; the breakdown truck had left. No flashing amber lights bounced off the dry-stone walls and lent an eerie perspective to the gnarled bushes and twisted trees of Scotland Lane. And it was almost silent too, except the sound of a breeze creeping through those bushes and trees.

The truck had stood upon the brow of a steep hill. The road cascaded down the hill and narrowed as it crossed a stream in the valley below. In complete contrast to the darkness of the brow, the valley was alive with the violent amber light of an intense fire; and the ferocious noise of the flames, the cracking, the smouldering, the popping, and the shattering of toughened glass, utterly slaughtered the silence.

It was a black Mercedes, its tail-lights still glowing. Its front end mangled by the bridge parapet, its shiny paintwork creased, torn and now blistered by a heat that sent embers rising high into the black sky on a ripple that looked strangely inviting. The driver's door was wide open, and she too had succumbed to the heat; her hair and clothes now almost entirely consumed by the fire, skin blackened, charred, fat bubbling, streaming down into the footwell where it sizzled on the bare metal like beef juice in a baking tray.

Chapter Thirteen

Things Really Can Get Worse

— One —

MONDAY MORNING RATTLED AROUND too damned quickly. Eddie popped another propranolol to quieten the bopping ticker in his chest. He flicked away the cigarette and slammed his way into the reception at the crime division and major crime unit building.

At least he'd had a proper deep sleep last night; finally the demons in his bed had seen fit to leave him alone and Eddie's mind had climbed out of the perpetual fog and back into a world that was as normal as he was ever going to achieve. Things were calming down; he took less propranolol and zopiclone, despite a sweet hankering that had developed for more zopiclone. And he wondered why that might be.

The only thing to change in his life was his mission to put James on an even keel again. That, and Ros leaving.

He stopped on the spot, the door still open; one foot in the building, the other outside. That was it. It was Ros. The reason for the nightmares and the dancing heart, the reason for the anxiety attacks. A part of him laughed. Surely that was bollocks, he thought.

He loved Ros, he worshipped her, couldn't wait to be with her, and was desperately sad when she left.

Yet he could not deny that his heart murmurings had abated somewhat, and that his sleep was better now than it had been for some time.

What did his body know that his mind hadn't latched onto just yet?

Eddie shook free of the thoughts, promising to spend more time later analysing that particular conundrum.

He'd let it go for now, but he couldn't let go of his habitual hatred of Mondays, despite having spent most of the wet weekend walking in circles around the lounge wondering what the hell he could do next that didn't involve watching shit on television. Life seemed noisy and full of crap as it was, without inviting it into his lounge. Instead of the television, he'd found an empty McDonald's coffee cup far more appealing, and had stared at that instead.

Eddie resumed walking, and the door closed behind him. "Morning, Moneypenny," he said to the receptionist.

"Eddie, someone to see you." She nodded towards the three plush leather chairs partly obscured by unnecessarily expensive potted palms.

Eddie saw something that looked like an extra from the Rocky Horror Show.

It stood up and smiled, then met him in the middle of the floor, hand outstretched.

"What the—"

Moneypenny snorted.

"Mr Collins?"

Eddie grunted. In front him was a skin-and-bone manikin wearing a pink blouson and tight black leggings that disappeared into knee high black platform boots with chrome buckles up the sides. Over his shoulder he carried a red satchel with hearts and skulls scattered all over it, and around his neck was a silver chain with a blue and pink enamelled yin yang. Eddie turned to Moneypenny, "Is this a piss-take?"

"Mr Collins, I'm Sidney. Your new secretary. You can call me Sid."

Eddie stared. "You're kidding, right?"

"They said you were shi– they said you needed a hand."

"You're from the redundancy pool, is that right?"

"I worked in CPS Liaison for four years—"

"They dredging the bottom now then?"

"I beg your—"

"Wait there," Eddie said. And then, to Moneypenny, "Is Jeffery in yet?"

Moneypenny nodded, she couldn't speak with her hand pressed over her mouth. And then Eddie barged through the double doors and bounded up the stairs.

Sid smeared Chapstick across his lips, "You know those palms are crying out for Baby Bio."

Within minutes, Eddie was back, jaw clamped tightly shut, eyes slits of exasperation and a demeanour that plainly said, 'keep your distance'.

"Everything alright, Mr Collins?"

"One question."

"Yes?"

"Can you make coffee?"

"Ah yes, you see I worked for Costa before—"

"Just a yes or no will do." Eddie turned and headed for the doors again, Sid following behind, his boots echoing on the floor as he scuttled round Eddie like a lapdog eager to please.

"I make a wonderful espresso, and if you like cappuccino, well I'm your man, and when it comes to exotic—"

"Shut up." As the doors closed, he could hear Moneypenny howling with laughter.

— Two —

"So how are you feeling?"

As they walked up the path towards his house, Charles looked at the police officer and didn't know whether ignoring the stupid question would be too rude. Yes, it would, he decided; the officer was only trying to be helpful. "Got a headache like you wouldn't believe."

"I would. Looks like someone face-painted you with a plum."

Charles nodded. He'd seen the reflection in the mirror. Not pretty.

"Look, Charles…" They both stopped walking. "I have a bit more bad news I'm afraid."

"More bad news? What the hell could be worse than being burgled and beaten up?" His lips twinged a tiny smile, but that's as much as he dare manage right now. The officer, after all, sounded serious, and Charles wasn't in the mood for tempting fate.

"After you went to hospital. Well, they broke in again over the weekend. Took your boiler."

"My boiler? Why?"

"Worth a lot in scrap metal these days."

"Jesus—"

"But they didn't turn off the water first."

"Huh?"

"Your house. It's flooded."

Charles hurried up the garden path and opened the front door. He stepped inside and the carpet squelched under foot. "Oh my good God." He stared at the lounge, all the wallpaper hanging off in strips, water dripping from the light fittings, the ceiling collapsed over in the corner where Steph's seat was. Her Lladró figurines lay smashed on the hearth, broken plaster all around them.

"It's not safe here. We had to turn off the electric."

Charles cried. "What am I going to do?"

"You got anyone you can stay with?"

— Three —

Eddie left Sid with Melanie in the main CID office so she could issue his temporary pass until the permanent one came through. He figured that it would give him just enough time to beat Jeffery to a pulp and make his getaway.

Instead, he'd found himself in the tiny kitchen in the CSI office, staring into the soap-splashed mirror over the sink, and looking into the bags beneath his eyes. He was wilting like a daisy kept in the dark. He tried to smile but the happy muscles weren't working and so he sighed and poured himself a good strong Kenco.

"Eddie?" It was Kenny, calling from the main office.

"Shit!" Eddie gasped and spilt the coffee, "Bollocks." He shuffled quickly out of the kitchen and back into his own scruffy, smelly little office. It was about the size of a kid's bedroom, had one tiny window that looked out across a thinly wooded area and then the M62 motorway.

The window was barely large enough for Eddie to squeeze the top part of his body out when he lit up a cigarette. Below the window, on a flat roof, a pile of cigarette butts spun in a vortex alongside screwed up paper and some dead leaves. Life in a microcosm.

The clock said 07:50 and already Eddie ached to be away home. But then he thought about that for a moment, and he thought about Jeffery interrogating him about how life was now that Ros had gone back to Scotland. Life was quiet again; a little too quiet. Maybe, now that he'd come to know what it was like to share his life with someone, it was also too lonely.

A year ago that would have been bliss, but... well, maybe in a few months' time he'd come to know that feeling of bliss once again, but for now it was definitely just plain lonely.

Out of it all, though, came the thankfulness that he'd known her after the horrid two years of thinking she was gone forever. But that thought, the getting to know her thought, had planted something in his mind that troubled him. What did it say about him? Maybe he wasn't so easy to live with; certainly not so easy as he'd thought.

But it didn't make sense. He was a pussycat.

Kenny knocked on the door, peeped his head around. "Eddie?"

"What the fuck do you want?"

"Can I ask you something?"

"Ask me and then I'll tell you if you can ask me."

"Eh?"

"Kenny, I'm busy."

Kenny stared at the empty desk.

"I'm thinking of policies and procedures, alright?"

"Yeah, right." Kenny crept into the office. "Here, you been nicking my coffee?"

"What? What do you take me for?"

"A thief."

"Be careful. I'm doing your appraisal soon."

"Really?"

"No."

"Yeah well—"

Then Duffy was in the office too, James followed and closed the door.

"You're gonna have to get a bigger office," James said.

"What the hell is this, *Mutiny on the Bounty*?"

"We've had a talk, and decided we want our team briefing," Kenny said. "You've been doing this job long enough and we ain't had a briefing in ages."

"Briefing." Eddie folded his arms and nodded. "You I can understand," he looked at Kenny, "because you're one of those sad bastards that actually enjoys this job, but you," he nodded at Duffy, "you surprise me."

Duffy smiled, "You… a briefing. This I gotta see."

"Briefing, right. Sit down then." Duffy and Kenny moved boxes and files, and sat on a stool each, and that left James spinning in a circle. "This isn't musical chairs, James. Use the damned floor."

"Oh, why me?"

"Because they have bus passes." Eddie reached into a drawer and pulled out a slim wad of paper. He stared from the trio back to the wad, licked his finger and pulled off the first sheet. He read it, "Irrelevant," then screwed it into a ball and tossed it towards the overflowing bin. He read the second page, said, "Irrelevant," pulled it off, screwed it up and threw that in the bin also.

"Hang on a minute," Kenny said. "You're supposed to read them to us."

"Oh right, sorry." Eddie peeled off the next page, stared at Kenny as he screwed it into a ball and threw it somewhere near the bin. "Irrelevant."

"Typical."

"Oh wait," Eddie said, "here's something." He cleared his throat and sat forward. "Following analysis of figures from scene visits and evidence recovery over the last six months, I can confirm," he stared at them, "you are still shit."

Kenny tutted.

"Briefing over. Now get out."

Kenny opened the door and stepped out, saying, "Got some more policies to look over?"

"After the crossword, yes."

James got to his feet and dusted off his trousers.

"James. You and Duffy are reviewing your evidence from the Tailor murder with DS Khan." Eddie ushered them all out into the main CSI office.

"Why?"

"Why? Because you didn't fucking solve it, that's why. Pull your finger out, James, and you," he pointed to Duffy, "start being some use to me or you're out."

Duffy laughed, "I'm winding down to my retirement, mate."

"You've been doing that since you started."

Kenny looked up from his desk. "What about me?"

"Go find a window to lick."

Eddie turned, about to go back into his own office, and stopped so suddenly that he almost fell over.

"I got my temporary badge. Looks great, don't you think?"

Eddie's shoulders drooped. "Kenny, this is our new admin assistant, Sid. Forget licking the windows, show him where we keep the kettle and anti-depressants."

Kenny's mouth slowly closed, and eventually he said, "Erm, would love to but I got shit to do." And then he whispered, "Fucking bender."

Eddie watched him leave the office, and looked around to find Duffy and James had left too. "Stay there," Eddie said to Sid, and ploughed through the door as though it didn't exist. "Oi," he shouted to Kenny.

Kenny stopped and turned.

"Bad mouth him again and I'll put you through that fucking wall. And then I'll start disciplinary against you. Okay?"

Kenny seemed confused. "What?"

"You heard me."

And then he understood, "I wasn't bad-mouthing him. I was bad-mouthing you, you prick." Kenny laughed and walked away.

Eddie stood there, stunned. "Ah. Right. That's okay then." With slightly reduced gusto, he headed back along the corridor, wondering if there was anything he had to do that would take him away from the office, even if were just for an hour or two; effervescence wasn't something he could tolerate this early in the shift.

Sid smiled at him. "So where do we start? You'll have to give me a bit of a crash course but I'm quick, oh yes, I'm not kidding you. You tell me how to do something," he clicked his fingers and pointed to his head, "it's in there for life. Talented long-term memory. You ever watch You Bet? I successfully identified twenty episodes of *The Bill* after a five second sound bite."

Eddie stared at Sid, walked back into his office and closed the door.

Within thirty seconds, the door opened and Sid poked his head in. "Got a minute?"

Eddie nodded, reclined in his seat and folded his arms.

"Not a good sign, is it?"

"What?"

"Folding your arms. It means you've already put up the barriers."

Eddie put his hands in his lap. "Better?"

"Much. Thank you." Sid closed the door behind him. "I guess you clocked me, haven't you?"

"Say what?"

"Oh, never mind."

"Well, what's up? If Kenny's offended you—"

Sid shook his head. "No one's offended me. But I feel like I should explain myself to you."

"You don't need to do that." Eddie sighed, "Look, I apologise for the way I behaved downstairs; it was very immature. I was taken by surprise—"

"See, this is what always happens. People feel awkward and start apologising, and before you know it, political correctness kills the atmosphere. Please," he said, "have a laugh, but make sure you're having a laugh with me, not at me."

"I would never—"

Sid held out his hand. "I'm not saying you would... I'm just saying in general."

Eddie nodded and finally relaxed. "Can I ask you something?"

"I don't date people from work," Sid's smile developed into a chuckle.

Eddie too was smiling. "What do you describe yourself as?"

Sid squinted, still smiling. "That's very gracious of you to ask; thank you." He cleared his throat, "I am a cross-dresser. Simple as that. Nothing more, nothing less."

"Gay?"

"Nope. Is that a problem?"

"I don't give a shit whether you're gay, straight, a tranny, or whatever. I don't give a shit if you're black, white, Asian, blue, or fucking green. I hate everyone equally." And then Eddie leaned forward slightly, and asked, "Is 'cross-dressing' and 'transvestite' the same thing? I mean," he winked, "standing up... or sitting down?"

Sid laughed along with him, and then he became serious. "I'm straight," he said. "I used to be a dancer. It was hard work, long hours, shit money... a bit like working here.

"But the only decent clothes I had were those I bought for the stage, and they were women's clothes. I looked great in them, felt good too. I'm only five foot eight but when I dress like this, I'm a giant, and I'm invincible." He paused a while, watching Eddie, "I've never bought a pair of boxer shorts since."

"That's all well and good, but you're out of that door if you make bad coffee."

———————

"So that's how the monthly stats are collated."

Sid looked up from the computer screen, "You sure?"

"It's how I've been doing it," Eddie said.

"And the overtime sheets are wrong as well."

"As well?"

Sid sighed, "And your evidence—"

"It's basically alright; just the details to sort out."

"Details? This is going to take weeks to put right."

"Yeah well," Eddie patted him on the back, "best crack on then, eh?" Eddie closed his eyes and began walking towards his office when the phone rang.

He was about to pick it up when Sid shouted, "Ah ah!"

Eddie's hand recoiled.

Almost ceremoniously, Sid cleared his throat and then answered, "Good morning, major crime unit crime scene investigation, Sid speaking, how may I help you?"

Eddie sighed and sat on the desk, watching Sid's face turn ashen.

He held a hand over the mouthpiece, and whispered, "It's divisional control."

"Christ, are they still there?"

"They've found a burnt-out car on Scotland Lane." He swallowed, "There's a body inside."

Eddie took the phone from him and watched him fall into his chair, wafting air over his face. "Welcome to CSI, Sid." He took notes, consulted Sid's computer terminal, and then hung up.

"That is awful, can you imagine—"

"That's your first mistake."

"What is?"

"Imagining what it's like. Don't imagine what it's like."

"But—"

"No buts. And you'd better get used to this; we never get invited to anything good, okay?"

"Oh my," he sighed, "I need a stiff one."

Eddie printed the log off, "For now, you'd better make do with a whisky."

"Now is not the time for jokes."

"Second mistake; now is the perfect time for jokes." Eddie grabbed his jacket off the nail behind his office door. "It would be inappropriate to laugh your bollocks off at the scene."

"You so need therapy."

"Tried it; didn't work, Sid. I'm going before Cagney and Lacey get back." Eddie left the office, but before the door had even swung closed behind him, he poked his head back through, "And don't eat all the Valium while I'm out."

Chapter Fourteen

Mr Whippy...

— One —

THE LANE WAS SO narrow that he had to pull over to let the fire truck through.

It was like walking into Narnia.

And it took Eddie by surprise how different it all looked out here now that the shadow he'd lived beneath for so long had gone. The sunlight looked more like warm tungsten after the flat bland white of a fluorescent tube that winter sunlight provided. The world out here in the countryside bloomed and turned the twisted veins of trees to the clothed beauty of green woodland. Eddie sat in the van with his shades on, looking out across the fields to his right, the hedgerows with blossom trees, and for a moment, he disappeared.

Ros had always been his woman, but now she wasn't around anymore. And when she left, everything turned an under-exposed vision of black and white, something he'd grown accustomed to, something he viewed the world with and thought, subconsciously, would never really change. That's how it was when something awful happened and you were left to deal with the aftermath. Black and white – monotone. Drudgery. Despair.

He looked around at the dry-stone walls, the fields, the woodland. This was picnic country, and it was almost warm enough too, he thought. No breeze, just birdsong on the air – that, and police radio traffic.

And it was radio traffic that burst his thought bubble, and Eddie sighed and threw the shades on the dashboard, kicked open the door. The source of the radio traffic was standing by the side of his van.

"CSI?"

"No," Eddie said, "Mr Whippy."

Up the lane stood Benson and the accident investigation bureau's Huggy standing next to him, holding some fancy piece of equipment. Eddie sighed, and walked towards them and the brow of the hill.

A traffic officer, red-faced from his walk up the hill, passed Eddie, speaking into his radio, "Mercedes 230. Yankee Kilo Six Three…"

Eddie watched him pant towards a guy with a dog, who stood at the cordon beckoning him urgently like a kid trying to get the teacher's attention before he pissed his pants.

"What are we doing here, Benson? This is divisional shit, surely."

Benson turned and his jaw stopped mid-chew. "Aw what the fuck are you doing here? I thought once you'd got promotion I'd never have to work with you again."

"Count yourself lucky I don't mind stooping to your level." Eddie nodded at Huggy. "Well?"

"Yes, I am thanks."

"I mean what are we doing here?"

Huggy nodded towards the car. "Deliberate is that."

"What is?"

"The fucking fire," Benson said.

"No way would a new Merc burn like that," Huggy said.

The wonderful countryside odours that Eddie had delighted in upon his arrival were slain by man-made toxins, a choking stench of petrol and oil, of death in a twisted caricature of a Mercedes hearse.

With aching thighs, Eddie stood next to Huggy and Benson and peered open-mouthed into the car where a black charred corpse sat among the rusty springs of the driver's seat, a ring of rusty metal in the form of a steering wheel just ahead of it. Eddie had told Sid not to imagine a person's demise, but he was doing that very thing right now, and he knew the other two were as well. Hard not to. And it was hard not to imagine how the family would take the news.

— Two —

Terry sat on the leather couch, elbows on knees staring rigidly at the carpet. Out in the hallway, the clock chimed eight, and that brought him from his reverie.

He stood, marched to the window and peered out onto the large driveway. His silver Jaguar stood alone, as he'd expected it to. No sign of Liz. He turned, stared at the untouched cup of tea, and then dialled her work. She should have been home at 6am, maybe seven at a push.

During the conversation with one of her colleagues, Terry's mind wandered into her demeanour the evening she left; how reticent she'd been, how determined to punish him, it seemed, for doing something wrong. But when her colleague reported that she hadn't even shown up at work, despite her calling ahead and telling them she'd be in, Terry's mind let go of the conversation altogether and he dropped the receiver. His eyes immediately began to water, he went cold and his mind panicked so badly that he couldn't even find the house keys.

She's dead, he thought. He just knew it. You'd see films or hear stories where people get a sudden jolt when they feel the passing of a loved one. Terry didn't get this; instead he got a weighty feeling in his stomach. He thought it might be called dread.

Terry locked up, climbed inside the Jaguar and through watering eyes, steered towards Stainbeck police station, four miles away. Less than three minutes after the dust had settled back on the driveway, the house alarm sounded and the curtains in the house over the road opened.

The next thing he knew, he was standing at the front counter with a police officer saying, "sir? Sir, are you alright?"

He blinked awake, felt dread nudge him, and then whispered, "I want to report my wife missing."

— Three —

Benson gave Eddie the bird from his car window as he drove away from the scene. Probably heading for the nearest bacon butty, thought Eddie. He turned back to the road, watched Huggy climb the last twenty yards of the hill ready to set up his equipment.

Eddie saw them first, and he called Huggy over. "Seen these?"

Huggy bent and peered at the road surface. "They look almost metallic," he said. "But they're not from a wheel rim or anything like that."

"So what then?"

"Dunno," he shrugged.

"Fat lot of fucking use you are. What about these then?" Eddie pointed to a faint black mark a couple of feet to the side of the metallic ones. "And there's an identical one the other side too."

Huggy looked at Eddie, "You've got the eyes of a shit-house rat, Collins."

"And you've got the face and smell to match. So what are they, wheel-spin marks?"

"Could be."

Eddie sighed, "I fucking despair."

"Well they're not obvious, know what I mean? He didn't even touch the brakes so far as I can tell. Probably never saw it coming."

"I know he didn't touch the brakes; no skid marks. But these aren't skid marks, are they; they're wheel-spin marks."

Huggy stood, peered back down the hill and set off walking. "I'll have a look, see if there's any tread pattern left on the tyres."

"When can you examine the car?" Eddie shouted.

"It's on my list."

———

Eddie took the camera from the van and set up scales alongside the marks. He took location shots with a bright orange numbered marker alongside each mark, then closed in on them, kneeling down to get the detail. And as he tried to stand, he spotted something else in the long grass to his right.

"Shit-house rat eyes indeed." Eddie walked towards it, and as he closed in he could see it was the white cap of a medicine bottle. He bent and, with gloved hands, carefully picked it up. It looked fresh, no signs of weathering on it or the small brown bottle; and the label was clear and clean as though it had only been printed yesterday. It said, 'Rohypnol – ELIZABETH SHAW'.

After their initial exam, Eddie called up for the fire service to return with specialist rescue equipment. Looms of brown wiring hung like webs across the open car doorway, and the fire fighters had decided the best way of removing the remains of the body was by removing the roof first.

It took another three hours of delicate cutting to extricate the body from the car. It had melted into the wire of the now naked seat structure; the plastic seat adjusters had warped and then melted, flowing into the crisping skin, as had the steering wheel.

The driver's feet had fused to the remains of the carpet, the shoes and clothes had disappeared among the blackened debris of fallen ceiling furniture, the headlining, overhead consoles. Body fluids had leaked and seeped everywhere, and soon everyone's gloved hands were slick with congealing grease. Even the tarmac of the road surface had bubbled and pooled and run in short rivulets towards the bridge before solidifying into searching black fingers.

— Four —

Terry's world swam in and out of focus and he struggled to get the key in the door. An echo came from his left, and when he looked, he found it was a police officer, and then he remembered. And then the echoes disappeared and the officer said, "Here. Let me."

"Terry? Terry is everything alright?"

He turned towards the shrill voice and then his eyes looked away as the neighbour from across the road hobbled over the gravel towards them.

"Oh my. Terry?"

"He'll be fine," the officer said. "Just need to get him inside."

"Have they been back?"

"Sorry?" the officer said.

"The burglars. The alarm's been going off again. I tried to contact Elizabeth, but…"

Terry's eyes had clouded over again, and his hands trembled as he passed the keys over to the officer.

"Thank you, we'll look into it," The officer opened the door and ushered Terry inside.

— Five —

Eddie didn't even see Miss Moneypenny as he strode through the foyer. She smiled at him, as she always did these days, but he was lost in another world. And at first he didn't recognise it. No, this was no Narnia, or anything quite so fictitious; this was real, yet it was as abstract as you could get. This was an emotional place, and that explained why it felt so foreign to him right now.

He ascended the stairs, carrying his evidence, the camera, and his notebook, but his mind was elsewhere. It grappled with it, this feeling; and it took him until he reached the office to finally identify it.

Coming from inside, he could hear music, and floating around the edges of that music, a high, squeaky voice was doing its best to slaughter the song.

Eddie stood outside the office door listening. Ros had played it often, it was one of her favourites and each time he heard it his mind took him back to when he was part of a couple. It was as though it enjoyed torturing him, this one half of a couple; it was as though it were poking fun at his situation now. That of a single man made single by virtue of the fact that he was an arsehole – and only an average arsehole at that, had a plaque above his front door to prove it. She'd left him to be with her mother. She'd left him not to be with her mother, she'd corrected. Of course, the evidence was plain to see. She'd left him because of the plaque.

And he could see now what the feeling his mind had been grappling with was. He could see it clearly because it had produced a rather fetching plaque of its own stretching right across the office door and engraved in English script: LONELY AVERAGE ARSEHOLE.

Lonely.

That was a loud word, and if it had a colour it would be black, and if it had a smell it would be smoke, burnt body smoke. Kind of ironic, he thought.

Eddie kicked open the door.

Kenny had his feet up on the desk reading a newspaper, Duffy was picking his nose and defacing a poster about drug abuse, and Sid was singing *Stairway to Heaven* at the top of his lungs.

They all stopped. They all stared at Eddie.

"Turn it off."

Sid hit mute and smiled at Eddie. "Coffee?"

"Where's James?"

Kenny slowly put down the paper and swung his legs off the desk, "He, er, he left early."

Eddie stood there, looking around the office, and he nodded slowly. "Left early." He threw the evidence bag containing the bottle of pills he found on Scotland Lane onto Sid's desk, and growled. "Send that to FDL. Please."

"FDL?"

"Fingerprint development lab."

"Oh. I see," he said. "And what form—"

"I need to see you, Eddie," Duffy cautiously walked towards him.

Eddie's cheeks throbbed. He stared at Duffy, and said to Sid, "Microsoft Word, Crime tab, Articles for Forensic Examination, FDL, Form 88."

"Form 88, right."

"What's rattled your cage?" This from Kenny.

"What's rattled my cage? Have you seen—"

And then Benson appeared in the doorway, "Eddie I need a CSI—"

"Button it, Columbo. Go grab a fig roll, I'll be with you in a minute."

"But I need—"

Eddie turned. "Don't fuck with me today, Benson!"

"What the hell is up with him?" Kenny said.

"You lazy-arsed fuck," Eddie shouted.

"See, this is why I need to see you," Duffy said. "I've been offered early retirement and I'm taking it."

"Oh great," Kenny said, "down by another member of staff now!"

"We won't fucking notice!" Eddie screamed. "Good," he said to Duffy, "get your stuff and fuck off."

Duffy looked at Eddie, his mouth open. "I've worked in this force over thirty years, and I've never been spoken to—"

"Firstly," Eddie began, "you've *been* here over thirty years, you've *worked* maybe three months. Secondly, I am shocked that you've never been spoken to like—"

"Jeffery never did!"

"Jeffery was blind as a fucking bat!"

"Shall we calm down," Sid said. "I'll make us all a nice cup of—"

"You still here?"

Sid took the exhibit and almost sprinted for the door.

"Eddie," Benson whispered, "I really need—"

"One more word! Just one more word, I dare you!"

"Time of the month?" Kenny said.

"Yeah, you have some hyper mood swings, lad," Duffy said. "Frankly it's why I'm going. You're an arsehole."

Eddie stopped dead. He looked at the office as though through new eyes; he saw his dishevelled staff with their dishevelled ways and for a moment he felt like quitting all over again. His breath came out hot and fast, and he realised that Duffy was right. He was an arsehole, and only an average arsehole at that.

"This is about Ros, isn't it?"

Eddie looked at Kenny, expecting to find a sick grin on his face. But there was none. He was being serious, and Eddie blinked, looked away.

"We've all lost someone—"

"Don't," Eddie said. "Just please, don't."

Benson walked up to him then. "Eddie?"

"What?"

"We got an address for the burnt stiff. I need someone there."

"Let's go," he walked from the office.

Kenny stared at the fig roll in Benson's hand. "Are you in the biscuit fund?"

Chapter Fifteen

...The Stairway to Heaven

EDDIE DROVE AND AT first, much to his relief, there was silence in the van. He found his mind wandering to happier times but it was inevitable that Benson would ruin it all.

"I'm only going to say this once."

"Don't bother saying it at all. Just give your arsehole a rest."

"You think you're the only one—"

"I said shut up."

"Wait till you see this fella. Then you'll find out what it's like to lose someone in a truly shit style."

"This is supposed to be helping?"

"Just wait. At least you know Ros is okay." He snatched a glance at Eddie, but Eddie was resolutely staring forward, avoiding any chance of eye contact. "Look into his eyes."

"What do you need me for, Benson? I was having an office meeting."

Benson raised his eyebrows. "Meeting? Sounds like you were in the process of losing all your staff."

"I live in hope."

"You might think you're a fucking superhero, can do all this shit by yourself," Benson paused as he watched Eddie roll his eyeballs. "You know something?"

"Oh do enlighten me."

"I liked you more when you were a pisshead."

"I was never a pisshead – no idea where that rumour came from. Anyway, flattery will get you nowhere. Now why am I being forced to endure your flatulent company?"

Benson sighed, faced front. "She's burnt to a crisp. You work it out, smart-arse."

Eddie could hear the chatter of a police radio coming from the kitchen as an officer made strong-smelling coffee.

In the lounge, next to Eddie, Benson stood in front of Terry.

Terry was in an armchair, his face pale, eyes just watery shimmers that looked at nothing and no one, just staring into some kind of nothingness.

Eddie understood what Benson had said, about looking into the eyes of a man who had lost a loved one in a shit style. It wasn't pretty. But the turmoil inside Eddie's mind, turning incessantly like the dead leaves and the cigarette ends on the flat roof outside his office window, wasn't exactly comfortable either.

Benson had obviously thought that seeing the misery on someone else's face might make his own feel insignificant, but it didn't: two miseries didn't make a delight; it merely compounded his own and made him feel anxious to be away from here so he could...

"We're going to need something of your wife's, Mr Shaw. Hairbrush, toothbrush. Something like that."

"Oh Jesus."

It was a mumble, lips parted barely enough to break the dry-skin seal they'd made. His eyes closed for a moment and the tears that had shimmered there rolled down his white cheeks. Eddie swallowed and looked away.

"You can't identify her, can you?" Terry looked up at Eddie. "Why?"

Eddie felt like grabbing Benson round the neck and forcing him to do his job, forcing him to tell the guy all the gory details of how his wife had literally become part of the driving experience they say you get by owning a Mercedes. Tell him how her body fat was now acting as an excellent rust inhibitor in the footwells.

"Tell me!"

"The car caught fire."

"Jesus Christ."

And then Eddie saw fit to offer some comfort, "It's likely she was unconscious before it started."

"And you know this? Can you stand there and tell me without doubt that you *know* this?"

Eddie stared at him; and it almost turned into a juvenile competition. So much for offering comfort; he might as well have offered the old guy outside and punched him in the guts. And right now, the anxious feeling, the need to be away from here had become quite hot; hot enough to make his palms sweat. And anyway, what would he do if he were away from here? He'd sit in a puddle of self-pity just like he always did, and he'd marvel at how that puddle got bigger the more he thought about Ros. If he wasn't careful, he'd drown in it.

"I'm sorry," was all he could think of saying. But it was enough for Terry to relent and break the eye contact. Any other time, Eddie would feel proud that he'd won the competition, but not today. Now he felt like shit. He left the room, left the remains of the conversation for Benson to fuck up; he'd done enough of that all by himself.

He made for the stairs and crossed paths with the officer who carried a tray of hot drinks. He could hear Terry in the lounge sobbing. Good ol' Eddie, he thought, always there with a shoulder for the grief-stricken to cry on.

It was a fact of life that shit things happen. It also seemed a fact of life that most shit things happen to good people. The old fella down there in the lounge seemed like a decent sort, if you excluded the minor outburst – which of course you could, under the circumstances. And he'd suffered one of the shittiest things Eddie could imagine – and where shit things were concerned, Eddie had a splendid imagination mostly supported by a substantial portfolio of shit experiences.

As he neared the top step he conceded that the grief of the man downstairs did indeed knock his own "grief" at Ros leaving into a cocked hat. But it still didn't make it easier to bear; in fact it made it worse. Ros was still technically reachable; it's just that she'd deliberately put many miles between them. And really, it might as well have been death, might as well have been an unearthly plane, for all the grief he felt.

She hadn't sent him the text message as she'd agreed to. And she hadn't responded to any of his. And really, there were only so many one-sided messages you could send before you began feeling like a stalker.

Yet it seemed absurd to have delved to this level of self-loathing and sorrow so quickly after she'd left. It seemed that his own grief came and went in waves, a lot like the topography surrounding the burnt-out Mercedes: up one minute, down the next; menopausal, as Kenny had suggested. It had been the song; that had been the trigger.

Eddie dropped his kit inside what was obviously the master bedroom, the other rooms up here being a study, a large house bathroom, three other smaller guest bedrooms, and a walk-in closet. And then he found himself in the en-suite as Benson made the floorboards behind him creak.

"You okay?"

Eddie touched the large twin sink below a wall-length mirror, a toilet at either side, nice neat towels in nice neat chrome rings fastened to the wall. Both toilet lids were up, and for a moment Eddie thought that strange, but let the thought disappear. "You know, I put gallons of bleach down mine, but it still looks like Silverstone. This place," he said, "it's like the Hilton on fucking steroids. Immaculate."

Above the sinks, and on the wall nearest the long frosted window, was a mirrored medicine cabinet. Eddie opened the doors and peered inside. The right side was full of pile cream, boxes of Rennie, Gillette deodorant and body spray. The left was full of women's toiletries, arrays of tiny bottles of candle oil and a further array of medicine. Eddie leaned in closer, spun a bottle so the labelled showed, "Rohypnol," he said.

"Formality then. Grab her toothbrush, let's get the fuck out of here."

In between the twin sinks, on a shelf of polished white tiles heavy on the left side with perfumes and moisturisers, and aftershaves and a proper shaving brush and soap set on the right, was an ornate lead crystal toothbrush container. Inside the container were two toothbrushes, one red, one blue.

Typical, he thought. In this bathroom they have separate everything, including toilets! But toothbrush holders? No, only one of them! "Which one? You need to ask him which one."

Benson sighed, "Red and blue, Einstein; you work it out."

"We need to be sure. I'm not playing guessing games with something like this. We either do it right or I'm walking and you can mop up the shit and tears."

"Keep your hair on, just take them both. He'll have a spare."

Eddie shook his head. "You're kidding, right? Just go ask him; I ain't authorising two items for analysis."

Benson sighed, fiddled with the change in his pocket. Feet never still. "Look," he said, "take the hairbrush; I wanna be away from here."

"Mars bar addiction biting again?"

"I feel uncomfortable here, that's all."

"Why? What makes you feel like that?"

Benson shrugged.

"Come on, spill it."

"Nothing to tell."

"Bollocks."

"Can we just get on?"

"There is no hairbrush. It's toothbrush or nothing. So go ask him, and while you're down there feeling uncomfortable, I'll make a start with some fingerprinting."

"No need, DNA'll do."

Eddie shook his head, "I want fingerprints to compare with the bottle from the side of the road."

"What?"

"You might be happy fucking up your own job—"

"Okay, okay." Benson left the room and Eddie began powdering the bottles of Rohypnol. "I'll ask which is hers. But we're taking both."

Kenny strolled around the body, marvelling at the charcoal, the layer upon layer of deep burning, and marvelling too at the tears in the flesh up by the thighs as her legs had gradually straightened out after being bent in a burning car for so long, how the charcoal had turned to black dust and how tiny crescents of red meat shone out like fissures in molten lava.

The smell was pungent. If you'd closed your eyes, you could have been standing by the side of a barbecue where someone had put plastic plates and rubber hose onto the grill just after the chops had begun burning.

In the corner of the mortuary, DS Khan stood chatting to Prof Steele as though nattering over the garden fence about football, exchanging the odd laugh as Steele fastened a plastic smock behind his back and tucked his greens into a pair of Dunlop wellies.

Kenny nodded at the mortuary tech; a man who looked perpetually bored with seeing the insides of people's bodies and still smelling death and excrement even after a dozen showers before leaving for home. The mortuary tech nodded back, but the acknowledgement was as cold as the room, as clinical as the mobile spotlights hanging from the ceiling, or the stainless table the corpse lay on, and as friendly as the grisly smile on its face.

By an empty table, two DCs were standing looking at the body and then at each other with eyes that said they'd drawn the short straw as exhibits officers yet again.

Khan and the Prof ambled over and the tech straightened up a bit, trying and failing to look interested. "You know we might struggle with DNA here," Steele said, seemingly to anyone who would listen.

"Why's that then?" Kenny asked.

"Because it'll be like beef burger juice by now," Khan laughed and looked at the Prof for confirmation. A nod came and Khan folded his arms.

"Might help," the Prof added, "if you could use dental records."

"We can't get DNA at all?"

"Should be able to satisfy your need for toxicology analysis," he shrugged, "but... well, I'll try of course, but I can't guarantee anything suitable for DNA extraction. She's been sitting inside a 250-degree oven for two hours."

"It'd help if we could," Kenny said. "We've got a name already—"

"From?"

"The car. Well, from the husband actually. Eddie's getting a DNA exhibit from her house right now."

The Prof looked at the body, looked at Kenny, and said, "I still think dental records might be your only hope."

Chapter Sixteen

When Pizza and the Past Collide

AND STILL IT WAS quiet enough to hear the buzzing inside his ears. At least he thought it came from inside his ears, supposed it could have been filling the room for all he knew. But no, when he moved about the noise remained constant. Just a drone, a zuzz from too many years listening to too much music too loudly. And he'd been chewing his thumb nail for so long that the skin around it had turned white and wrinkly.

It was getting dark now, beyond twilight and he hadn't really felt the need to get off his arse and go and switch on the light. Hadn't felt the need to pull down the blind either. He was content to sit at his favourite window seat and stare out into what used to be beautiful countryside, but was fast turning into various hues of grey with lots of black and the odd twinkling light from Woodlesford over the river and canal down there.

There were two things floating across the zuzz right now, vying for attention in his cramped mind. And though he was reluctant to allow either in, they kind of forced themselves on him. The first was Duffy, and how he'd volunteered for early retirement on account of Eddie winning the Arsehole of the Year award for the second consecutive time.

Initially Eddie had shrugged and told Duffy to naff off if he didn't like the way he ran things around here, but he conceded that may have been a tad rash. And why was it a tad rash? It was a tad rash because his judgement had been clouded by the second thing floating across the zuzz right now: Ros. And the way she had abandoned him, and the way it made him feel inside; like he was scum, like he didn't even deserve to be consulted on the matter. That it was fine for her to pack her hot water bottle and just fuck off without so much as a look back over her haughty shoulder. Well, no, even that wasn't right. She'd booked a table, was going to tell him he was history over a bowl of vegetable soup with croutons.

If it hadn't been for her and the way she had just gone and left him to be a single person all over again, then maybe he'd have had more sympathy for Duffy. Perhaps he could even have conceded that he wasn't the best boss in the world – unlikely, he acknowledged, but he could have pretended.

Anyway, she was gone and he was history. And if history had taught him one thing, it was that he could only rely on himself; if he wanted to function at all with anything resembling normality, then he had to forget her, he had to knuckle down, crack on with the job and stop crying into his beer and taking out life's shittiness towards him on everyone else.

There, he'd done it, admitted it. "Dad would be proud," he whispered.

And then there was a knock at the door.

He would come back to the Duffygate thing and how to resolve it after pizza.

Eddie grabbed his wallet and opened the door, hand already extending in readiness to receive the pepperoni delight with extra olives when his eye caught on that there was no box on offer, that the pizza delivery guy seemed to be vehicle-less, and that he also wasn't wearing his usual yellow sweater and red trousers. In fact, his was a lot older, uglier and smellier.

Eddie stared. "Dad?"

"Hello Eddie."

Eddie was startled. They'd last seen each other twenty ago at his mum's funeral. They had shaken hands, if he remembered correctly, after sharing a single malt in celebration of a lost mother and wife in the local pub, The Three Pointers near the cemetery, and Eddie had driven away into oblivion, holding onto a blame he pointed squarely at the old man. "I'm taking a wild stab here, but you're not moonlighting for Frankie's Pizzeria by any chance, are you?"

"My house is flooded."

Eddie blinked.

"You gonna invite me in or what?"

"That's not a rhetorical question, is it?" Suddenly Duffygate was a long way away. "Come in, I didn't want a quiet relaxing evening anyway."

The old man took off his flat cap, gave a wan smile, begrudgingly, noticed Eddie, and trudged inside just as a faded red Corsa squealed to a halt outside the door. Eddie sighed and though his stomach grumbled, his appetite had receded into a tight little knot somewhere approaching his anus.

A youth wearing red trousers, a yellow sweater and a baseball cap on backwards climbed out and approached Eddie carrying a boxed contribution to Eddie's impending heart failure. Eddie saw the decals on the car. They'd peeled off because no doubt this youth was racing around town at warp speed six. They now said Rank Pizz. "You got any spare garlic bread with you?"

"I have, Mr Collins, yes."

"I'll have it. And you got anything spare with mozzarella on it? I need to freshen my dad's breath a bit."

Eddie hadn't put the main light on. He'd made do with the lamp in the corner of the room. And there was good reason: though it was an old cliché, when his dad ate it reminded him of a bulldog licking piss off a nettle, and there was no need, thought Eddie, to put himself through that trauma just yet.

But now, coffee in hand, blinds down and main light on, Eddie could see his dad quite clearly and without any fear of being traumatised, and he could see the string of cheese hanging from his white-bristled chin. But what was most startling was how the side of his face was a shocking purple colour. "You look like Mikhail Gorbachev. What's been going on?"

"Who's Mikhail Gorbachev?"

Eddie sighed, "He used to work down the chippy... Never mind who he is! What the hell happened to your face?"

Charles rubbed his cheek and grimaced, looked up to see if Eddie was watching his reaction.

Eddie was watching alright, and he wasn't impressed.

Charles began with the burglary, "Aggravated burglary, the copper said to me. And then his sergeant said it was robbery now, that they'd reclassified how… well, I don't know, that's what he said." He told about the Chewing-Gum Thug and his buddy, and the rings and watch they stole and the slapping they'd given him. "And as if that wasn't enough of an insult or an injury, they came back while I was laid up and nicked me bleedin' boiler!"

He'd gone on at great length about how it left his house flooded, how the hospital stay was like a trip into Victorian England, how the insurance company were dragging their heels, and then asked, "What's happened to your phone?"

"Why?"

"Cos I tried ringing you. I needed you."

"It's in the bin."

"Why?"

"Cos people kept ringing me."

By the time Charles had finished his tale, Eddie had forgotten all about Duffygate, and had forgotten all about the old guy who'd lost his wife to a rather vicious car fire. Eddie had other things on his mind now, and even though he sat there looking like calmness personified, he was boiling inside. His nostrils flared a little; that was the only giveaway. "You're staying here now."

Charles whispered, "Thanks. Just for tonight, son, till I get things sorted. I don't want to put you out."

———

Eddie had cleared some of the junk out of the spare room, found some bedding that wasn't too badly stained and tucked the old guy up for the night. He hadn't told him that someone had been shot dead in that room – it might have scared him – and he hadn't mentioned that the old bedding was covered in a rather graceful if somewhat gruesome arc of blood or two; some of it hadn't washed out too well.

And then Charles had surprised him with a question that he hadn't foreseen. "You got a woman?" he said, just like that.

Eddie had heard the cistern filling and instantly knew what he was talking about. "Not anymore."

"I saw a box of... you know. Women's things," Charles had nodded back towards the bathroom, "thought you might have a really bad case of piles or you—"

"Well I haven't. Not anymore."

"Piles?"

"Woman!"

"Oh. Sorry to hear that."

"Goodnight, Dad." And that was almost the end of their first meeting in almost two decades. A strange encounter, he thought, but there was nothing new there. They'd always been a strange pair, a combination of elements like mercury and water, beautiful in their own right but reluctant to mix. And the tampons were just another thing of hers he hadn't got around to disposing of; and he wondered if he'd left them and the other assorted oddments belonging to Ros as a reminder, something to help him feel more... normal? Attached?

An hour later, as Eddie stretched out on his bed listening to some Pink Floyd, he became aware of a presence.

"Son?"

Eddie looked up.

"You locked the doors?"

"You saw me do it."

Charles nodded in thought. "Just making sure." He continued to stand in the doorway, his fingers tapping at the frame.

"You okay, Dad?"

"What? Me? Yeah, I'm fine." He didn't look up.

Eddie turned the music off and climbed from the bed. "You don't seem fine."

Charles smiled, but it was fake. He nervously licked his lips, and didn't know where to look. "I er. I'm just a bit, you know, nervous."

"I get that." Eddie approached, then he shared the doorframe with his dad. "You not slept well since it happened?"

Charles shook his head. "I slept okay in hospital. But I think that was down to the pain meds, really." Another fake, twitchy smile.

"You want to spend the night here?" Eddie nodded to his own king-size bed. He bit his lip; part of him was expecting Charles to laugh and walk away. But instead the other part was right.

"Would you mind? Just for tonight. Just till—"

"It's fine. You don't need to explain."

Charles entered the room, "I feel like a toddler creeping into his parents' bed," he laughed. "How weird is this?" He pulled back the duvet and sat on the edge, his back to Eddie.

"It's okay. It'll take some time, Dad. You've been through a trauma; you need time to recover and get your head in order." Eddie turned on the bedside lamp, and then turned off the main light. "You need time to get your strength back."

"I'm an old man," he said. "How much time have I got?"

"Don't be daft."

There was a long silence before Charles whispered, "The road to recovery starts tomorrow. I've had enough of feeling like this."

In the space of a month it seemed he'd swapped his dream woman for his old dad. Eddie sighed a big sigh. Not exactly a fair exchange, was it?

Chapter Seventeen

More Questions Than Answers

— One —

"WHAT LITTLE WAS LEFT of her lungs was full of tar, really greasy black stuff it was."

Benson looked at Khan, "Surprised you could tell, if she was so badly burnt."

Khan shrugged. "It proves she was still alive when the car caught fire."

"Any chance of DNA?" Jeffery adjusted his tie.

"It's not looking good. They took samples but she was like a lump of pork scratchings, so it's unlikely."

"Where's Collins?" Superintendent Cooper looked at his watch and then up at the wall clock. "You did mention the briefing to him, didn't you?"

Benson nodded, "I emailed him. You know what he's like, boss, no respect."

Jeffery looked embarrassed.

"Tox results are due back in today," Khan continued, and read from the report in front of him, "'Inconclusive as to the possibility of stroke or heart failure—'"

"You think she swallowed a handful of those tablets Collins found?"

"Won't know until tox comes back."

"Pound to a pinch of shit she was swimming in them," Benson said.

"Anyway," Khan said, "we finally got X-rays of her mouth so we can at least compare dental records."

Cooper nodded, chewed a nail and then said to Benson, "Get back over to Terry Shaw's house, have a word with the neighbours, make sure everything checks out, dig around a bit, find out if she went off the rails. But be tactful. And then get over to the garage, Huggy's been annoying me already this morning. See what he's found. And get Collins to get a CSI to meet you there." And then to Khan, "You go check with the work colleagues… cross the Ts etc., okay?"

"Boss."

"If we get nothing, we can wrap this thing up, pass it back to division and hand over the body for burial."

Eddie hit the card reader and slid into the foyer, hoping for a quiet day of deep contemplation at life's ability to completely piss him off without even trying. On top of that, he had some thinking to do about his dad. Was it fair to kick the old guy out? No, of course not. And would it be the right thing to do even after the boiler had been replaced and the damage repaired?

When he'd landed on the doorstep last night, he'd looked about two degrees away from petrified, and furthermore, Eddie thought, he must have been desperate if he'd gone to the trouble of tracking him down and asking for a room for the night.

Desperate? That word almost made him laugh, but it was still true. How desperate must he have been to come looking for me? "Desperate indeed." It would take a special person to go back and live in that house knowing what the local scum had done, knowing they could come back and do it all over again any time they pleased. Poor old sod would never get a moment's peace.

Eddie's wish for a quiet day was declined at the first hearing. Just as he was nodding a greeting to Miss Moneypenny's cleavage, Benson appeared in front of him like an impenetrable barrier. Eddie allowed himself his second sigh of the morning. "What?"

"You missed the briefing."

"What briefing?"

"If you'd been there, you'd know what briefing."

Eddie thought about that for a moment, then decided it wasn't worth wasting his time over. He sidestepped Benson and headed for the doors, and the stairs to a strong coffee and a silent office.

"It was a suicide."

Eddie stopped and turned. He hadn't yet worked out what Benson was going on about, but he guessed the comment was aimed at him, since Miss Moneypenny's chest was incapable of holding a civilised conversation. He knew that because he'd already tried.

"The burnt stiff. Prints on the pill bottle you found matched those you lifted from the house."

"Oh, you mean the prints you didn't think were worth taking?"

Benson grimaced. "And she was full of Rohypnol."

Eddie stepped closer, intrigued. "Any idea why?"

"Not yet, but I'm going to speak with the neighbours and Terry Shaw again, see if I can shed some light on this lot and file it away. Maybe whichever SOCO you sent depressed the living shit out of her."

"Okay, I haven't had my coffee yet, which means I'm technically still asleep. So you'll excuse me for asking this question: what the fuck are you on about?"

"They were burgled a week ago. Some SOCO covered it last Thursday, and I don't know about you, but an hour with one of you sad bastards would see me reaching for the Gillette too."

"I know this is a difficult concept for you to grasp but burglaries are for divisional SOCO, we're major crime unit CSI, and we only do serious—"

"Yeah, whatever. Same conclusion though."

"She was burgled, and a few days later she turns up chargrilled. No one checked into it?"

"Cooper's call."

"No wonder you lot are called defectives." Eddie left Benson, and headed straight through the double doors, up the stairs, and into the main office where he saw Francis Cooper, thumbs tucked into his trouser belt, glaring at him.

Eddie was going to turn right, and head for the seclusion of the CSI office – that little part of the building just big enough for a mop and a bucket – and the chance of a coffee, but Cooper's glare ate into him; and he felt compelled to find out why he looked so hostile.

"Boss," he said. "Knicker elastic snapped?"

Cooper removed his thumbs from the belt. "Why weren't you at the briefing?"

"I just heard all about it from Columbo anyway." Eddie spied Jeffery peering out through his office window, and waved.

"Don't you read your emails?"

"There's a delete button on keyboards for a reason, you know."

Cooper stiffened, "I get the feeling you're not taking this very seriously."

"I get the feeling no one knows what the fuck is happening around here."

Jeffery's door opened.

"I beg your pardon?" Cooper leaned in, whispering. "You need to watch—"

"The burnt woman," Eddie said, "she was burgled a few days ago. No one bothered to check if there was a link?"

"Francis," Jeffery approached, a humble smile on his pale lips, eyes darting between Eddie and Cooper, hoping to defuse whatever was about to erupt. "Eddie's not himself in the morning before his first coffee."

"You mean he's usually less arrogant?"

"He means—"

"Eddie!" Jeffery stared hard at him.

Eddie took a breath, "I'll go and get that coffee now." And he walked away.

"I want to see you, Collins," Cooper called after him.

And Eddie waved over his shoulder, "Busy. Got work to do."

"Sorry about that," Jeffery fidgeted.

"Get him on a tight leash, Jeff. I'm keeping an eye on both of you."

It never happened like that. Coincidences like this were lies – they weren't coincidences at all. Not really. You could analyse the figures, collate all kinds of stats from happenings like this and you'd find that coincidences rarely happened.

Eddie marched up the corridor to the broom cupboard, mulling over how blind Cooper and his cronies seemed to be.

"No way," he mumbled, "would someone turn up dead days after being burgled without some kind of link." He pushed through the door into G34 and silence greeted him. He sighed with gratitude, headed for the kitchenette and that coffee he'd been promising himself for hours.

"Eddie?"

Eddie closed his eyes. Too good to be true.

"Eddie, that you?"

"No." Reluctantly he carried his stolen coffee into the office. It was deserted except for Sid.

"I knew it was you."

"I'm happy for you." Eddie glanced around the office, noted the shiny desks and the smell of lavender and potpourri. Sid had too much time on his hands. Sometimes Eddie hated efficient people. "Where is everyone?"

"Well, let's see."

Something more pungent had a fight with the potpourri and won by a knockout.

"What's that smell?"

"Ah!" Sid jumped to his platformed feet, and clunked across the carpet as quickly as he could to meet Eddie, holding out his hands. "This!"

Eddie looked at Sid's nails. "You painted them black."

"You like?"

"Stunning. Just fucking stunning."

"That was sarcasm, wasn't it?" Sid returned to his seat a whole lot slower. "I can tell sarcasm. That was sarcasm."

"Where are they?"

"You think I should have left them red, don't you?"

"Sid. I couldn't give a toss if you pulled the bastards out." He sipped his coffee. "Now where is everyone?"

Sid lifted his nose in the air, swivelled his chair so he wasn't facing Eddie. "Kenny is on a training course. James is still sorting out some stuff for the DS on the Tailor murder. And Duffy hasn't turned in."

"He phoned in sick?"

"He phoned to say he's posted you a letter."

Eddie shook his head. "Let's hope no jobs come in eh, seeing there's only me here!"

"Actually, I'm glad you are here." Sid regained his previous enthusiasm. "I still need you to go through these with me," he prodded a pile of papers. "I don't mean to pester you, really I don't; but I do need to know how to process the monthly stats."

Eddie perched on the desk, gently placed his cup down and asked, "Do you know how to use IBIS?"

"Yes. Why?"

"Do me a favour and see if you can find out who attended a burglary on Connor Road last Thursday will you?"

Sid began tapping the keyboard. "Connor Road."

"Yep."

"There are two Connor Roads. Alpha-Alpha or Charlie-Alpha?"

"Alpha-Alpha."

"Thursday."

"Yep."

Sid looked up, pleased with his efforts. "It was Roger Conniston."

"Right, good." Eddie stood and was about to walk when Sid cleared his throat and pointed again at the stack of papers.

"Please," he said.

Eddie sighed, and then a smile burst onto his face. "Okay," he said, "let's do it!"

"Really?"

"Absolutely. But first, would you like a drink? Tea?"

"Oooh, yes please."

"And what about a Jaffa, you want a Jaffa?"

"Why not. And a fig roll too."

Eddie pointed at him. "You wait right there," and walked quickly toward the kitchen, leaving Sid smiling to himself, a look of relief and satisfaction colouring his face. He admired his nails again as Eddie clattered a pair of cups together in the kitchen before creeping through the door and out into the hallway, closing it quietly behind him.

— Two —

The phone rang just as Benson pulled up outside Terry Shaw's house. He scrabbled around in his jacket pocket, took out the phone, and said, "Yes, boss?" He listened, and as he did so, his gaze wandered over the flowers stacking up against the wall next to Shaw's gate.

In the study, Terry was keeping the little shredder on full throttle, feeding into it handwritten notes, printed documents, old photographs, and even newspaper cuttings from another file he'd found tucked away underneath the bottom drawer of Liz's desk. Some of the newspaper cuttings drew his attention for far too long as he studied them, beginning with the date, and then the headline, and then the story.

Her handwritten notes confirmed to him what she'd spent her time pursuing since April; how far into it she'd gone, how much detail she'd unearthed. As he fed the machine, the shaking in his hands began to subside, his heart rate finally began to calm a little and he allowed himself a long blink and a pronounced sigh.

And then he screamed as the doorbell rang.

— Three —

"But that's absurd."

Benson looked at Terry's face, and tried to read perhaps more than was on offer. "I've just had it confirmed. Why is it absurd?"

"It just is. She was perfectly happy; I see no reason…" and then he trailed off.

Benson didn't break the silence, not yet. He studied Terry's hands, noticed them shaking, and noticed a healing cut on the right palm. He hadn't shaved either, looked dishevelled. But that's perhaps as it should have been, right? Man loses his wife of twenty-eight years in such a horrific way. Bound to take its toll, right?

"I see no reason why she'd do such a thing."

"Her system was filled with Rohypnol, Mr Shaw. There has to be a reason."

Terry stared at the wall behind Benson, no emotion, no trembling lip, hands now curled into fists in his lap.

"I'm gonna need details of her GP. And her dentist."

Nothing.

"Mr Shaw?"

———————

Benson returned to his car and took the chill out of the air by sitting with the engine running and the heater on. It wasn't a cold day, quite mild really, but being in Shaw's company for a little over twenty minutes had goosepimpled him quite badly. There was just something odd about the man. Okay, he reasoned, he'd suffered a bereavement, and was due a large amount of slack because of it, and he was dishevelled, silent. But his eyes were alive still; they refused for the most part to look at Benson, content it seemed to peer off into the distance, avoiding contact as though afraid of giving something away.

Benson shuddered and pulled out a Mars bar.

Two things happened just as his teeth contacted chocolate: a scruffy man who wore jeans and tatty trainers, a hoodie with a hole in the elbow, and who was carrying a small, wilting bunch of carnations, stood at the memorial and bent to add his own contribution; and Benson's phone began to ring. It was Khan.

Benson looked up as the hoodie began walking away. He left the phone ringing on the front passenger seat next to a Mars bar with teeth indentations, and climbed from the car. "'Scuse me," he called. The hoodie stopped and turned, and Benson produced his very best "I'm friendly" smile.

Chapter Eighteen

The Yellow Pages

— One —

"WHAT BRINGS *YOU* BACK here?"

Eddie stopped at the door leading into the SOCO office and said to the sergeant behind him, "In order to appreciate how good life is, it's often wise to remember how fucking shit it was before." Eddie barged through the door and heard the sergeant mention something about being as poetic as ever.

Peter McCain looked up from his desk as the door closed behind Eddie. He didn't smile a greeting, just mumbled, "What brings you back here?"

"Can't you be more original?"

McCain sighed and put down his pen. "Okay," he said, "fuck off."

"That's better; I knew you had it in you. Fat bastard."

"Look, I'm busy, what do you want?"

Eddie stopped himself from saying what he really wanted, he even considered rubbing McCain's nose in his failed attempt to get the job Eddie now had, but for once he pulled back on his ever-present desire to tell it how it was. Today he wanted information, and not a fight. "I just need to look at a report. Connor Road, Thursday."

"Burglary?"

Eddie nodded, "Yep."

McCain folded his arms. "Why?"

"It might have a bearing on a job I'm working on." Eddie could see the gears whirring in McCain's head; he could see him constructing and then deconstructing objections.

Obviously, he failed to come up with any that wouldn't sound pathetic – or he was genuinely busy. He nodded towards a terminal, "Log on, help yourself."

Eddie sat, punched buttons and watched a pixelated egg timer. The silence was crushing. He tapped his fingers. "You want a drink?"

McCain look up, squinted at Eddie. "Erm, yeah. Tea."

"Good. Make me a coffee while you're there."

The machine kicked in and Eddie selected a crime scene program called CIS, typed in the address and watched the story unfold. Terry Shaw had reported the break in when he and his wife arrived home from Cornwall at 6am on Thursday, finding the kitchen window badly damaged. Attending officers linked a previous call to the same address the day before, but they'd filed it as no further action, false call good intent, having attended the house and discovered the alarm sounding, the neighbours gathering, but no signs of forced entry.

Eddie attempted to bring up the SOCO's report but failed. He tried the password again, and again the screen laughed at him: Password Not Recognised. "How the fuck…"

McCain sighed and looked up.

"Why won't it let me in?"

"Because you're a knob."

"Well that was helpful."

And then help did arrive. The office door opened and Roger Conniston walked in, and threw his camera kit on the desk. "Eddie," he said, "what brings—"

"You do, as it happens." Eddie stared at McCain, grinned, and then turned to Roger. "Go back to the burglary on Connor Road."

"What, now? I've just got back in for a meal!"

"No, Jesus! It's like talking to Lloyd Christmas. In your mind, Roger, in your mind."

"Oh."

"What was she like?"

"Alright," he shrugged, "Atmosphere was a bit tense."

"What do you mean? Between them, just her, what?"

"I don't know; I got the feeling they didn't like each other very much."

Eddie thought about that for a moment, pictured Terry Shaw's face, the tears. "Okay, what about the burglary, anything unusual?"

Roger slipped out of his jacket. "If this is twenty questions, can I at least get a drink first?"

"No."

He slumped in his chair. "No, not really. Kitchen window was forced, laptop and some paperwork taken. Nothing stood out. Why?"

"Nothing stood out?"

"Well, if it means anything, the electricity box in the garage had been tampered with."

Eddie looked at Roger with interest. "Go on."

"The burglar turned the power off, and then cut the cable for the back-up alarm."

"But the alarm went off, right?"

"Yeah, why else would he cut it?"

Eddie nudged the computer mouse, password not recognised still on the screen. "Come here," he said to Roger, "bring the IBIS log up for me."

After a lot sighing and "aw, do I have to-ing", he brought the log up and Eddie read it while Roger made himself a drink. "'Time of call: 0228. Time of arrival: 0231. Alarm sounding. All windows and doors secure and in order. False call, good intent.'" Eddie turned to Roger, "How the hell could they not catch him in there?"

"There was no way that window was in order; it was butchered!"

McCain yawned and asked, "Why are you so interested in this?"

Eddie took a drink from Roger's cup, "Because," he said, "the woman he spoke to is dead."

"So?"

"So. Don't you think it's a bit coincidental that they're burgled, the alarm power is cut, the window is in good order yet it's actually butchered. And then she turns up dead?"

McCain's eyes screwed up and he shook his head, "It's unusual, I grant you. But my question stands: why are you so interested in this?"

"You haven't changed at all have you? You're still a short-sighted narrow-minded prick. It's my job. It's our job – all of us."

"Since when did you turn into the caped crusader?"

Eddie chose not to answer; he was being Mr Restrained this morning. Instead, he put on his jacket and turned to Roger, "Email your report to me, would you? And send me the log too." Eddie's phone began to ring, and the third sigh of the morning fell out of his mouth, "Roll on retirement," he whispered.

— Two —

The hoodie turned to faced Benson, a shifty, untrusting look in his narrow eyes. He nodded, "Yeah?"

Benson left the car door open, could even hear the phone still ringing on the seat, and approached the hoodie. "You know the Shaws well?"

The hoodie buried his hands in his pocket and took an almost imperceptible step backwards, checked left and right.

"DI Benson," he smiled again, adding an extra measure of reassurance this time.

"Known them over a year. I'm a cleaner—"

"You work for them? Sorry, what's your name?"

"Matthew Stone." He seemed to relax a little and the tension disappeared from his face, eyes became normal again.

"Can we go somewhere and have a chat maybe?"

"Why?"

"Please," Benson said. "Ten minutes."

Benson scraped the silent phone and the Mars bar off the seat as the youth clambered in. He tossed the Mars bar onto the back seat.

The phone began ringing again as they entered the café and ordered tea. Benson scowled at the screen.

"What do you want with me?" Matthew seemed calmer now, but still fidgety, "I have to get back."

Benson looked from the kid to his phone again. He switched it off, sipped his drink.

"You think Terry had something to do with this?"

"What makes you say that?"

"Why else would you bring me here?"

"Nice couple to work for?"

Matthew stroked the handle of his mug, appearing reluctant to talk openly, even though he was away from the neighbourhood, in neutral surroundings. He sighed and said, "They cancelled my contract. I don't clean for them no more."

"Why did they do that?"

"You tell me."

Benson winked, "Get caught with your hand in the till?"

"Fuck off. I might look like a scrote but—"

"Hey, I'm sorry, okay? I was just messing."

"Yeah, well I don't appreciate it."

There was a silence between them for a moment, and Benson took the opportunity to munch half a blueberry muffin and let the kid calm down a bit. "They didn't give you an explanation?"

"Paid me a month in lieu and showed me the door."

Benson finished off the rest of the muffin. The lad did look like a thief, it was true, but he had about him an air of honour, just the right amount of protest at the insult. "You ever pick up on something in there, maybe a bit of animosity between them?" Benson watched, but the kid had begun playing with his cup handle again. "Matthew?"

He looked up, something like a grimace on his face, "Up until recently they were great."

"Go on."

He shrugged, "I don't know. Something happened between them. Lots of arguments, conversations they didn't want me to hear. Big awkward silences. It was uncomfortable being there sometimes, and that was unusual, to be honest. They were great people, very kind to me and my Lucy."

"Lot of marriages hit difficulties—"

"No, this was different."

"Why?"

"They just weren't like that. The first week in April, they were great. I cleaned for them on the Friday, nothing unusual. When I came back on Monday, it's like a different fucking house." He shrugged again. "It never got better from then on; in fact it got worse. Not long after that he cancelled my contract."

"You think something happened over that weekend?"

"Ironic really."

"What is?"

"They went to a wedding."

After he dropped Matthew back on Connor Road, thanked him for his time and finished the Mars bar that had grown soft and a little hairy on the back seat, he rang Collins and headed for Fox's garage.

— Three —

Behind a large red tarp suspended from a rail, was a row of cars in the SOCO bay. Fox's had upgraded their status over recent months, doing more and more recovery work for West Yorkshire Police until most of their business was concerned with it. Pulling crashed vehicles from glass-strewn streets where culpability needed proving was excellent business, as was recovering vehicles that had been stolen and then found.

Benson swept aside the tarp, and he and Eddie ducked in as a wave of rock music thundered out. "Huggy!"

From behind the burnt Mercedes, a face smeared with soot popped up, and a row of white teeth greeted them.

"Turn that shit off," Benson shouted, following Eddie into the bay.

"Oi," Huggy wiped his hands on a rag and came around the car, "that's Thin Lizzy is that, *Killer on the Loose*. Quality."

Eddie lit a cigarette and blew it at Benson, "What you got, Huggy, I've places to be and people to annoy."

"Skid marks, remember. The brakes tested okay. But come an' look at this." They followed him around the car, its bodywork twisted and charred, and stood at the engine bay, crumpled bonnet propped up with a piece of wood. Huggy held up a blackened aluminium casting. "Okay, first thing, the tamper-proof seal on the throttle housing's been broken." Proud of his detective work, he smiled at Benson and Eddie.

They looked back with blank faces.

Huggy sighed. "This," he said, "is a throttle housing, right?"

"Get on with it."

"I bolted it onto a main dealer's demonstrator car, started the engine and the rev counter went straight up to three thousand."

"It was stuck open?" Benson asked.

"Screwed open. Somebody made the engine run fast deliberately."

"But surely she couldn't drive a car that was revving its arse off all the time?"

"No, no, this was done at the roadside. Two-minute job."

Eddie crunched the remains of his cigarette out, "It's automatic transmission, right? You could screw the throttle open, lean in and put it in gear—"

Huggy was shaking his head, "At that engine speed, it would've taken your head off before you could pull it back out of the car."

Eddie took out another cigarette, ignored the glares from Huggy and Benson, and similarly ignored the no smoking signs on the walls, and asked, "There isn't a coffee machine in here is there?"

Benson asked Huggy, "Is that all?"

"Nope, there's—"

"Wait a minute, the marks on the road."

"What marks?" Benson asked.

"If you'd stuck around at the scene, you'd know." Eddie walked to the back of the car. Near a steel pillar was a trolley jack. "On the road surface at the top of the hill. They looked like wheel-spin marks."

"They jacked the car up," Huggy rushed to the jack, "engaged 'drive' and then lowered the jack."

"See," Eddie looked at Benson, "I told you he wasn't as thick as pig shit."

"Ah," Huggy walked away from the jack, "but the throttle ain't your only problem."

"Oh good, just when I thought I'd got it sussed."

"Come here, look at this."

Benson and Eddie crowded in with Huggy at the open front passenger door where curtains of corroded wire hung down like an electrical veil from the tops of the door and screen pillars. The roof, removed by the fire brigade, was propped against the wall. Beneath the dashboard another thick nest of wires stared at them, laughing. Huggy looked at them, grinning like a fool, nodded to the wires.

"Ah yes," Eddie said, bewildered, "I see it now."

"One thing that bothered me about this was the extent of the fire. So I checked the inertia switch."

"Yeah, I'd have done that too."

"The what?" Benson asked."

"If a modern car is involved in a collision, the inertia switch automatically shuts off the fuel pump. Stops it from going up in flames." He looked at Eddie and Benson. "This one didn't."

Eddie, unlit cigarette dangling from his mouth, leaned in and caught the stench of acrid, toxic fumes, the smell of human flesh, and that cold flat unwelcoming odour of damp. He lifted a loom of wire, its insulation melted away, and looked at a small charred plastic lump.

"It's the relay for the switch," Huggy said, "it's been bridged."

Eddie massaged his temples. "Okay, I'm officially confused now. Stop being so cryptic and speak English."

Huggy's smile dropped away and he planted his hands on his hips. "What's up with you?" he said. "You're not looking too good."

"Few rough nights, that's all."

"Kids?"

"Just the one."

"How old?"

"Sixty-seven. Now can we get on or shall we all join hands and sing the Hokey Cokey?"

Huggy looked at Benson, Benson shrugged, nodded at the relay. "The bridge makes the relay useless." Huggy pointed at the base of the relay. "If the relay trips because the car is involved in an accident, the fuel will stop pumping. This bridge wire across these two terminals here on the relay, makes sure the fuel keeps pumping."

Eddie asked, "And could that have been done at the roadside too?"

"I can't see it, no. Getting to the relay and then bridging it would've taken an hour."

"She's not going to sit there for half an hour and watch someone tamper with her car."

"And," Benson said, "he's not going to expose himself for that amount of time out in the open."

Huggy took a step back, leaned against the wall and folded his arms, pleased it seemed, with the way his investigative skills had been received, "I can't tell you how or where this was done," he said. "But I'm telling you now, somebody wanted this car to burn."

Eddie lit the cigarette and began walking to the tarp, "Better play *Killer on the Loose* again, Huggy."

— **Four** —

Eddie watched Cooper as he sipped slowly on a frothy coffee, sitting behind his expensive, *expansive* desk like Lord of the Manor. He had two screens as well, two great big computer monitors staring at him, swish wireless keyboard and pictures on the wall. How the other half live, he thought. Eddie had one shitty monitor running off a steam-powered computer that worked when it felt like it and just shut down when it didn't, a keyboard with the letters A and T missing, a mouse that only worked if you hit it first, and the only things he had on his office walls were stains from the damp. Oh, and shelves of files.

Night and day.

And then he looked across at Benson, reclining in a chair, staring out of the window and chewing his nails. It seemed if there wasn't something in Benson's mouth, then he was anxious, or he just shut down like Eddie's computer. Maybe his jaw was hard-wired to his brain. His gut was making a valiant attempt to break out through his shirt, a hairy white mass gradually creeping through the gap between the buttons. Eddie retched and patted the cigarette packet in his trouser pocket.

"So what's he like?"

Eddie looked back across to Cooper, surprised he'd at last woken up and decided to address those who'd waited patiently, and completely coffee-less.

"Who?"

Cooper tutted, "Terry Shaw. What's he like?"

Benson sat up in the chair, considered an appropriate answer and eventually said, "He's okay."

"Thanks. *Hardly Wire in the Blood* is it?"

"I only know him as a widower, boss. He's distraught. I've never felt the need to doubt him. And he's not known to us, no previous convictions; not on any of our systems."

Cooper peered at Eddie through the gap between the two screens. "And I gather, because of the fire, there's no chance of knowing who tampered with the car?"

"Only a good detective could tell you that," he stared at Benson. "I'll get you the Yellow Pages."

Cooper sighed, and asked Benson, "FSS made a positive ID yet?"

"Yep. They weren't sure if they could get useable DNA from the body, but it seems they have. Samples from the PM match DNA taken from her toothbrush."

"And her fingerprints were on the Rohypnol bottle."

"Definitely her then." Cooper tapped his front teeth with a pen, "You think Terry Shaw could do this?"

"Nah. From what Huggy said, you'd need knowledge of that particular car, and you'd need access and plenty of time because it wasn't done at the scene."

Eddie piped up, "I want to go back to Terry's house."

"Why?"

"To have another look at this burglary scene; something's not ringing true here."

Cooper sat back, crossed his legs, "Go on, I'm listening."

"I went to see the SOCO who examined the burglary scene. He said the kitchen window was butchered, but the officers who attended linked it with a previous call, false alarm they said it was."

"And?"

"And the alarm wires had been tampered with."

"There's no suggestion the burglary and the car are linked. The car was outside."

Eddie stood up, "Listen," he said, "there's bad luck and there's bad luck. You ring for a pizza and dial the wrong number by mistake, you're guaranteed to get the only arsehole who thinks it's funny to take your order. But... burglary and murder? That's dying in hospital with the bedside TV stuck on Big Brother. It doesn't get any worse than that."

Cooper watched his thumbs spinning in his lap, then looked up, "Benson?"

"I have no idea what the fuck he's talking about."

Cooper sighed, "What do you think about him going back to the Shaws?"

"Let him go and see if he can find anything. Tell you the truth, I'm getting a strange feeling about it all too. I bumped into a kid who used to clean house for them, and he said things went off the rails after they went to a wedding. We need to dig a bit deeper, boss."

"Just let me take another look."

Cooper rubbed old hands through grey hair. "Tread carefully."

Chapter Nineteen

Fiery Jack

IT WAS THE KIND of day that, upon reflection as he drove home, Eddie derived satisfaction from as well as a stinging kind of guilt. Neither ruled, both were equals. The satisfaction came from trying his best to do what was right for the late and very crispy driver of a Mercedes Benz.

So, he'd done well by Mrs Mercedes, and tomorrow he hoped to do more good too, this time for her husband. But the stinging guilt came from two altogether different sources. One was his office, the people in it, his staff, were so disheartened that they avoided him. He wasn't totally stupid; he allowed himself a little credit in that respect. He knew when people body-swerved him, and he knew because he'd done it himself a thousand times, and still did it when he didn't want to be near certain people – usually those in authority.

But it saddened him that his staff – former workmates if you will – body-swerved him so much they were probably in a different postcode. He made it his mission to try harder to be liked. He decided, though, at least in the back of his mind, that he wouldn't promise. No one likes breaking promises.

And as he pulled the Discovery onto the small driveway next to his dream cottage, the one he almost left last year for an idyllic life in the country when he knew full well that idyllic life didn't exist beyond the wishes of the heart, he remembered part two of the guilt trip.

Eddie opened the front door of his cottage and stood on the threshold listening to a regular thump-thump noise coming from somewhere within. "Dad?" Guilt trip part two was the sixty-seven-year-old child he moaned to Huggy about. And he shouldn't have moaned at all because over the last twenty years, the sixty-seven-year-old child had been no trouble at all, and shit, he was here out of desperation – already decided upon. The least he could do for his old dad was to be sympathetic.

The thump-thump grew louder the further into the house he stepped, until, standing in the centre of the lounge, it was all-encompassing. Eddie lit a cigarette, exhaled, and headed towards the murder room – or perhaps he ought to rechristen it his dad's room.

He stood by the doorframe and grinned so wide that the cigarette almost fell out. A mirror leaned against the far wall in the same spot that a poor young lady had been shot to death not so long ago. The mirror was positioned in front of a treadmill, and on it, wearing very short shorts and a white vest with a tear up the seam, was Dad, running and panting for all he was worth.

"What the fuck…"

Charles hit a button and stopped running. He carried on panting, though, and turned around, ill-prepared it seemed for the ridicule he should have expected. "Just don't say anything."

"Moi?" Eddie belched smoke into the room with each gasp of laughter.

"And if you must smoke that filthy stuff, do it somewhere else, not in here."

"What you so worried for, you're hardly likely to die young, are you?"

"I mean it!"

"What the hell do you think you're doing? I hope you've got a defibrillator nearby."

Charles mopped at his glowing head with a tea-towel and finally stepped off the machine, barely able to stand upright. "I wanna look good again."

"Again?"

"Very funny."

"Anyway, that's the embalmer's job."

"Up yours," Charles muttered as he limped to the bathroom.

"What d'ya want for tea?"

"A good fry up!"

"I should've known," Eddie blew smoke into the room and then headed for the kitchen. "I'll give it two weeks," he shouted.

"Bollocks!"

And while eating his good fry up, Eddie suddenly realised his dad had moved in. There was no official ceremony as such, just the fact he'd ordered and had delivered in the first day, a running machine. The old guy was settled and he was happy; and it lent a certain pride to Eddie's evening. Yep, today had been satisfying on several fronts.

"So why did she leave?"

Eddie swallowed some sausage and noticed Charles had Brylcreemed his hair especially in honour of the fry up. "Who?"

"The woman. The one who stayed here with you."

"None of your beeswax."

"I'm only concerned."

"No, you're just nosey."

"How long did she stay for, this woman?"

"This woman was called Ros." Eddie stared at his dad, looking for a sign that he was sufficiently satisfied and would carry on dribbling food down his chin. Charles wasn't eating, though; he was looking directly at Eddie, waiting for answers.

Eddie put down his fork. "Her name was Ros, and she lived here for about eight months."

"What did you do to piss her off?"

"I used the tact and diplomacy I inherited from you."

"I get it, you were bossy. You were always bossy—"

"End of subject. Eat your bacon."

"You know," Charles whispered, "you can always talk to me. If you need a bit of advice."

"I don't need advice about women from my dad."

"What's that supposed to mean?"

"It means… Never mind. Just eat."

"Or if you just need to talk, get things off your chest."

"You want to be homeless again?"

"Just saying."

"Well don't."

The bedside clock told Eddie it was two-fifteen. And what's more, it looked bloody happy about it too. Eddie was far from happy. He thumped the mattress, punched the pillow again, probably for the hundredth time in the last two hours and sighed the best sigh of his day so far. Seeing as the heart palpitations had settled down since Ros had left, he thought that maybe he'd be granted a good night's sleep every now and then too.

Just went to show how much he knew, didn't it?

He thought he'd done a reasonably good job of putting Ros to the back of his mind until his dad had brought the subject up over dinner. 'What did you do to piss her off?' he'd asked. Normally a remark like that wouldn't bother him, and at the time, he didn't think it had, but now, when he should be several fathoms below the surface, the question was nudging him, keeping him awake wondering what the answer to that very simple question was. What *did* I do to piss her off? Or in simpler terms: Why did she leave?

He turned on the bedside lamp, saw the quilt was screwed up into a pile with the cover gaping open, twisted into a damp cyclone next to him.

All this had been resolved in McDonald's, or in the car park afterwards, but obviously it hadn't been resolved because she couldn't give a straight answer to that very straight question either. She'd done what his staff had done and body-swerved the issue, dressing it up in fancy terms like a politician would. So you go away happy, thinking everything's been addressed, and when you finally get home and sit down with a brew, you realise nothing has changed, no answers were proffered; and confusion still reigned.

And then to almost come clean as she boarded the train – to admit that the tale about her mother dying was just that – a tale. What was all that about? Why did she feel the need to lie? Why did she feel the need to leave so suddenly? And if she'd admitted the mother thing was a lie, what was the truth? And what else was she keeping from him?

Eddie climbed from bed and shook out two sleeping tablets from the near-empty bottle, swallowed them with water and lit up a cigarette. He lay back down, took a lazy drag and watched the smoke spiral up to the ceiling.

It was then that he heard a kind of shuffling from the hallway, and he turned his head to see Charles stooped in the doorway, looking as though he'd soiled his boxer shorts. Eddie belched out smoke and then struggled to laugh without coughing.

"What you laughing at, you moron!"

"What the fuck have you got on your face?"

Charles touched his face, his eyes widened before closing in resignation as he remembered. "It's a mud pack."

"A what? You look like Mrs Doubtfire."

"You got any Fiery Jack?"

"I thought I was being haunted by an anorexic pimp."

Charles feigned a smile, "Very funny." He groaned. "My back's killing me; have you got any or not?"

"You mean you didn't bring any with you in the two Eddie Stobart trucks you hired?"

"Fat lot of help you are!" He lurched into the room, trying to waft away the smell of cigarette smoke and giving up almost immediately. "Anyway, I'm leaving all my furniture there, the charity people are collecting it next week. I only brought the essentials, stuff I actually need."

"Really? You need a running machine?"

"That's different. I'm making a new start. Besides the treadmill, I'm travelling light. I've come to the conclusion that modern life is all about gathering as much shite together as you can, just so some poor bugger has to sort through it all when you're dead."

"So you're doing me a favour?"

"In a way. But I'm doing myself one too; I feel lighter without it all."

That got Eddie thinking. His dad had a good point there; he got the same feeling of being unburdened when the phone hit the bin.

"Zopiclone?" Charles rattled the pill bottle. "What are these?"

"Nothing. I just like the taste. Kind of like a Walnut Whip. But without the walnut. Or the whip."

Charles looked at the label, then glared at Eddie, "Here, these are—"

"Sleeping tablets. Yes, I know."

"Why are you taking sleeping tablets?"

Eddie groaned, drew another almighty drag on the cigarette. "This might come as a bit of a shock to you—"

"And don't get all sarky on me, it's a reasonable question."

"For a five-year-old, yes it is."

"Well?"

Eddie grinned, then began laughing. He couldn't stop, and pretty soon, he reached the point where he threw the cigarette into the ashtray and rolled off the bed holding his stomach.

Charles tutted, looked at the ceiling. "What?"

"You! How the hell can I take you seriously with a fucking mud pack on?"

Charles glared. "I'm concerned for you. Idiot. I've always been concer—" And he stopped there, swallowed and looked away.

Eddie stopped laughing. He sat up, retrieved his cigarette. "Really," he said. "It's funny then how I haven't seen you since we buried Mum. We stopped seeing you before Kelly and me got married."

"And you never called round if I remember rightly."

"Cos it was so frosty we needed thermal underwear!"

"It was your mum," Charles said. "She didn't take much to her. To Kelly."

"I met Kelly years after Mum died."

"I know that, I know that! But we still... we still talk."

Eddie flicked ash. "Seems like you didn't think too much of me either. I never heard a word from you after Kelly left."

"I know, I'm—"

"And Becca too." Eddie looked up at Charles, but somehow the face pack and the boxer short combo just didn't strike him as funny anymore. Charles blurred and then rippled. "Go to bed, Dad."

"We need to talk about this."

"Why? It's two o'clock, and besides, the Walnut Whip is kicking in."

"Son."

"Don't," Eddie spat. "This isn't a rehearsal for some Jeremy Kyle shit; I ain't prepared to dredge up a dead past just to make you feel good inside."

Charles sighed, shoulders slumped. "You want me to leave?"

"Just go back to bed."

"So have you got any Fiery Jack or not?"

Chapter Twenty

Doc Martens and Leather Gloves

IT TURNED OUT THE Walnut Whips didn't work. Not until it was time to get up for work. As he arrived at the office, Miss Moneypenny's chest was just a yawn-induced blur, and by the time he'd made it all the way out to Terry Shaw's house, his head was about ready to fall off and roll around the van's footwell.

The last hour had been a redundant microcosm of echoes and dodgy vision, and he was pretty sure he'd insulted at least two detectives and an SIO before he'd even blundered his way into G34 for his van keys. No one else had been there; it was blissfully silent and the urge to lock himself in his own office and grab half an hour's kip was brutally strong.

When the phone rang and Benson asked which SOCO had been dispatched to a dentist's surgery in Leeds, a posh one, he'd said, top-drawer dentist's, Eddie had sworn at him, then pointed him in the direction of divisional SOCO and slammed the phone down.

And on the desk, leaning against the wall, was a letter. A white letter, handwritten address, backwards sloping writing with big flowery loops, the kind a woman might write. Eddie didn't see it.

The van's heater was still not working, so by the time he stepped into cold morning air outside Terry Shaw's house, and endured a less than warm reception, Eddie had more or less woken up. Blinking felt like someone rubbing his eyes with 240-grit emery paper, and his brain had become a ball of tightly compressed cotton wool. Looking back on it, perhaps his opening line to Terry Shaw, 'Have you got any coffee on?' may have been the wrong approach. It could explain the frostiness.

Half a cup of coffee later and Eddie was standing in the kitchen alongside Mr Shaw who, now that he'd also had time to come around a bit, seemed a little more amiable.

"I don't get it," Terry said.

Eddie made no attempt at enquiring what it was he didn't get. Instead he looked at the 'butchered' window frame and marvelled at how a copper could walk right past it and say it was in good order. The plastic was gnarled, torn as though a drug-addled idiot had tried to break in with a chainsaw. He took out his brushes and flicked aluminium powder all the way around it.

"I don't understand why you're doing all this again. Are you saying the first man was incompetent?"

"Roger? Incontinent maybe, but he's good at his job."

"Do you think this," Terry nodded at the window, "has anything to do with my wife's death?"

Eddie had expected the question; it's exactly the one he would have asked about ten minutes ago. Unfortunately, he didn't have an answer prepared. "I don't know."

Terry snorted, a sign of derision that would have angered Eddie on a normal day doing a normal job. But today was different. Today he was trying to work out an answer to that very question. And so far he was drawing a fat blank – so his answer was in essence, totally correct, and Terry's derision understandable.

"Look, you're going to have to ask the coppers, all I do is make a mess in people's houses."

Nothing from Terry. Eventually, he opened a drawer, took out a cigar and said, "Do you mind?"

Eddie looked into his tired face and saw something he hadn't seen the last time they met: resignation. It was an acceptance of his wife's fate, and that of his own. Widower. It made him appear weaker, had given him a ten-year head start on where he was a few days ago, and it made Eddie swallow and offer a smile that began as pity and then quickly turned to one of respect. Without wishing to diminish Shaw's status, Eddie was almost a fellow widower – of sorts – and he knew how heavy those extra ten years were, especially when you were lumbered with them overnight without warning. "Only if I can light up as well."

Terry gracefully nodded, "More coffee?"

"Talked me into it." Terry got to work, and Eddie looked back at the window. "Anyone moved this window lock?"

"No."

"You keep all your windows locked when you're away?"

"The downstairs ones, yes."

Eddie stopped admiring the chainsaw sculpture, and stared up at the ceiling. And within minutes he'd set up shop in Terry's study, peering out at the conservatory roof below.

Terry entered the room, placed Eddie's coffee on the desk and leaned unobtrusively against the doorframe, flexing his right hand, rubbing at it with the thumb of his left. "Why are we in here again?"

Eddie took out a new squirrel-hair brush, charged it with aluminium powder, flicked the excess off and brushed along the inner windowsill. Like watching an image slowly develop on photographic paper, the outline and then the detail of several Doc Marten footwear marks developed on the white gloss paint. "Because of these," he said.

Terry came forward, suddenly interested, watching as Eddie photographed the footwear marks then lifted them with a large clear adhesive sheet.

Eddie took a sip of coffee, then opened the window and saw indentations that were consistent with a tool, probably a decent sized screwdriver – having being used as a jemmy between the casement and the frame.

"They came in here too?"

"Looks like it." Eddie took self-adhesive scales from the camera bag, got some good close up images of the marks before filling them with a silicon casting medium. He stood back and gulped on his coffee. "You said they went into the garage too?"

Terry nodded, "This way."

The garage was a cold concrete and breeze-block cube with a shiny, grey-painted floor. In it were mowers, strimmers, trimmers, petrol cans, a power wash, ladders dangling on hooks on the wall, a shelving system with a few boxes on it, yet strangely devoid of bric-a-brac; a freezer and a good-sized wine rack. Along the far wall ran a metal-framed work bench with a thick wooden counter top below the electricity cupboard.

"He used one of my screwdrivers for the switchbox cover. Turned the power off and then cut the siren wire."

"And where did the screwdriver live?"

"Toolbox under the bench."

Eddie stopped in the middle of the floor, crouched down and shone the torch across the glossy sheen of the garage floor, hoping to see footwear marks in dust, namely Doc Marten footwear marks. Not surprisingly there were none visible because the police, the alarm people and no doubt the Shaws, as well as Roger, had trampled whatever was there into oblivion. "So... I mean what did they take from you? It seems an awful lot of trouble to go to just for a poxy TV or DVD player."

"My wife's laptop."

"Did it have MoD secrets on it?"

Terry looked quizzically at him, "I'm not sure I follow."

Eddie walked to the bench and sank to his knees, brush in hand. "Well, this is the kind of thing you'd expect if there were high-value goods taken, but a laptop?" He kept the rest of the sentence to himself because it wasn't his place to say what he was thinking: that this whole thing seemed far too elaborate for a fucking laptop with someone's family tree or bingo sites on it.

Normally, burglars break in through the easiest point of entry and take something they've had their eye on, something they can see through the window – such as the lovely big flat-screen TV stuck on the lounge wall – or keys to the shiny new Merc on the drive; or they break in blind and have a look what's about. But if an alarm sounds, they scoot pretty quickly, taking the twenty quid that was left out for the window cleaner, or the iPad left out charging on the kitchen worktop.

In Eddie's experience, normal burglars never broke into a property, disabled the alarm, walked by the whizzo TV, the Merc keys, the twenty quid, but take time to root out a laptop to take. Laptops were ten a penny – go up to Chapeltown or Hyde Park, he thought, and the students are practically giving them away by leaving doors and windows unlocked and open.

In cases like these it was the information they held that made a laptop valuable. "Just wondered if there was some important information on your wife's laptop."

Eddie turned and saw Terry shrug. "Not that I'm aware of. She does voluntary work for drink and drugs rehabilitation – behind the scenes stuff, raising funds, buying, that sort of thing. Not sure what good that kind of information would do a burglar."

"Any famous or important people on that list?"

"I wouldn't know. She never spoke of it in specifics, just generalisations. Data Protection and all that."

Eddie gazed at the floor for a moment. Data Protection was important, he knew that. But unless you worked for the Intelligence Services or the SAS where those kinds of big secrets really were important, you could guarantee that almost every spouse of everyone with a bog-standard secret to tell would be indulged.

"You know…"

Eddie looked back at Terry just in time to see him deflate and look away, jangling the loose change in his pocket.

"What?" Eddie asked.

"Nothing."

"No. Go on."

Terry took a breath and it seemed as though he were mustering the strength to say what he had to say to this complete stranger, without having his chin wobble and the tears begin again. "I've never felt as selfish in my life," he said. "You cry hard because you look forward to the reaction you get. Do you know what I mean? You want people to know what you're going through, what you're feeling." Terry's eyes began to flood anyway, "There's nothing more comforting than being the star of the show."

Eddie swallowed. He was about to say something, anything, something mundane and harmless like "I know, yeah", or "It'll get better", when Terry turned and just walked away, closing the door from the garage to the hallway behind him. And then Eddie let out the breath he didn't even know he was holding, and mimed phew.

For a moment he dwelled on Terry's words and tried to unearth their meaning. He was sure there was one. How abstract was that! His wife was dead and he wanted to be the star of the show? Didn't make sense; but then it suddenly did. He, Terry, was the only one left now, the only one people could see, and he supposed it was important to him that people could see what he was enduring, to empathise.

But empathy was a talent not gifted to Eddie. He preferred not to think too long and too hard on other people's problems when he had a fair old bunch of them to go at by himself. And there, that one thought, that selfish thought, almost caught a hold before it slid down the vortex rubbish chute inside his mind to be lost forever. And it was lost; it didn't get the chance of a second hearing because Eddie was occupied with the newly replaced wiring in the electricity box right now.

Below it, on the dusty bench, was a screwdriver. It was part of a set, Terry had said; and Eddie crouched to see where the rest of the set lived. He powdered the under-bench cupboard doors, and the metal cantilever toolbox on the shelf inside, and found a healthy array of leather glove marks.

What lay behind the toolbox stopped him dead in his tracks.

Chapter Twenty-one

Boiling an Egg

COOPER SHOOK HIS HEAD, "There could've been 300 people at that wedding."

"Just let me check it out. If I hit a brick wall I'll bin it, but let me cover this." Benson stood rock still, keeping his eyes on the old man, listened to him sigh – a weakness he was eager to exploit, "Something went wrong with that relationship and it started that weekend."

"You don't know that."

"Matthew Stone said there was a dramatic change in their relationship—"

"You sure he isn't being dramatic? He's a cleaner, a sacked cleaner at that. He's not going to know everything there is to know about what went on in that house."

"He knows more than most!"

"And there could be any number of reasons why Shaw would do this, if Shaw did this. What's his motive? Maybe something happened after Stone was fired."

"Exactly!" Benson was beginning to warm up and felt uncomfortable in Cooper's office. He had little time for Collins, but when he'd said no one had any vision, well it was beginning to feel like Collins was enlightened. "The wedding's the obvious place to start. If nothing else, it gets me talking to people who know them a lot better than we do."

"I don't know."

"So what then?" Benson took a step forward. "Go on, what's your master plan?"

Cooper glared at Benson, fists resting on the desk, his cheeks throbbing as he clenched his teeth. And then he began to soften, and his shoulders slumped. He blinked, "Okay."

"Thank you."

"But don't spend all week on it. Don't get drawn into gossip, I need motivation. Nothing else."

"Yes boss." Benson hid his smile successfully, and watched Cooper groan into his seat.

"So where's Collins now?"

Benson slackened his tie and slumped in one of the chairs facing Cooper's desk. "He's gone over to Terry Shaw's gaff."

"Oh yeah," Cooper massaged the back of neck. "I'd forgotten about that. He doesn't believe in coincidence, doesn't our Mr Collins."

Benson shifted in his seat.

Cooper looked at him. "You do, I suppose?"

"No idea. It can't hurt to check it out though."

"And where's Khan?"

"I sent him to divisional SOCO. Liz Shaw's dentist has been burgled too."

Cooper raised his eye brows. "Coincidence?"

Benson shrugged, "We'll soon see."

"Keep me posted."

"Boss."

"I want you to go back there and see him anyhow."

"Who?"

"Lord Lucan. Who do you think?"

Benson said nothing, looked away.

"Offer him an FLO. This is going to be a long wait for him."

———

Benson drew up behind Collins's van and killed the engine, and thought on his latest action: go and see Shaw, offer him a family liaison officer. Shaw was a wiry old bird and despite the tears he'd cried and the soft creamy centre he liked to promote, Benson suspected he was hard as nails on the outside; not a façade as such, but something approaching it. He anticipated another cold reception and another glance at what it was like to have your heart ripped out and still be forced to carry on living.

He got out and locked the car. As he walked along the driveway to the front door again, he attempted and failed to straighten his tie, momentarily trying to make a good impression before realising he didn't care one way or the other. He had a job to do, and right now he was concerned with doing it, not fannying around on the periphery, hoping not to upset the walking dead.

Benson knocked. He waited only seconds before the door opened and Terry Shaw stood there looking reasonably human for a change. Except for the tears, he looked like any other millionaire who'd just got out of bed. "Mr Shaw."

"Inspector Benson," he mumbled, wiping his eyes with a handkerchief. "What is it today, more character assassination; would you like to sully my wife's memory further by telling me she was a drug addict and part-time prostitute?"

Benson sighed. "Can I come in?"

Terry opened the door wide and stood back, "Be my guest. There's already one of your men here. I can set up an office for you in one of the spare rooms if you like."

Benson followed Terry down the hallway, the smell of cigar smoke heavy in the air mixed with that familiar feeling of dread, a déjà vu moment from yesterday.

Once in the lounge, it seemed neither was inclined to sit. Just being civilised was sufficient without getting comfortable too. "When can I bury my wife?"

"We'll be as quick with our investigation—"

"When? I have a right."

"We can't release your wife's body until—"

"Until your investigation is complete, yes, yes. You said that already. But how long will it take? I mean, you've even sent people back to go over old ground so it seems you're not making much headway are you?"

"Old ground?"

Terry stared, not impressed by Benson's lack of knowledge. His eyes said something about the left hand and the right hand not talking any more.

"Where is he?"

"He's done the kitchen again. And now he's in the garage. Again." Terry folded his arms.

"I assure you we're working—"

"How did they do it? Come on, tell me, I want to know. And while we're on the subject, tell me why. Why did they do it?"

Benson's shoulders squared off and he stared at Terry Shaw. "Not interested in who?"

Terry glanced away, "That was my next question after you'd blundered your way through the others."

"We've appointed a family liaison officer for you."

"No, no, Inspector Benson. I'm not going to be mollycoddled by someone feeding me drips of irrelevant information—"

"It's not like that."

"Come on! You don't want someone looking after me, inspector. You want someone looking *at* me."

Eddie was on his way out of the garage and into the hallway when he practically fell into Benson.

Shaw was a few yards behind him. "Are you all done, Eddie?"

"All sorted. Thanks again." Eddie opened the front door and stepped out, admiring the way Terry made no comment as Benson bade him goodbye and closed the door. Together they walked up the driveway. "I see you made a good impression again."

"Shove it," Benson said. "What did you find?"

"Glove marks, and—"

"Knew it'd be a waste of time."

Eddie stopped at his van. "What you doing now?"

"I have people to interview, Collins, leads to follow up. Detective work, they call it."

"Ah right, you mean you've found a new coffee shop?"

Eddie drove away, and Benson watched him. "Tosser," he whispered.

———

Without even realising it, Eddie found himself in his new favourite Starbucks car park, a cardboard cup of coffee burning his hands.

It was his favourite because it was the only one he knew of. McDonald's, he'd decided, was out of favour these days on account of the bad memories they held for him. Starbucks – a new start.

It was his first real coffee of the day and with each sip he felt the tension receding and he also found his thoughts becoming clearer. He knew they were becoming clearer because at last he understood what the problem in the office was.

It was him.

Eddie lit a cigarette and wound the window down a few inches. There was no option other than to bow his head and apologise to his staff, try to rally a bit of team morale and inject some energy back into them. And he had to do all this and still seem viable as a boss, and not come over as weak. Eddie took a last drag on the cigarette, flicked it through the window and engaged first gear. Within the hour, he found himself trudging towards the office door. He paused, straightened his back, tucked his exhibits under his arm and strode forward with purpose.

He stepped into the office, a warm smile on his face, ready to begin building bridges. Sid was at his desk sipping something from a china mug, a small tea plate with an assortment of biscuits by his side. He stopped sipping every now and then to text someone. Beyond him was Kenny, sitting in front of his computer with his arms folded, face red, cheeks throbbing and a mound of exhibits cluttering the floor around him.

"Fuck's sake!" Kenny yelled. "Let's increase the amount of computer work we do, but keep the same old steam-powered computers we've been using since Jack the Ripper took an interest in open air surgery. Jesus!"

Kenny's outburst attracted Eddie's attention for two reasons. Firstly, he was surprised to see Kenny doing any work at all. Usually if Eddie was preoccupied, he'd be the one playing games on his phone or watching TV. And secondly, the reference to Jack the Ripper was at first amusing, then intriguing. It made Eddie think of Terry's garage.

James was sitting at his desk reading a newspaper.

"Sixteen exhibits to enter and this thing's boiling a fucking egg!"

Eddie coughed. "You need a hand, Kenny?"

Everyone looked up. Sid slowly put the phone away and James slid the paper into his desk drawer.

"Where've you been?"

"I've been working, Kenny."

"Why don't you work at getting us some new computers?"

"It ain't going to happen. Get used to it. We get everyone else's cast-offs, you know how it works around here. It isn't *CSI Miami*, so get used to it."

Kenny shut his mouth.

"James, help him instead of sitting there like a prick."

"I've been doing a statement."

"Very good, I'm happy for you. Now get off your arse and help your colleague."

Sid was smiling.

"And you," Eddie said, "get Duffy on the phone and tell him to get his arse in here in the morning, my office eight o'clock sharp."

"Yes, Eddie."

Eddie disappeared into his office and slammed the door. They all looked at each other. Then Eddie's door opened again. "Make it half eight."

"Yes, Eddie."

Eddie slammed the door again. Stood on the other side of it breathing hard. There, he thought, it's really not so hard being pleasant to them after all. I should try it more often.

"Eddie?"

Eddie sighed. He threw the exhibits on his desk and opened the door, remembered his smile, and stepped back into the main office. "Yes, Sid."

"I'm so glad you're in a good mood."

"Why?"

"I really need you to show me how—"

"Stop. Who said I was in a good mood? Why do you think Duffy's coming in tomorrow — he's a computer whiz-kid, he can show you how to do all that shit."

"Well, I was hoping—"

"Good," Eddie reached for the door handle, "we all need hope, Sid." He closed the door, picked up the phone and punched in the number for Killingbeck SOCO. As the phone rang, he shouted, "Sid!"

The door squeaked open an inch and an eye surrounded by black make-up peered in.

"Still upset with me?"

The eye looked away.

"Fix me a coffee, would you? Good and strong."

The door opened and so did Sid's mouth, ready with a strong protest, but Eddie looked away.

"Roger," he said, "it's me, Collins."

Sid closed the door.

"I went back to Connor Road."

"And?"

"Point of entry was the kitchen window, right?"

"Is this going somewhere, because I'm a bit—"

"Kitchen window, right?"

Roger sighed, "Yes. Kitchen window."

"The kitchen window was unlocked from the inside."

"They never told me that," Roger whispered.

"Did you ask? Did you even look?"

There was a long pause before Roger finally spoke. "You found another point of entry, didn't you?"

"Upstairs. Study window over the conservatory."

"So why make it look like they got in downstairs?"

Eddie licked his lips. "I don't know. And that in itself is enough to piss me off." The door opened and Sid walked in with a mug of dark coffee, gently placed it on Eddie's desk and waited, as though hoping for a thanks or at least a nod. A tip maybe? He smiled a little as Eddie covered the mouthpiece and looked at him, "Any biscuits?" Sid's smile faded and he left the office.

He said to Roger, "Don't worry about it, I've apprised Jonathan Creek. He's on standby."

"So why did you ring?"

Eddie sipped coffee.

"You asking for my opinion?"

"I wanted to see if you knew why they'd created a second point of entry."

"Strange you should say that."

Eddie leaned forward, "Why?"

He grinned. "I've absolutely no idea, but—"

"Useless piece of—"

"But one of your lot, a DS Khan, has been over here asking about a break-in at a dentist's I went to."

"And?"

"You're gonna like this."

Eddie slapped his desk, "How will I know if you never fucking tell me!"

"Doc Martens. And leather gloves. He took all the patient records. No computers or monitors, just the records. Didn't even root through the drawers for petty cash."

Eddie stared at the stains on his wall, but didn't see them. He saw the Doc Marten footwear impressions all over the sill of Terry's study, and he saw the leather glove marks on the toolbox under Terry's bench.

The phone said, "Eddie?"

Eddie gently put down the receiver and reached inside his jacket pocket for his cigarettes.

Why would the same guy turn over a dentist's and break into Terry's house?

Eddie opened the window and breathed smoke out into the early evening air. For a change, the Leeds skyline looked almost serene, and if he thought about it really hard, he could have been anywhere in the world right then: he could have been in Montreal or Sydney. And then he looked down at the spent cigarette ends on the flat roof below his window. And then he heard a series of sirens scream along the motorway beyond the clump of ill-looking trees and shrubs around the security fence, and realised there was no place on earth as shitty as Leeds. But at least it tried.

Eddie finished the cigarette, and had almost succeeded in sinking into one of those rare moments of thought, the clarity of which seemed to impart a knowledge he never knew he had. There were no sirens, there was no shitty skyline, graffiti, or the smell of petrochemicals any more. He was scraping away at the question, "Why would you break in twice?" and slowly getting towards that little treasure box where he knew the answers were, when the phone rang.

The smell came back, the graffiti slapped him in the face, and Leeds shouted at him.

Eddie sighed, closed the window and picked up the phone, "What?"

It was Khan, "Mr Cooper's office. Briefing."

"Fuck."

Chapter Twenty-two

The Letter

— One —

BENSON STARED AT HER chest for as long as he could safely get away with it. It was quite magnificent.

She cleared her throat.

His eyes travelled north. For a moment he blushed and looked away, cursing his inability to work out how long 'safe' actually was.

"She was a lovely woman."

"When did you last see her?"

"About six or seven weeks ago, at a wedding."

"Did she seem okay to you?" Benson looked at his notes. Her name, Louise Walker, stared at him as though taunting him.

He wondered if perhaps Cooper had been right; this was the third bored housewife he'd interviewed and none of them had any first-hand information about Liz Shaw. It was all hearsay, gossip, and bollocks, and all quite meaningless. The only plus side was the company – at least this company.

"Is this when I'm supposed to say she seemed fine, nothing out of the ordinary?"

Benson shrugged, slid the pocketbook away. "Supposed to?"

"There was something bothering her."

Benson's eyes were drifting south again.

"I remember that much. She seemed defensive, on edge about something. But that wasn't really until mid-way through the evening, about the time Terry was feeling off-colour."

Benson waited. "Go on, Louise."

"I don't know. I got the impression it was something to do with Claire, but I never got around to asking her."

He took hold of the pocketbook, "Who's Claire?"

Louise smiled at him, as though she thought he was staring at her chest again, "Claire Whitehouse. Or Claire Holden, as she is now."

Benson belched as he reached the door. He straightened his tie and pushed the bell. And he waited.

He stared at his reflection in the glass door, considered himself to be aging well – still had all his own teeth – but wondered why things had taken a downward spiral with the wife. These thoughts kept his focus on his reflection, when behind his back, a red Ford Escort crept into view, visible only for a short time as it passed the entrance to the driveway. It paused, the driver stared right at Benson, appeared to look at Benson's car parked at the kerbside, and then it drove away at speed as the door opened and Benson's reflection disappeared.

Benson turned to look as a late fifties woman, sophisticated, well-to-do, answered. From his jacket pocket, he slid the small well-worn black wallet and showed his ID. "Mrs Holden?"

The woman leaned forward, squinting at the wallet. "That's a Tesco Club card."

"What?" As he fumbled with the wallet, she smiled at him, and he said, "Ever wanted to press rewind?"

"Every day."

At last he found the warrant card and held it out for her inspection. "Sorry," he said. "DI Benson. Major Crime Unit."

"What's this about?"

"Elizabeth Shaw."

"Elizabeth? What's happened?" She swung the door wide, "Come in." She led him to a large, spacious and airy kitchen that was as cold and uninviting as a mortuary, and then asked again, "What's wrong with Elizabeth?"

"Please," Benson began, "sit down, I have some unpleasant news for you."

"Oh, you sound just like DCI Barnaby."

Benson didn't have a clue who DCI Barnaby was, but he waited until she'd perched her backside onto a dining chair before saying, "We think Mrs Shaw died in a car accident a few days ago."

Claire Holden brought a hand up to her mouth, and looked through Benson as though he wasn't even there. "Oh no… how did it happen?"

"Not sure yet, we're still—"

"What do you mean, you 'think' she died? Are you saying she's still alive?"

"No, no. I mean her identity hasn't been confirmed yet."

"How did it happen?"

"Mrs Holden, we're still conducting—"

"Yes, you're right," she drifted off again, "I know, you can't say anything more. She was a good friend. How's Terry?"

Benson sighed, "He's not good." He offered no more, simply waited until Claire's eyes had focused again, and said, "You saw her at a wedding six weeks ago. Apparently she was fine until you showed up."

Not for the first time today, he wondered if he was merely being someone's entertainment. It seemed as though she lived her days with little or nothing to keep her mind ticking over, and today she'd hit the jackpot – plenty to think about now. She looked like a woman perpetually waiting.

No doubt the hubby would be at work, or playing golf, or laying into the secretary at some crummy hotel, yet here she was, Claire Holden, would-be socialite, dutifully keeping the house neat and tidy for a husband who couldn't care less.

"I wish you'd come to the point, inspector, instead of beating around the bush." This didn't appear to be an angst-ridden statement. If anything, it was in jest. Her eyes sparkled as though she was enjoying tormenting her new playmate.

He studied her, noted how on the surface she was behaving as anyone would after hearing of their friend's possible demise, but beneath the veneer she didn't seem overly distraught. "Were you close friends?"

"Not really, no. Back in the day we were, but you know how the years amass and the exchanges grow fewer. Actually, the wedding was the first time we'd met in well over a decade. I'm sorry about it, her death I mean, of course I am." And then she looked at him, showed a glimmer of a smile, "But if you're expecting tears..." She climbed out of the chair again and returned moments later, sliding a plate of doughnuts towards him. They appeared almost instantly; it was as though she kept them handy just in case a fat policeman were to call. Benson's mouth watered.

"Hungry?"

"Always am." And as if to confirm it, his stomach groaned. "See?"

Before Benson had swallowed the first mouthful, she placed a cup of tea at his side and retook her seat, arms crossed at the wrists, staring at him, a sliver of playfulness lurking in her features. "She thought there was something going on between me and Terry. She came around soon after the wedding, accusing me of sleeping with him." The sliver grew into a smirk. "Alan blew his top."

"Were you?"

"Sleeping with Terry? No. Actually, we were friends, that's all."

Benson raised an eyebrow.

"It's true. Me and Michael, he was my boyfriend back then, would hang around with Terry and Liz, and a friend of his, bit of a lech, actually. This was way back in the seventies and early eighties.

"We were all students, well, apart from his friend—"

Benson held out a hand, hurriedly chewed, as he delved into his jacket for the pocketbook and pen. "You know the name of this friend?"

"No, sorry."

"What's Michael's surname?"

"Tailor."

Benson stopped writing. "Michael Tailor?"

"That's right."

"How're you spelling Tailor?"

"Is something wrong, inspector?"

"Spelling it like that?" He swivelled his notebook so she could see. She nodded, "Is anything—"

"Did he have any middle names?"

"Erm. It was a long time ago."

Benson stared at her.

"Oh, it was George, that's right. Michael George Tailor."

Benson wrote "George", then seemed to drift away, pen held in a hand that was doing nothing, eyes holding a gaze but seeing a dead man lying in a puddle.

"Inspector? Is everything alright?"

Benson snapped back, quickly smiled, and then reached for another doughnut. "Sorry," he said, "these are delicious."

She peered at him out of the corner of her eye, and Benson continued.

"Liz was with Terry at this time?"

"Yes."

Benson scribbled, dabbed away the sugar with a napkin as he did so.

"We were a tight-knit group, actually. Well you had to be, living in Leeds at that time. And after what happened to Shaney McGowan…"

Mid-chew, Benson asked, "Shaney McGowan?" The name rang a bell, but he couldn't place it.

Claire nodded, "Yes, we knew her. She was a bit of a live wire, actually. Very popular with the lads. Including Terry."

"Are you saying Terry and Shaney had a fling?"

"I don't really want to speak ill of her but she had a bit of thing for most good-looking lads." Claire shifted in her seat, looked uncomfortable about what she was about to say. She licked her lips, "One thing you should know, and I feel awful about it now, but…"

Benson eyed her. "Go on."

"Before the end of her visit, I told Liz about Terry and Shaney." She almost winced, and then busied herself examining her fingernails so she had an excuse for not looking at Benson. "I didn't want to but when she started shouting the odds…" She trailed off, staring into space.

"Don't worry about it," Benson soothed. "Liz didn't know about Terry and Shaney back then? At university?"

Claire shook her head, covered her mouth with her hand.

"What happened to her?"

"You don't know what happened to Shaney McGowan?"

Benson shrugged, "Why should I?"

"She was murdered."

"Unfortunately we deal with a lot of murders—"

"Not like this one, surely."

Benson looked confused, took a sip of coffee, and stared at her. "1979?"

"Mrs Holden—"

"She was killed by The Yorkshire Ripper."

* * *

Eddie slid into Cooper's office and saw the old man stretching his aching back. Khan, a wad of notes in his lap, was sitting by the window. Jeffery was frowning. He wore a frown whenever he saw Eddie these days, and Eddie sighed in response to it, wondering if this was a real briefing or just another chance to fuck him over and score points in front of the head.

Cooper gently eased himself back into his plush chair.

Eddie asked, "Where would I be able to get a chair like that?"

"Try Staples," Cooper smiled at him. "Now sit down." He looked at Khan, "Where's Benson?"

"Out interviewing bridesmaids."

"For God's sake. Get onto him, tell him I want him back here. We need his input on this—"

"He could be anywhere."

Cooper raised his voice, "I don't give a shit. He knew about this, he should be here." He stared at Khan, daring him to answer back once more. Khan took out his phone, and Cooper turned to Eddie who'd been forced to sit next to Jeffery, "You got anything exciting to tell me?"

"Er, yeah. Apparently the number of women having breast enlargements has risen by sixteen per cent in the last—"

"That would be a 'no' then, would it?"

Eddie leaned forward, elbows on knees, "The burglary doesn't make sense. I mean, the kitchen window was a false point of entry. He actually climbed onto the conservatory roof and forced his way in through the study window."

"Why?"

"No idea. I've never come across a burglar who'd conceal his access by creating a false one."

Jeffery cleared his throat, "So that he could come back again? Something he forgot to take…"

Khan, phone to his ear, snorted at Jeffery.

"That's the only explanation," Cooper said.

"Ah, no it can't be," Eddie said. "If he forgot to take something, how could he arrange the second point of entry? If he forgot to take something, he wouldn't know he'd need to return, would he? He planned it; he knew he would need to go back so that's why he protected his original entry."

"But what for?"

Eddie shrugged.

Khan looked at the phone as though it had grown testicles. Eddie stared into space, still wondering about the burglar's tactics, and Jeffery studied the dirt he'd found under a thumbnail.

"Jesus," shouted Cooper, "look at you. I don't know whether to brief you or ask you to sing Kum Ba Yah."

"Battery's dead!"

"Last of the boy scouts, eh?" Eddie held out his phone and Khan snatched it, dialled Benson's number and put the phone to his ear. "Can I have a chitty for Staples, Jeffery?"

Cooper shook his head, tapped his fingers on the desk.

———————

Benson stood in the hallway, licking the last of the sugar off his fingers. "You're sure, Claire? About Shaney McGowan and Terry Shaw?"

Claire folded her arms and stood up straight, pulling her cardigan a little tighter, "Like I said, she wasn't shy about flaunting herself." She took a step towards the door, ready to open it, when Benson's phone began to ring.

He took it from his pocket, saw the caller display, and switched it off.

"I can't believe I told her about them. I mean, I just blurted it out. A reaction, I suppose, to the confrontation." She paused. "I feel awful now." She opened her mouth as though wanting to say more, but then closed it again.

"Go on, Claire."

"You don't think it had any bearing on Liz's death do you? What I told her…"

Benson could see she was feeling awkward, the meandering steps towards the front door, the folded arms, twitching fingers. He opened the door himself and turned to her, "Liz definitely didn't know about Terry and Shaney back then?"

"Don't think so. Not from me, anyway."

"I shouldn't worry about it. Sounds to me as though their marriage was failing anyway – otherwise why come here and accuse you of sleeping with him?" Benson nodded, smiled his thanks and then stepped outside. Before the door closed behind him, he turned and said, "Oh, just one more thing."

"Yes?"

"Did you get those doughnuts from Asda or Tesco?"

— Two —

Jim tugged the black holdall off the passenger seat, threw it over his shoulder and then locked the Escort's door. He began walking across the pavement to his front door when his neighbour's door opened. Jim looked away, hoping to avoid eye contact.

"Alright, Jim? Haven't seen your Sam in a while."

Jim turned the key in the front door, hitched the holdall up his shoulder again, intending to ignore the neighbour. But then he had second thoughts. He made a smile grow on his face, and nodded a greeting, "She's probably wrapped around some other mug. She'll be back when she runs out of luck."

The neighbour laughed and walked off.

Jim opened the door and slammed it hard behind him.

— Three —

Eddie returned to Cooper's office with a fresh coffee and took up his original seat just as Benson, face an unhealthy shade of red, stumbled in.

Cooper pointed to a seat. "Here he is, rebel without a salad."

"Sorry, boss."

Khan kicked Benson's seat just as he was about to bend his knees, "Don't ever reject one of my calls again."

Benson stood up again. "Your call?"

Eddie smiled.

Benson crouched and leaned into Khan's face. "Speak to me like that again, boy, and I'll pull your fucking tongue out of your arsehole."

"Alright, alright, can we please get a move on before I die of old age?" Cooper watched Benson finally take his seat. "Right. We know Elizabeth Shaw had alcohol and Rohypnol in her system. Her GP prescribed Rohypnol in March for insomnia."

"You don't choose to take a relaxant before driving though, do you?" Eddie said.

Benson cleared his throat, "From what I've just found out – which is why I was late, by the way, a little thing we sometimes do called making enquiries! Things haven't exactly been rosy between Mr and Mrs Shaw recently."

Cooper folded his arms, "Go on."

"Six weeks ago she found out that Terry had slept with someone else while they were at university together."

Khan, keen to be back inside the briefing, and keen to make it appear that Benson's threat hadn't unnerved him, said, "University? That must've been over thirty years ago, Christ's sake."

Benson stared at him, grinding his teeth. "Does that matter? Betrayal is betrayal. You find out your partner's been lying to you all this time, it's going to hurt."

Eddie put down his coffee, "So what you're saying is he waits six weeks after the wedding, then kills her because she won't shut up about some student he dipped?"

Khan laughed, and Benson made a move to get out of the chair.

"Sit down," Cooper said.

Benson's chair creaked. "All I'm saying, boss, is she just found out he had secrets. Their relationship crumbles over time—"

"I can't see it," Eddie said. "Shaw is no mechanic; his nails are spotless; there's a toolbox under his bench with more dust on it than your Slimfast application. There's nothing to suggest that he tampered with that car—"

Benson shouted, "I'm just coming up with theories, alright? You want to come up with any better ideas, don't hesitate to join in. If not, give your arse a rest!"

"What's the name of this bird he was pumping?" Khan asked.

"Shaney McGowan."

"Okay," Cooper said, "go speak to her, see if she can't—"

"She's dead, boss. Murdered by The Yorkshire Ripper in '79."

Eddie spat coffee out. "The Yorkshire Ripper?"

"What?" Cooper asked.

"The dusty toolbox in Terry's garage?"

"What about it?"

"There were three books hidden behind it. I mean well hidden, tucked up nice and tight for some reason. They were all true crime books. About The Yorkshire Ripper."

Cooper's mouth fell open.

"I have something too, boss?"

Cooper turned to Khan, "Well go on, then!"

"You asked me to get Liz Shaw's dental records?" He cleared his throat, "I went to the dentist's, very posh place, top end service, over the far side of—"

"Get to the point!"

"The patient files. That's the only thing he took. The burglar, I mean. The dentist's was burgled. And that's all he took. The files."

"Coincidence," Cooper said.

"Nope," Eddie said. "It's not. I spoke to the SOCO who attended that dentist's, and he told me the burglar was wearing Doc Martens and leather gloves."

"So?"

"So? Don't you read reports?"

"Don't get cocky, Collins."

"That's the same combination that was found at Terry Shaw's burglary."

"Coincidence."

"Bollocks."

"Has the footwear bureau linked the scenes yet? Do the footwear marks belong to the same shoe?"

Eddie and Khan shrugged. "They've not said so yet."

"Until they do," Cooper said, "it's coincidence."

"Boss," Benson said, "it's no coincidence."

"You need to start opening your eyes, Cooper," Eddie stood. "Otherwise we're all pissing in the wind."

"You need to sit the fuck down, and let me think a minute."

"Boss?"

Cooper breathed out a long sigh, and then turned to Benson. "What?"

"One of the lads that Shaney McGowan and the other group of kids at university hung around with was a guy called Michael Tailor."

Cooper looked confused for a minute, and then his eyes widened fractionally, "The guy in the muddy footpath?"

"Yet to be verified, but there can't be too many Michael George Tailors around."

"It's him alright," Eddie said. "James found Doc Martens there too."

"Public place," Khan said, "bound to be Doc Martens there."

"I'm just saying, that's all. It adds weight."

"Weight, my arse."

Eddie rose from his seat again.

"Oh for Christ's sake, sit down!" Cooper's face was glowing crimson. "This is not musical chairs!"

Eddie said, "We need to get those books, boss. If Liz Shaw hid them there—"

"I said shut up."

"No you didn't. You told me to sit down, you never told anyone to shut up." Eddie took a sip of lukewarm coffee, blew a kiss at Khan.

"Well now I'm telling you to shut up."

"What harm can it do? Benson can keep him talking, I'll go get the books."

Cooper rubbed his chin, "I don't know. Terrence Shaw has been very cooperative. If you start badgering him, he'll get nasty."

"Aw bless," Eddie said. "Last I heard we were investigating a woman being burnt alive, and you're worried about a suspect getting nasty?"

"We have to look at it, boss."

"Let me think."

"Those books were hidden. I don't know why, but if there's something in them relating to Shaney McGowan, we need to see it."

Cooper tutted, rubbed his forehead.

"You said yourself he was scared of something," Benson said. "We could be there first thing, when his guard's down."

"So far that's two people dead from the same seventies crowd at university. Terrence Shaw is another one of that crowd."

"That's right," Benson agreed. "We've got Liz missing or dead, we've got Michael Tailor dead—"

"So who's outstanding in this crowd?"

"Terry Shaw, Claire Holden. And there's someone else too, but Claire didn't know his name. He used to hang around with Terry."

Cooper drummed his fingers and that was the moment Jeffery chose to rejoin the meeting. "Sorry I'm a bit late—"

"A bit," Cooper said. "We're done. You missed it."

"Boss," Benson said, "we need to warn Claire Holden."

"About what?"

Eddie almost laughed, "That her old friends are being popped off one by one!"

"So what, you want me to put a guard on her twenty-four-seven? On yer bike."

"She should be informed."

"Then inform her," Cooper was sighing, shoulders sinking closer to the desk. "And if you must, ask Terry Shaw about this missing friend of theirs."

"And the books?" Eddie stood firm, he was resolute, determined not to leave this office until he'd got an all-clear to get those books.

"Tomorrow morning," he eventually said. "Now go on, piss off."

Benson and Eddie marched for the door.

Khan watched them leave. "Boss?" he raised his hand, like an unsure student, "what do you want me to do?"

Cooper looked up and whispered, "Get out."

Back in his own office, Eddie sat down in his squeaking chair with a hot mug of stolen coffee in his hands. And that's when he spotted the envelope on the desk. The white one, partially covered now by files. He stared at it for a moment before putting the coffee down. There was something about the letter that stopped him thinking about the job; it pulled his attention to it, and when it snagged his eyes it snagged his brain also, and Eddie nearly fell of his chair.

The handwriting, that's what caught his eye. It was familiar. "Ros."

He reached for the letter, examined it, studied it and noticed the postmark was from almost a week ago. "Nottingham. Fuck's she doing in Nottingham?"

And then he put it down. He slid it away with the very tips of his fingers.

Eddie pushed his chair away from the desk until it hit the wall behind him. His mind filled with horrors too numerous to contemplate. The horrors filed themselves, sorted themselves, discarding the outrageous ones, the improbable ones, and the impossible ones, until he was left with a gnawing fear that refused to abate. "She's found someone else," he whispered. "No, that's not it. She'd have told me that face to face if she had." A small childish gasp expelled itself from his mouth, "It was never her mother who was dying… it was her."

He tried to cross his legs but the desk got in the way. So he put his fingers to his mouth instead, began chewing. In the end, Eddie simply reached for the envelope, went straight past it and opened the cigarette packet instead.

Leaning out of the window, absorbed in remorseless thoughts, he puffed away, and knew that he couldn't carry on unless he knew. The catatonic state of his mind would endure for as long as he felt disinclined to stay out of that damned envelope. It was the horrors that stopped him, the fear of what he might find inside.

He flicked away the cigarette, longed for a whisky, but drew himself back inside and closed the window. Retook his seat.

It stared at him.

Chapter Twenty-three

There's no Such Thing as Fate

— One —

"How was work?"

Eddie stared at him. "Did we get married while I was out?"

"I can't take an interest now?"

"You could if it was genuine. It's the kind of question a spouse asks, just so they can tick the 'I-give-a-shit' box."

"You're in one of *those* moods, eh?"

Eddie laughed, and a couple of faltering beats from his heart stopped him. "I'm not in any kind of mood. Yet." Maybe it would be a good time to hunt around for a second-hand defibrillator for himself.

"Tea's nearly ready," Charles left the lounge. "Chicken and chips with beans."

Eddie smiled to himself and kicked off his boots. It really was just like being married. And that was the trigger to take him right back to Ros again and the letter she'd sent to him. It was folded, unopened, in his back jeans pocket. It was a cowardly thing to do, he'd decided. There could be nothing in it that she couldn't have said to his face. Except…

The house smelled of roasting chicken, and that was the last meal he remembered her cooking for them. She was so natural, nothing gave away the game going on inside her head, the way she was planning just to leave him. And she'd even kept a clear mind for the occasion; no wine with her meal, just bottled water. He didn't think it was strange at the time, but now he did. She must have been fretting inside, a bundle of jagged nerves ripping into her self-confidence; a thousand questions gnawing at her decision. But hats off to her, she'd gone through with it.

He remembered the give-a-shit box, and how she'd pretended to give a shit and ultimately failed to give a shit. That box was right next to the competition box. The competition box was usually opened just after asking the how-was-work question, and it was there to outdo him. Whatever his day had given him, hers was always worse. If a pigeon had shat on him, she'd been shat on by two. It was a natural thing; it was a cry for sympathy. And that's where Eddie's big failing was: sympathy. He'd never been good at expressing it… whoa, just a minute, he thought. Here I am not only blaming myself, but inventing new and crooked ways to blame myself.

Eddie held his head in his hands. All those things he'd just thought about Ros; they were all bollocks. She was a saint, and he was saying bad things about her to lighten the load, and to make losing her easier to deal with. He identified that, and he tagged it, and he filed it. Ros wasn't that bad really; she wasn't into mind games in the same way his wife, Kelly, had been.

As he went into the kitchen, he began blaming himself for her leaving too.

Charles handed over the plate. Steam rose from the chicken, but the beans looked like they'd been scooped straight from the tin. "Thanks."

Charles thrust a knife and fork at him. "You okay, son?" Eddie smiled and walked back into the lounge but Charles didn't follow him.

He sat, put the plate of food on his lap and waited. Still nothing. "Dad?" No reply. Eddie sighed, dumped the food on the coffee table and went back into the kitchen.

Charles had his back to him, staring out of the window at a landscape greyed and robbed of detail by the onset of a dusk with an accompanying mist that glided up from the river. Charles's reflection in the glass looked odd, as though his face was shiny.

"What's up?" Eddie made no attempt to touch him.

"I'm fine." Of course that was a lie. His voice was thick, creaky, and off-kilter, as though he'd tried hard to sound natural and neutral, maybe even happy. But it came out all flat, like a crying man trying not to cry.

"If you're going to stay here," Eddie said, "then you're going to have to learn how to cook the beans. Okay? These are stone fucking cold."

"Sorry. If you bring them back in, I'll—"

Eddie sighed. "Dad. What's up?"

Still he didn't turn. "It'll only take a minute to warm them—"

"Stuff the beans. What's the matter?"

There was a substantial pause before he answered. "The house contents weren't insured. Not that I could replace the... the rings anyway. And the watch. You never can replace sentimental things, can you? I mean, it's not the things themselves that holds the value, is it? It's the memories, see." Charles rubbed the hem of his cardigan between his thumb and index finger. "It's the memories that handling them would bring back. Now that I can't hold them and feel them, the memories have gone. It's like they stole those too." His chin wobbled. "I feel violated, son. I'm not sure I could ever go back there. Not now. Not after that. Even if the insurance company fixed the damp, put me a new boiler in, and redecorated the place, it'd still feel... I'd still feel..."

"Vulnerable?"

"Easy prey. But not only that. I could never settle at night knowing they could be back. I'd be a nervous wreck."

"So stay here. I thought we'd been through all this." They hadn't. They'd grazed the topic only slightly and Eddie had assumed all the things that went unsaid were already agreed upon.

"Listen, son," Charles finally turned, and in the dazzle of the fluorescent light, Eddie could see the puffy eyes and the dampness beneath them, and the slowly receding bruises, "I haven't got no idea how long it'll be before it's repaired. It might take years, by which time, the bastards will've broken in again, or some bleeding squatters will have taken over."

Eddie swallowed, thought of reaching out to his dad, but he didn't because it would have made it worse. The last thing someone blubbing needed was a hug. He folded his arms and slowly grew angrier.

"I'm sorry. I should—"

"You should come and sit down and learn what it feels like to eat cold beans." He was smiling, and he hoped Charles would do likewise, but he didn't. His cheeks grew wetter. And now, well disguised though it was, the anger was beginning to glow in Eddie's chest.

"You don't seem to get it. I could be here years."

Eddie shrugged, amplified the smile, "That's fine with me." He stared at his dad's face, tried to read it to see if he'd got the message wrong somehow: maybe he was saying he wanted to borrow the money for the house so he could move back in as soon as possible; perhaps he hated being here.

But he took notice of the nuances in Charles's eyes and the worried cardigan hem, and eventually they confirmed it: he was shit-scared to go back. Those arseholes, the ones who were slowly making Eddie angrier and angrier, were the ones keeping Charles from making the decision to stay – from accepting the invitation to stay of his own volition. They'd not only robbed him of his wedding ring, and even of his dignity, they'd robbed him of his freedom to choose too.

This explained many things about his dad that until now he'd considered as eccentric behaviour. The running machine, and the face packs, of Charles saying he wanted to 'look younger'. Of course he did; he wanted to feel younger too. He wanted to be able to defend himself against those arseholes.

Eddie decided to save that particular conversation for later, but it had to be aired.

And now Eddie squeezed his hands into fists and rushed at Charles.

Charles took a step back and Eddie embraced him until the old man cried properly. Eddie ground his teeth, kept to himself the prickle of hatred that tingled the skin on the back of his neck; hatred towards those people who'd made his dad cry. "Tell me about the robbery again, Dad. All of it. Don't leave anything out."

— Two —

Though it was dark, Eddie could see the old place quite clearly. The street lamp was directly outside his old bedroom window, just as he'd remembered. Eddie had always been a complainer, he kidded no one about that little fact, least of all himself – and what he remembered complaining about most of all in his teenage years was the streetlamp shining in through his bedroom window.

It seemed a trivial thing now. But back then it had been as serious as a nuclear disaster – it lived in Eddie's world and it consumed him. It was his power play, his way of pushing the boundaries, of stretching his adolescent muscles. After all, his parents didn't care, he'd decided; they thought he was just an angry teenager with nothing better to do than sleeping and playing with himself. That's what he'd assumed. The truth, he'd later learned, was that his folks couldn't afford blackout curtains for his room. And when he found that out, Eddie felt less than six inches tall. He felt appalled by his selfish behaviour.

On the small driveway was a skip with rolled-up carpet draped over the side like a giant's tongue, and beneath the skip was a stain from the water that had trickled its way out.

He flicked away the cigarette, tried and failed to flick away that constant needle of guilt that stabbed him each time he came back here – which was rarely. He took out his torch, turned the key and squelched into the hallway.

"Oh my good God." He stared at the lounge, at all the wallpaper hanging off in strips, water still dripping from the light fittings. The ceiling had collapsed over in the corner where his mother's seat was. Her Lladró figurines lay smashed on the hearth, broken plaster all around them.

Of course, they'd turned the electricity off, and it seemed at last the insurance company had pulled their finger out, judging by the three dehumidifiers stacked in the kitchen, waiting for a time when the electricity could be turned back on, or until they could arrange for a generator to be rigged up. In the meantime, the place was cold, obviously as damp as a leaking cellar, and echoey. Hostile. It felt nothing like home now; all the pictures had been taken down, the ones that hadn't just pulled their hooks out of the damp plaster anyway; and the whole house had a cloying, musty smell.

Eddie felt a chill as he mounted the bare wooden stairs, the torchlight bouncing from wet wood, tracing the dried stains of long-dead rivulets that had cascaded down the walls and stairs. As he neared the top, he saw a huge black hole in the ceiling, bare wooden laths like a dead animal's ribs exposed to the torchlight, and fingers of wet loft insulation hanging down to snare the unwary.

He understood why Charles had been so teary about it. Your house was your safe place, especially when it had been your home for more than forty years, and to see it like this was seeing a sick relative with only a fifty-fifty chance.

The landing was no better, again bare swollen wood, shiny in places, buckled doors and frames, spawled plaster and bare brick. Not really a home any more, just the memory of one.

Eddie stood in the doorway of his old bedroom, marvelling at how small it now appeared to him and how orange the wallpaper was thanks to the damned streetlamp. And, he laughed, how bloody horrible the wallpaper was! Things back then seemed so normal, but now... now they seemed like bad taste and poverty – always a bad combination.

Ironically the best room left in the house was the bathroom, barely touched by the flood of water from above. And when he entered his dad's room, he found that this too had fared quite well. The boiler was in the attic, directly above the stairs, and so most of the damage was in the stairwell and the hall ceiling. The whole house reminded him of the aftermath of a fire scene after the fire brigade had extinguished the blaze and rushed off to the next three-nines call. All they left behind was the dripping of cold, black water and the smell of destruction. Here it was the same, torchlight scattering from puddles, echoes of wet footfalls, and unpleasant smells.

This was the room they'd hidden his Christmas presents in. Their wardrobe floor was false, raised off the floorboards by a couple of batons screwed to the sides. It hadn't been meant as a secret hidey hole, just a way of removing the lip inside a homebuilt structure so shoes would be easier to put away. But he'd found them, every year for a dozen years, hidden presents, little parcels of love from an odd couple to their equally odd boy.

Eddie blinked, and wiped the memory; he wasn't here for a comforting trot through an old family album.

The bed was still there, covers pulled back, probably not even touched since Charles got out of bed the night they robbed him. In the corner, next to the wardrobe was a musty old green armchair that his dad would snooze in, and a dressing table with one of those ornate wooden chairs, something like a Louis XIII or whatever, standing before it – far too ornate for a house like this, but perfect for making Mum feel like a queen. On the dresser were the three mirrors that his mum used as she put on her lippy and sprayed lacquer on her hair. Small doilies lined up on the mahogany, hair brush, scissors. Memories lay behind dirt-smeared glass as though hiding from the present.

Eddie swallowed.

He tried not to see her in her dressing gown, or in her slip if it was summertime, smiling at him from each of the three mirrors.

He stepped closer, rested a hand on the back of her chair like he used to when he was a petulant teenager, and he cast his torch one last time over the dresser, letting the light bounce from the bevelled mirrors and smear rainbows across the ceiling.

His mood had mellowed. The house was a sad and damp crypt of a long-dead childhood, but Eddie chose to glide through now and into the past where a childish happiness had reigned for a while. He looked at his mum, returned her smile and felt the warmth of her hand on his, "What's up, Eddie?" she'd said.

With a croaking voice, he said, "I miss Ros, Mum."

"But that's good, son. Once you've finished missing her, you can let her go and rest easy."

"But I want her back."

Steph smiled at him again and shook her head slowly. "No," she whispered, "you wanted her because there was no one else around, silly. You wanted her because it seemed like fate had drawn you two together, when really it was a case of wanting what had been denied you both for so long."

Eddie looked away, hating the sound of truth; it cut an even bigger hole, a deeper hole, than the guilt ever could.

"Remember Eddie, there's no such thing as fate."

"She lied to me."

Steph laughed, "Of course she did. She wanted to protect you."

"But, Mum—"

"Miss her. And then let her go."

He closed his eyes, and drew in a long trembling breath. And when he opened his eyes again, the spectre of Steph was gone.

And then he saw it.

Chapter Twenty-four

The Books

— One —

THERE WAS SOMETHING SO underhand about this that it brightened Eddie up. Slightly. He appraised Sid as he approached, saw him blowing onto his nails again, inspecting them in the glare from the overhead lights. Today, he wore black from top to toe. Leather, the whole ensemble. "What have you come dressed as today?"

Sid did his best pout and ignored him thoroughly.

"You look like a roadie for Kiss."

"This is the height of fashion." Now Sid studied Eddie, and for a moment Eddie felt quite uneasy. "You look like a tramp."

"Phew, for a minute there I thought you were going to insult me."

Sid squinted, "I'll try harder next time."

"Here," he handed over a small plastic universal container.

Sid held it up to the light and tried to rattle it. "Urgh, chewing-gum."

"Get it off to the lab."

Sid placed his hands on the desk and looked up at Eddie. "What's the small word?"

"Now."

"The other one."

Eddie appeared confused. "Twat?"

"Please."

"You're welcome," Eddie strode away.

After Sid had finished tutting, he shouted, "What crime is this relating to?"

"I don't know. Littering. Just get me a name and address."

— Two —

Eddie slammed the van door, looked up at the sky that spat rain in his face, and promptly stood on a snail. The crunch made him wince. He pulled another drag on the cigarette and grabbed the kit box from the van. Benson waited by a gatepost, hands deep in his pockets, watching, brow creased against the rain.

"No, you stay there," Eddie said, "I can manage."

Benson didn't move.

"Tosser," Eddie hurried past him and up the gravel of Terry Shaw's driveway, squinting against a steady blizzard of blossom. Behind him, Benson approached.

"You let me do the talking. Do what you have to do, and I'll keep him on our side."

Eddie puffed on the cigarette. He'd seen Benson's attempts at diplomacy before, even had to photograph the injuries that it had caused. This was going to be good, he thought.

Benson rang the doorbell. "This is what I'm good at. You won't hear a peep from him."

The door opened, and Eddie flicked away his cigarette.

Terry, hand shaking on the door handle, stood in the relative shade of the hallway, his slippers and nose poking out into the diffused sunlight. Eddie was still getting wet and the blossom sticking to his face and hair made him look like an extra from some shambles of a wedding party. "And today you're here because..?"

"Mr Shaw," Benson began. "Can we come in?"

"No."

Eddie nodded, this was going well. He peered around the door and met Terry's anguished stare. "Sorry to drop on you again," he said, "I know this is pretty shitty."

Benson sighed.

"If you could just let us in out of the rain before his clothes shrink and we have to take him to A&E again, I'd appreciate it."

"What do you want, Eddie?" Shaw had the courtesy to step aside, and Eddie wasted no time grabbing his kit and marching past.

Benson followed rather more cautiously, and it was he, Benson, who caught both barrels from Shaw's never depleted arsenal. "You've been here every day since it happened!"

"I know, Mr Shaw—"

"I've given you free run of my house, and still you're no further forward. Still," he shouted, "you won't let me have my wife's body." He pointed out through the open door, "You should be out there!"

"You were right. Not a peep."

Shaw faced Eddie, "What?"

Benson mouthed, 'wanker' at Eddie, "Mr Shaw, we are doing—"

"I want to see Mr Cooper. This is going too far."

"We'll be out of your way in no time."

"Give me his number!"

Eddie closed the door to the garage behind him, and the ferocity in Shaw's voice dropped to being merely violent. And though he was here on a serious mission, Eddie found it hard to muffle a giggle. In fact, it was one of those occasions when Eddie found it nearly impossible not to laugh so hard he could have pissed his pants. The more he thought about how serious it was, the more he wanted to laugh. And the more he heard Terry ripping strips off Benson, the more he wanted to howl. "Not a peep," he laughed as he headed to the work bench.

And he continued with little fits of giggles as he rigged up the camera and photographed the bench, the cupboard beneath it, and then the toolbox. Gently, he pulled the box aside and photographed the books as a collection, and then one by one as he pulled them out and fingerprinted them. From each glossy cover, he developed several good quality marks which he lifted with rubber tape, labelled, and dropped into a small brown pre-printed envelope.

He took from his kit box three large translucent bags, and lowered each book into its own bag. And even after all that, he couldn't help snorting at the wonderful shade of crimson Benson's face had turned out in the hallway.

And then Benson himself walked into the garage. "What have you found?"

"*Famous Five Go Berserk*, Stephen King's *The Shining*, and a well-thumbed edition of the *Kama Sutra*." He slammed the lid of his kit box, nodded towards the hallway door. "Jack Nicholson's quiet."

"I gave him a big cuddle."

"Smothered him then."

"Come on, let's get the fuck out of here."

"Loved your appeasement tactics."

"Shut up."

When Terry walked in soon afterwards, the atmosphere turned heavy and sullen, almost prickly, as though there was a storm brewing. And Eddie almost laughed again.

"What are they?" Shaw pointed at the books in the evidence bags.

Eddie stood and humbly whispered, "I can't tell you that."

"What are they?"

"Evidence," Eddie said.

"Of what? What's he talking about?" Shaw turned to Benson. "What's he mean 'evidence'?"

"Come on, I'll write you a receipt." Benson began walking to the door, but Shaw stood still.

"But I don't understand, he said he couldn't tell me, but I have a right to know."

"No. You don't have a right to know. Let's get that bit perfectly clear," Benson's tone as well as his raised voice said that he was through being Shaw's punch bag, and he was through playing softly with him. "I can tell you they are books, but that's all I can tell you, and all I *will* tell you. For now."

"For now?" Shaw looked puzzled. "Why for now?" He looked down at Eddie, "What's he mean 'for now'?"

"Mr Shaw."

"What's he mean?"

"Mr Shaw!"

Terry Shaw, as though slapped, suddenly came to, turned to face Benson. He whispered, "But I don't understand."

"Cast your mind back to your university days for me," Benson closed in, hushed his voice slightly. "You knocked around with a lad. You two were very close."

Shaw looked confused again.

"What was his name?"

Benson waited. Eddie paused in packing away the camera, that prickly atmosphere intensified, and Eddie chose to look at the floor rather than feel Terry Shaw's suffering.

"I have no idea who you're talking about."

Benson counted on his fingers. "There was you and Liz, there was a man called Michael Tailor and his girlfriend, Claire Whitehouse. And there was someone else, wasn't there? A friend of yours."

The silence grew until it was almost deafening. Eddie was getting cramp.

Terry Shaw shook his head, "I'm sorry, I have no idea who you're referring to. There were lots of friends back in those days, and even if I knew who you were talking about, I probably wouldn't recall his name. I mean," he almost laughed, "I hadn't remembered Michael's name until you just mentioned it." He swallowed, looked from Benson down to Eddie, and then walked out of the garage.

Eddie didn't feel like laughing any more. Now he felt like punching himself in the stomach for finding Terry Shaw's situation in the least humorous. Once back at the van, he lit a cigarette and felt ashamed.

— Three —

The door buzzed before Eddie had even got close, and single swipe of a boot opened it easily. With arms full of exhibits and his camera, Eddie was glad of the help. From the reception desk, Miss Moneypenny smiled, "Hi Eddie. Been busy?"

Eddie nodded a greeting at Moneypenny's chest, and headed for the double doors, "What on earth made you think that?"

Eddie pulled on a pair of gloves and slid the first book out onto a sheet of brown paper that covered his desk. The title read, *The Trail of The Yorkshire Ripper*.

He sat down, swallowed as though nervous, as though this were a significant step along the path as they searched for the Holy Grail. He opened the book, flicking through pages at random, stopping every now and then to read a particular paragraph or study a particular photograph. Eventually, he placed the book back into its bag, and took out the second: *Why They Missed The Ripper*. This one shared some of the gruesome pictures of the first, but was less scientific in its approach, more dramatic. But another thing it shared with the first book was that nothing leapt out at Eddie. No significant clues.

He sighed and threw the book back in its bag, and unceremoniously now, tipped out the third book: *The Ripper Years*.

More photographs of more gruesome murder scenes or of property relating to murder scenes. The caption below the one that now grabbed Eddie's attention read: 'Evidence Overlooked'. Eddie bent to have a closer look but could see no better. He looked around for the magnifying glass, his face crumpling, screwing up the longer he searched, eyes squinting. Eddie leapt on the door, yanked it open and shouted, "Sid!"

Sid arrived promptly, a little out of breath, and said, "What's up?"

"Magnifying glass." Eddie stared at him.

Sid said, "Excuse me."

Eddie said nothing, just stared at Sid.

"Eddie?"

"How tall are you?"

Sid looked confused, "In my heels?"

"How tall?"

"Five-eight," he said. "Why?"

Eddie squinted and slid by him and out into the CSI office.

"Eddie," he called after him. "Is this another stunt to get out of the overtime sheets?"

Eddie was gone, the office door slammed shut.

Chapter Twenty-five

Missing the Point

— One —

TERRY RAN SHAKING FINGERS through greasy grey hair and stared at his feet. "I don't know, you'll have to deal with it till I come back. I said I don't know. Could be another couple of weeks." He squeezed the bridge of his nose, "I haven't even buried her yet! Have some respect!"

The doorbell sounded, and Terry became rigid. "I have to go," he hung up the phone and stared at the frosted glass in the front door as though he could see right through it. Was it the police again? What did they want this time? It was getting beyond a joke, and he promised himself that this afternoon he would contact his solicitor; he'd get him to look into the legality of them holding Liz's body for so long, preventing him from laying her to rest, and also the liberties they were taking with his goodwill.

He snatched at the handle and yanked the door open, "Now listen!"

Jim smiled up at him. "Hello, Terry."

Terry froze. His chin shook for a moment and his face paled almost instantly. He looked beyond Jim, looked to see if anyone was watching, and hissed, "What the hell are you doing here?"

Jim walked into the hall, and hurriedly Terry closed the door.

"I told you not to come here." Terry pulled at his hair this time.

"And I told you I needed that money. I did what you asked."

"I'll give you the money when the police leave me alone."

"What's that supposed to mean?" Jim, several inches shorter than Terry, fronted up to him, pale blue eyes heavily recessed, seemed to drill into Terry's until he was forced to look away.

Terry swallowed, hands never still, "They're treating it as suspicious."

"Now wait a fecking minute, I followed every detail."

Terry prodded a finger at Jim's chest and snarled, "I'm a suspect, for Christ's sake. They're asking all kinds of questions. Questions that suggest they don't think it's a suicide." He pushed the finger, "You fucked up!"

Jim turned away, walked into the lounge and headed for the drinks cabinet. "We go back a long way. And you know me pretty good." He poured himself a large one, tipped the glass at Terry who stood aghast in the doorway. "You know that when I make an arrangement, I stick to it. See. I expect you to do the same. Only now I want one hundred."

"One hundred? You really think I'm going to double what we agreed after this?" Terry stuck out his chest, "You'll be lucky if you get anything from me."

Jim necked the drink, gasped an aaaah as it stung his throat. And then put down the glass and walked across the carpet to Terry, eyes fixed on him. And without slowing, he grabbed Terry by the throat and shoved him hard into the wall. He placed his other hand over Terry's petrified eyes. "Block it out, Terry. Everything you have. Block it out. And you go back to what we did. Picture the scene. Picture it, Terry. Do you see her?"

Terry held his breath, but already he could feel the heat growing in his chest. He squeezed in a breath, and slowly he nodded.

Jim tightened his grip. "Do you see her? Her hair glowing in the sunlight, swaying in the breeze? And her daughter, asleep in the pram? Oblivious to us. Do you see her?"

Terry let out a sob. He was close to wetting himself, and he was more afraid now than at any other time in his life, even back then.

Jim whispered in his ear, "Look at her. Take a good look, and remember what we did."

Terry began to cry and Jim took his hands away, and took a step back. Terry didn't try to hide his tears; he openly wept and then sank to the floor where he buried his face into his knees.

Jim nudged him, "Here," he said, "take this." He held out an envelope. Terry reached for it, and he took it using the very tips of his fingers. "You've got till Sunday. Then I get the police involved."

"Wait."

Jim opened the front door, and turned around.

"It was in the papers; Mick Tailor's dead. Do you know anything about it?"

"I know everything there is to know about his death. If you catch my drift."

Terry swallowed. "Why?"

"The less people around from those old days, the better. If Liz worked it out…" He paused. "I found out where Claire Whitehouse lives. Remember her? I went round to her place yesterday."

"You haven't!"

"Nah. The cops were there." He smiled, "I think they're onto you, Terry."

Terry tried to think tactically, but his mind was fogged by Jim's unexpected presence. He wondered if now would be a good time to tell Jim that the police were looking for him, that they'd identified the small university gang, the little clique they'd formed all those years ago. It seemed they had.

But when Terry looked up again, the doorway was empty.

———

Terry stared at it. Face unmoving.

He took another drag from the stale cigar, took another belt of whisky, and he continued to stare at it. He flipped the Polaroid in his fingers, looking at the back of it, expecting perhaps to see some clue on there. But he didn't, it was just the back of a Polaroid picture. And then he flipped it over again, and the image he had blurred because of the tears. "This wasn't the deal," he whispered. "This wasn't the deal!" he screamed.

— Two —

Eddie slammed the door and crashed into his seat, shoved the books and assorted papers aside, and then pulled a series of disks from his desk drawer. He opened the computer's drawer and slid the first disk in, fingers tapping impatiently as it loaded. "Come on, come on."

Once it had loaded he clicked on a folder and opened it. His eyes grazed each picture as he rapidly flicked through the entire album, stopping at one shot in particular. "Shit," he whispered. "How come I didn't see it?" He hit 'print' and ejected the disk.

In his haste to get out of his chair, it slid back and dinked the wall. He raced up the CSI office, Sid eyeing him, edging back all the time, and began sifting through Kenny's desk tray. "I lock the porn away."

"You did the PM for the burn-out, didn't you?"

"Why?"

"Why can no one just answer a fucking question with an answer these days? Did you photo the PM or not?"

"Copy disk is in the tray."

Eddie tipped Kenny's tray over his desk, ignored the protests as papers scattered across the floor, and found the disk. Within moments, he was back in his office, had loaded Kenny's disk and clicked on an image of the victim on a stainless-steel table, a body scale at her side. "Fuck me." He hit 'print'.

Eddie rushed along the corridor, barged through the doors in the main office and headed towards Benson's corner. Benson was typing with one finger of his right hand. His left hand alternated between picking up a coffee cup and picking up a Mars bar.

Eddie stood at his side, panting, "How tall was Elizabeth Shaw?"

Benson stopped typing. "Why, have you seen a coffin on eBay?"

"How tall!"

Benson put the cup down and slowly turned in his seat, "You are three-quarters mental; do you know that? What the fuck is your problem, Collins?"

Eddie thrust the printed pictures at him. "I'll tell you what my problem is, Columbo. Look at her feet."

He did, for several seconds, then looked at Eddie in the same way Sid had done a few minutes ago.

Eddie sat on the desk and folded his arms. Quite calmly he said, "You name one person who can drive a car without their feet touching the pedals."

Benson stood up, "Come with me." He knocked, and didn't wait for a response before barging into Cooper's office.

"Please come in," Cooper said, "sit down and make yourselves at home. Can I offer you some tea perhaps?"

Benson pushed both prints onto Cooper's desk. Eddie closed the door. No one spoke.

It took almost half a minute, with Eddie and Benson watching the balding crown of Cooper's downturned head, before Cooper broke the silence. "You didn't notice this at the scene?"

Benson stood back.

"I've had things on my mind," Eddie said.

"Things on your mind! Jesus wept!"

Benson said, "It was treated as an RTC, boss. There was nothing at that time to suggest—"

"Oh well that's alright then. So while we've been pissing about with the car, doing all this Top Gear shit, not one person could tell me the body had been moved."

Eddie and Benson glanced at each other. "Moved?" Eddie said. "You're missing the point."

Cooper looked back the images. "What?"

"The burnt female isn't Liz Shaw."

"We need to search the body's DNA against the database."

"I don't understand. The DNA from the body matched Liz Shaw's toothbrush."

Eddie's attention drifted from Cooper, "Then it wasn't her toothbrush."

Cooper stood, fists on the desk, "Then whose was it? Margaret fucking Thatcher's? This is just brilliant."

"The toothbrush came from her bathroom. I was there when Eddie seized it."

"Liz Shaw was about my height," Eddie said. "I know that because I saw a photograph of her and her husband standing together. They're both roughly the same height. And her husband is as tall as me, so—"

"Who the hell had an opportunity to swap a toothbrush?"

Eddie pointed to the print on Cooper's desk, "I've looked at the post-mortem photos, and whoever's on that table is a lot shorter than me." He paused, stared off into the distance, thinking, "That's why he protected his point of entry."

Cooper grimaced, "What are you talking about?"

"The burglary." Eddie clicked his fingers. "First thing a burglary victim does is tighten the security at the point of entry. He drew us and Terry Shaw to a false point of entry – the kitchen window – because he wanted to make sure he had easy access through the study window. Because he was coming back."

Cooper thought about it, and then smiled, "To put someone else's toothbrush in the bathroom so we could get DNA."

"Exactly," Benson said. "And take a bottle of Rohypnol."

"But how would he know we'd go straight for DNA? For all he knew we could've gone for dental records, or both." Cooper's voice trailed off to a whisper.

"That'll be the fucking coincidence you were talking about," Eddie shouted. "The dentist's got hit too, remember – patient files taken. The SOCO states he found Doc Marten footwear impressions, and leather glove marks. The same combination I found at Terry's burglary scene."

"Same guy," Benson said.

"Do you still think it's a coincidence?"

Cooper retook his seat. "Who's playing games with us?"

Eddie sat in his office, head in his hands, breathing shallowly, trying to supress the anger that tasted sour in his mouth, that burned a little inside his chest. It grew hotter until he punched the desk and swiped a tub of pens at the wall. But still he didn't feel better; still he had that feeling of being stupid, of overlooking something fundamental. But worse, he hated the feeling that someone was fucking him about, obscuring evidence. "What for?"

Eventually, he sighed, bent and picked up the pens, and put thoughts of a double whisky as far from his mind as he could. He had enough battles to fight right now without blunting his focus.

The books stared at him. He reached for one and then there was a knock at the door. He shouted, "I've gone out."

Benson let himself in.

Eddie fingered the book's spine, *The Ripper Years*. "Thanks for speaking up in there."

"He's agreed to fast-track the DNA and have it checked against the database."

"I've been onto the fingerprint bureau. The marks I lifted off these," he patted the books, "are all hers. Every one of them." Eddie pushed the book away. "Why would he want us to think his wife's dead?"

Benson leaned against the doorway and wiped away chocolate from the corner of his mouth. "Well it's not for the insurance. We've done some digging and he's fucking loaded."

"Better still," Eddie said, "who is it? Who is the body in the car?"

Benson shrugged. "We'll know one way or the other later today."

"Has he asked for the McGowan file?"

"He's tracking the Holmes Inspector for it." Benson came in, closed the door behind him, "Believe it or not, he's also going to the Chief Constable."

"What?"

"Apparently they've got to work out a strategy for feeding any Ripper shit back into the public domain without it causing a riot."

Eddie thought about it for a moment. Sutcliffe was out of the way, hidden from public view; and all the suffering he'd caused and all the national fear and revulsion he'd induced all those years ago had abated, died down to become a smoothed-over memory.

People shared tales about him, comfortable that something like him could never happen again, happy that they could mock him and analyse him without fear of retribution, could be brave once more and ponder the if-only scenarios safe in the knowledge that they would never be tested.

Terry Shaw had turned it all upside down.

The families of the victims would bleed again when this came out. And when, after a break of thirty years, they once again saw the headlines beginning with 'The Yorkshire Ripper', their whole lives would end and they'd be back there, reliving the horrid seventies like they never went away. "Why would it have to go public? We've kept things under wraps before."

Benson snorted. "Nothing as big as this before. If there is a Ripper connection here, it'll get out as sure as I've got a hole in my arse. Better manage it before it does, eh." He turned to leave, "And anyway; it's in the public interest."

Eddie nodded towards the books. "I know she hid them."

"If you find anything in them, let me know. Soon as you can, yeah?"

Eddie stared at the books, dragged *The Ripper Years* closer and didn't even notice Benson leave the office. He opened it again, flicked through the photographs in the chapter headed 'Shaney McGowen' and stopped at the black and white image he'd needed a magnifying glass for earlier. It showed nothing more interesting than a rag. Next to it was another shot of the same rag, but closer so it showed the word JAWS. It looked like a patch you could probably buy at the time the film came out, one of the many merchandising items fans could get their hands on. Well, someone had bought this and sewn it to a bandana. They had made it personal.

It was mostly blood stained, a dark smear, spatters of dark grey on a lighter grey background. The legend below the image read: *A bandana left at the scene of McGowan's murder in September 1979. Its owner was never traced.*

A tickle scurried down the skin on Eddie's neck.

There was a hand-drawn arrow pointing to that bandana. Next to it, an exclamation mark made with a pen that was heavy enough to break through the glossy paper. In the centre, right at the bottom of the 'A' in 'JAWS', he could see a small dark grey – possibly red – hand-stitched heart. Eddie grabbed his camera.

The heart, the heart was everything. Now the bandana wasn't only personal – it was unique.

He got in as close to it as he could, and then photographed it.

Over the page, Eddie studied the next image, and a confused look spread over his face as his mind processed the picture there. "Can't be." From the clutter within his desk drawer, he eventually found the magnifying glass he'd searched for earlier, and brought it down to the image. He looked up with surprise and then began to smile.

As he closed the book, he noticed a receipt stapled to the inside cover flap, with a date only two weeks after the wedding weekend back in April, so he knew it was a new book and not something Elizabeth Shaw had found, say, in a second-hand book store, or on a car boot sale. So the exclamation mark and the notes in the margin were definitely made by her.

Book in hand, Eddie closed the office door behind him.

Sid was hovering. He coughed.

"What it is, Sid?"

"Duffy didn't turn in this morning, Eddie."

"I'll sort it. You get on with your nails." The door slammed behind him.

Chapter Twenty-six

Scatter Cushions

EDDIE HAD LEARNED HIS lesson and bought pizza for tonight's tea. And after being asked how work was the previous night, he'd also thought about bringing flowers. The moment he closed the door behind him, he could smell something burning.

"Don't get mad," Charles said as Eddie clomped into the kitchen. He was wringing his hands together, moving from one foot to the other.

The fire had started on the hob. Ironically a pan full of baked beans now looked like a pan of ancient dog turd. The oven door was open and the last tendrils of smoke from the charred chicken were being sucked up by the extractor fan. There was water everywhere.

Eddie put the pizzas down, folded his arms, foot tapping, and stared at Charles.

"I didn't want to give you cold beans again, son."

"Cold beans I can live with. A dead pensioner would affect the resale value, okay?"

"I'm sorry." Charles stared at the floor.

Eddie sighed, "You alright?"

He nodded.

"Hey, are you?"

"I'm fine." His voice was whiny, throat closed up with tears.

"Come on, I bought pizza."

After the meal, and after sitting through almost two hours of the musical *Hello Dolly*, smirking at Charles who was enthralled by it, barely even blinking, Eddie reached for the remote and turned the television off. "So have you been doing any of that running crap today?"

"I'm sorry about the kitchen. I'll go clean it up."

"Leave the kitchen."

"It's not crap."

"The treadmill is new, Dad. You bought it two days ago, had it delivered here. You didn't have one at your house."

"So?"

"So you're on a health kick and I want to know why?"

"Can't a man take an interest in his health?" He got up, collected the pizza boxes and headed out of the lounge.

Eddie followed. "It's not like you. Why did you just start now? Got a yearning to be Arnold Schwarzenegger?"

"See, all you do is take the piss out of me. Don't you have people at work you can take the piss out of?"

"Of course I do. I'm a boss now; they give me people to take the piss out of. But why should they get all the special treatment?"

Charles dropped the boxes on the counter top, picked up the crusty turd and dropped it, complete with the pan, into the bin. "I'll get you a new pan."

"Sod the pan, Dad."

"I'm doing it because I need to be fit."

"Oh yeah, for the marathon, I forgot."

"Stop it!"

Eddie froze, saw the spittle fly from Charles's mouth, saw the wide eyes and the fists. He'd made a mental note to have this conversation out with him, to exorcise the exercise, he'd called it, but if there was a wrong way to go about it, he'd had the great misfortune to find that way at the first attempt. Good old Eddie. "Dad," he said, "what's bothering you?"

"You ever had some youth come into your room in the dead of night? It's not nice. You feel vulnerable, like you said. You feel... useless. I don't want to feel like that anymore."

Eddie's cheeks flushed. He felt ashamed of himself. "Ah. I'm sorry; I hadn't thought of it like that." Yes he had. Of course he had, but he wasn't going to let Charles know that. He wanted the old man to speak the words, to air them.

"It's okay," Charles whispered. "I'm being a stupid old man."

"Yes you are."

Charles looked up, the hurt in his face obvious.

"You're staying here, Dad. You've no need to feel like that anymore."

After a while, Charles said, "I appreciate the offer son, really I do. But I can't stay here. You need your own space, your own freedom."

"All I need is to know I'm not coming home to a burnt-out cottage," Eddie was smiling.

"I'm being serious though. What if you want to bring a young lady back?"

"I won't. Trust me."

"But you might."

"Then she'll have to take me and take you too, won't she."

"I'd seriously hamper your chances then."

"Like I have chances thrown at me all day long." Eddie lit a cigarette, exhaled and reached for the kettle. "That's how I broke my shitty stick, beating all those desperate women away all day. Gets wearying sometimes."

"You're killing your brain with that stuff."

"With coffee?"

"Smoke, I mean."

"It's alright; I work for the police, I don't use it." Eddie pulled out two mugs, threw coffee into them and grabbed the milk from the fridge. "And anyway, you've probably inhaled about twenty years' worth just from burning tonight's tea." Eddie turned around with a grin on his face and Charles was holding out his hand. "What's that?"

"Take it. This week's rent."

"Keep it. Buy yourself some jogging bottoms. And a new face pack."

"Just take it. Please."

"You're not here because I want your money, Dad. You're here because I want you to be." Eddie looked away, tapped his feet while the kettle boiled. "I understand you being afraid around there."

"I wasn't. Not until..."

"Yeah, well I used to go around there when I worked nights, and I didn't like it. And I had a whole force behind me. It's gone downhill big time, the estate I mean. You don't have to be embarrassed about fear. So once and for all I'd like you to stay."

Charles nudged him, but Eddie refused to turn around. He gripped his arm and pulled, but Eddie lifted the kettle to avoid a face to face. "You want a nip of whisky in here?" he asked. "I won't join you though, if you don't mind." Eventually, he had to put the kettle down, and Charles pulled harder this time. Eddie had tears in his eyes.

"What's up, son?"

"Got smoke in my eyes, that's all."

"Really?"

Eddie laughed and picked up his old dad, held him tight for the first time since he was a nipper. And Charles embraced him, shed a tear or two of his own. And when his feet were back on the ground again, he said, "Thanks for the invitation. But have you given it plenty of thought?"

Eddie nodded.

"I mean really, have you? I mean what about the future? You come home one day and I'm sitting in the lounge with an open sphincter, calling you Thora and mumbling sweet nothings into a scatter cushion."

Eddie laughed and sipped coffee.

"It could happen."

"It'll never happen, Dad. We don't have any scatter cushions."

Charles laughed and pretended to frown too, "How come you can't be serious just for one conversation?"

"Because making fun of it makes it easier to handle. I don't like talking about stuff, personal stuff."

"You think talking about it will infect you or make you out to be a weaker man?"

"It's nothing so deep, Dad. I feel uncomfortable about it, so I make light of it if I can't avoid it altogether. Know what I mean?" Eddie trudged back into the lounge.

Charles picked up his drink and followed. "If you've got me here for a while, then we might as well… you know, get to know each other a bit, eh?"

"Why? I'm happy the way things are."

"Tell me about her. The girl."

"Ros?"

"Aye, tell me about her."

"You mean begin the story with why she left me?"

Charles said nothing to correct Eddie's statement, just stared.

"That's a topic personal to me. It's off the table."

And he was sleeping better too. Maybe Steph had been right: miss her and then let go. He stared at Charles, and eventually Charles grew uncomfortable enough to avoid his gaze. "Sorry," Eddie said, "I just got to thinking about her for a moment." And he had been. Alex, his doctor, had told him to find out the cause of it all, that his body was acting in self-defence, trying to warn him about something bad – probably stress – and this was its only way to do that.

Was he right? Had the stress levels decreased since she abandoned him?

He thought they had, yes. Considerably, in fact.

And that made him happy. He'd finally uncovered the reason behind the panic attacks. Ros. But finding out that reason had opened a fresh box of questions, not least why would Ros make him feel anxious? Was it the fear of being in a relationship, or was it more specifically being afraid of being in a relationship with her?

The first thing he'd done after she'd left was throw away that pink quilt cover.

It occurred to him that the panic attacks weren't specifically aimed at Ros, they were an inbuilt fear of being taken over by someone else, of having their own ways of life thrust onto him whether he liked it or not.

He looked across at Charles and wondered if it could happen again.

Chapter Twenty-seven

The Grass at Hyde Park

— One —

WITH SOMETHING APPROACHING TREPIDATION, Eddie walked up the path towards the front door. He felt anxious not because he was afraid of the response he might get to the request he had, but because of the way he'd behaved towards the old guy the last time they'd met. He'd made up his mind to be a little more huggy, a little more touchy-feely, a real gem of a boss who was one of the boys.

Eddie knocked. No one answered; and that was even worse than being greeted with antagonism. To have no response was worse than having an ear-bashing. He turned, stared at the overgrown mess either side of the cracked concrete path on which he and several slugs now stood. And he wondered why he hadn't rung first to make sure he was home. He sighed and took a step or two back towards the gate, resigned to a wasted trip, and resigned to living through this feeling again on some other day – for which he would make an appointment first.

On the third of those steps towards the gate, he heard a muted voice say, "Who is it?"

Eddie turned, "It's me, Eddie." The door chain came off and then there was a key in the door. Touchy-feely, he reminded himself, be cuddly, be lovable. Eddie grew a smile as the door opened.

Duffy looked out.

Eddie closed the gap between them, "Why weren't you at work this morning, you useless little fuck?"

Duffy stared at him, mouth open.

Eddie could see the hurt in his eyes. "Okay," he said, "that's a bit too strong; I apologise. You're not that little."

"You shouldn't be here. I'm on sick leave. Stress."

"And I'm a caring boss, remember? I'm here to make sure you're not faking it." Eddie smiled wider and made to go inside, but Duffy held his ground on the threshold. "You serious?"

Duffy nodded.

"Oh come on, I was having a laugh."

"Some things aren't that funny, Eddie."

"You remind me of my dad. He's a stubborn old goat as well." And that's when Eddie caught himself. His dad was stubborn on the face of it. Tell him the sky was blue and he would tell you it was white. And fold his arms petulantly while he said it. But that was just his old dad, right?

Duffy took a step back inside the hallway, and before Eddie could raise a protest, he closed the door.

Eddie stared it, then at the step. If his dad had been there, he would have slapped Eddie across the face. He knew it. Because the sky was white – for him at least. Not everyone saw things the same way he saw them. This was a revelation of sorts. "A new management way of thinking, Eddie," he told himself.

He knocked.

The same muted voice as before said, "Who is it?"

Eddie kicked the step. He was about to shout 'Who the fuck do you think it is? Father Christmas!' when he checked himself, and understood the second chance he'd been given. "Hi, Duffy. It's me, Eddie."

Like saying abracadabra, the door opened. Duffy smiled – but only just. "Eddie."

"How are you, mate?"

He rocked his hand side to side, "So-so. Want to come in?"

"If you can spare a few minutes, yeah."

Duffy watched him closely, then said, "Well I can't, so go fuck yourself!" And slammed the door.

Eventually Eddie blinked, and then laughed loud enough that the entire street could have heard him. That really was the funniest thing he'd seen all week.

The door opened, and with a wide smile, Duffy said, "Come in, you prick."

Eddie sipped his drink. Duffy had called it coffee when he handed the mug over, but it was more like piss with scum floating on the top. He put it on the coffee table before him and made a mental note to leave it there. "So how are you, then?"

Duffy reclined in a threadbare chair in front of the unlit fire, and turned off the TV. "Like you care." He crossed his legs and showed off equally threadbare tartan slippers.

Eddie pushed the package away from him slightly. "Why else am I here?"

"I'm pissed off at you, if you must know."

"What, you can't take a bit of banter now? This is the police, you've been here how long, thirty years, and you hadn't worked that out yet?"

"There's banter, and there's banter. What you said was an insult, Eddie. You insulted me."

"It was a fact. All facts about you are insults."

"Is that from *Hello Dolly*?" Duffy shook his head. "I never had you pegged as a musical fan."

Embarrassed, Eddie carried on. "So you go sick?"

"Prove I'm not." Duffy folded his arms.

"Touché," Eddie reached for the mug, and caught himself just in time. "I went too far—"

"And don't think you can manipulate me here with one of your stupid gags."

Eddie nodded. "I went too far, and I said things I shouldn't have."

Duffy raised his eyebrows, and then squinted in suspicion.

"You're actually a good worker." Part of Eddie agreed with that statement, another part was rolling around holding its stomach. "Sometimes though, I notice you can be a bit…"

"Bit what?"

"Reluctant."

"Reluctant?"

"Come on, Dufflebag. Everyone has their off days, I understand that."

"Wait a minute; it's not so long ago that you were a washed-up piece of shit that could hardly pick up a brush!"

That stopped Eddie dead in his tracks.

"I'm sorry," Duffy said, "but it needed to be said. People won't respect you until you've earned that respect."

"You don't respect me?"

Duffy stared at him, and Eddie could see there was a lot of working out going on inside Duffy's head, a lot of turmoil. He hadn't expected to be on this particular topic, not in a month of Sundays.

"I was a washed-up piece of shit. But I'm not any more, far from it. That alone should command some respect. Don't you think?"

Duffy shrugged.

"Well forgive me for blowing my own fucking trombone here, but I think it does. And I'll tell you while we're on the subject of me, that I'm damned good at my job, that I work at it, and I work hard. And that's something else that should command respect. So when people like you go off on one saying that I'm a washed-up—"

"I'm sorry."

Eddie was breathing hard. He found himself leaning forward with tight, aching fists, and he found himself on the defensive and on the offensive both at the same time. "Yeah," he panted, "well…"

"I do respect you. It's just sometimes I don't like you. You can be a mean bastard, Eddie Collins."

"That's just me, mate. I don't mean anything by it."

"But it means something to me. It means something to other people you insult too."

"I need to understand people more. I need to appreciate they have their own point of view that might differ from mine. My dad would say the sky—"

"That's straight out of a management pamphlet if ever I heard it."

Eddie laughed, and reclined. "Actually, it's not."

"Sounds like it." Duffy slurped his drink and nodded to Eddie's cup, "Don't let that go cold."

"Right, I won't."

"Anyway, you were busy buttering me up with compliments."

"Ah yes, I was." He smiled across at the old man, and got a smile right back. "As well as being a good worker when you fancy it, you're also one of the most experienced in the office."

"Number one; I'm a good worker when my decrepit old bones allow me to be. I ain't as young as I was, lad, and I ain't as young as you are, so think on next time I'm being reluctant, eh? And as for experience, you'll find I'm one of the oldest left in the force, my lad." Duffy breathed in, proud of that particular fact.

And rightfully so, conceded Eddie. "I know you're experienced. In fact it's your experience that I need right now, with this case I'm working on."

Duffy squinted.

"1979."

"Wait a minute." Duffy wagged a finger at him, "Wait just one minute. You came here looking for information, didn't you? Nothing to do with a welfare check!"

Eddie swallowed, "Two birds," he said.

"Cheeky twat!"

"Can we please draw a line?"

"Round your neck!" Duffy sighed. "Drink your drink," he snapped. "And what about 1979?"

Eddie stared at the 'coffee', decided no job was worth strep, and pressed on, "Shaney McGowan. Remember her?"

"Hyde Park. Yes I do."

Eddie took the book from a plastic shopping bag, found the page where Duffy was standing by the cordon tape wearing flared trousers and a shirt with huge lapels. He passed the book over to Duffy who stared at the image for some time. "Fuck me," he whispered. "I was a good-looking fella, wasn't I?"

"Anything about that scene strike you as odd? Did you think it was The Ripper?"

"What's going on here? What you working on?"

"It's a long story. Please, did you think it was The Ripper?"

"See, now why can't you involve me in this case?"

"Can't. Contamination. You worked the original scene."

"That was thirty years ago!"

"Yeah, but you haven't washed since then."

"Aw, come on, this is something I'd like to sink my teeth—"

"You're off with stress, remember?"

Duffy tutted and looked back at the book, thumbing through the pages. "Well, she was found close to where one of the other victims was. Attacked with a hammer. Her nipper was in a pushchair not far away. Looked like they'd gone out for a stroll."

Eddie reached over and turned the page. He pointed, "This bandana," he said, "recognise it?"

Duffy yelled, "Hey, that's my photo!"

"I know. The bandana, Duffy."

"Course I recognise it. I took it out of her mouth."

Eddie watched Duffy. "You didn't think it was weird? The Ripper hadn't done that before."

There was anger in Duffy's eyes. "He hadn't attacked a mother with her child present before, either."

"I know. But the bandana?"

"I told the SIO that he ought to put it on the television news, see if it got a response. But he had his head so far up his arse that he could see his own heart attack coming." Duffy stared into nothingness. "Never found out who it belonged to. It was bagged and forgotten about."

Eddie sat back in the chair. "He never confessed to Shaney McGowan. Did you know that?"

"Of course I knew that. I was working these scenes while you were still shitting yourself."

Eddie took the book back, threw it inside the carrier, and stood. "Come on, we're going out."

"What? Where?"

"Hyde Park."

"But I'm on sick."

"Not anymore."

———

Eddie closed the door and lit a cigarette as Duffy walked around the front of the van. "Where now?"

Duffy swatted at flies and began walking along a path that passed in front of a graffiti-free war memorial. Eddie kept alongside and snatched glimpses of the old man, wondering what might be going on inside his head. Who knew what effect such a trip back into the past might have; stepping back in time to encounter the final scene in a young woman's life – re-visiting the time that changed a child's life forever?

More flies. They turned off the path, the sounds of traffic running along Hyde Park Corner diminishing with each step until it became barely noticeable. Within a minute blossom trees, beech trees, and hawthorns enshrouded them. An overgrown low brick boundary wall, painted in moss and scratched at by fingers of bracken, meandered away into the distance, swallowed by greenery.

Enclosed in this secluded pocket, they walked on damp grass that was long enough to make a shush noise as they waded through it. None of this was here in the seventies photograph. Back then the wall appeared to be only a few years old, and a dedicated gardening team kept the shrubs in shape and kept the grass under control.

Duffy stopped. He stood, it seemed, in the exact spot he had thirty years ago, surveying the carnage before him. "It never leaves you." He drew a deep breath that shuddered its way back out, and eventually said, "Pushchair was over there, under that tree." He turned, hands in pockets, "Shaney was lying here."

Eddie flicked away the cigarette. "Talk me through it."

Duffy pointed towards the low wall, "The head was nearest the wall. Her knickers were found at her side; apparently she'd had sex before she died."

"Did they find semen inside her?"

"Semen? There was the full cast of *Pirates of the Caribbean* in there! We didn't have DNA technology back in them days; best you could hope for was a blood group." Duffy scratched around, hands still in pockets, rattling change. "No footprints. Back then, you could bring vehicles up here but the ground was so hard we couldn't even get tyre impressions."

Eddie began to feel a little nervous. It was clear Duffy's memory hadn't suffered in respect of this scene – and he could relate to that. If he was sitting in the office talking about a job that was years old, he could barely remember it, but put him in the kitchen where someone was murdered, or in the bedroom where someone was raped, and he could nail it piece by piece, exactly what was found and where.

But now he was working his way towards the important piece of Shaney McGowan's murder, and the important piece of Elizabeth Shaw's disappearance. "Tell me about the bandana. You did seize it, didn't you?"

Duffy looked from the grass up to Eddie, "No. I wiped my arse on it. What do you think?"

"I got to be honest, you've done well, mate. I didn't expect you to remember as much as you have. Things change over time, it's not like a room in a house is it; it's grown—"

"This was The Yorkshire Ripper, Eddie. If you're ever unlucky enough to be so involved in a case like that, believe me, you'll never forget it." Duffy took his hands out of his pocket, "I'll have one of them cigs off you."

Eddie didn't know that Duffy smoked, but it didn't need saying. He just handed one over and then offered his cigarette lighter. And when Duffy had lit his, he took out one for himself as Duffy began walking away.

"Tell you something else that sticks in my throat." He turned and faced Eddie. "Some old kid said he had information about this murder. He worked in a garage about a mile from here."

"What information?"

"No idea. One of his staff found him dead in an inspection pit. They never got to interview him."

Eddie caught up with him, "Was it suspicious?"

Duffy shrugged, "I didn't do that scene, a colleague of mine called David Lloyd got it. Anyway, it was treated as an accident. Who knows, maybe he could have led us to him. Ripper's luck, Eddie. It was like a curse."

Together they walked through the greenery until it turned gradually more and more grey, until the sounds of shushing grass became tapping on tarmac, until the forgotten and constant groan of the nearby traffic came back to them and they automatically began speaking louder to compensate. "You remember the name of this guy?"

"The garage man?"

"Yes, the garage man."

"Dankmeyer Flenkenstein."

"What?"

Duffy laughed, "How am I supposed to know? Jesus."

Once the van doors cocooned them, and the noise had shrunk back to something easily ignored, Eddie asked, "Will you be in at work tomorrow?"

Duffy looked across at him.

"Could really do with you back on board."

He smiled, "We'll see."

— Two —

Eddie ascended the stairs to the main office feeling two things at once. He felt quite pleased with the progress he'd made with Duffy on a personal and a professional front, and hoped he really would be in at work tomorrow. It was important, he felt, to grow as a manager and learn to deal effectively with staff issues as well as his own. He couldn't stand the thought of Benson belittling him again, telling him he was losing his staff, and he couldn't bear to hear the whispers from those staff members complaining that morale was low.

Bastards!

And the other thing he felt, which was just as unusual as having a revelation that he was finally becoming a good boss – a people person – was excitement about a case.

They came along maybe once or twice a year, cases that got your juices flowing and rekindled some of the sharpness that everyday life and everyday cases blunted after a while; reignited some of the eagerness you felt when you were just starting out – when you thought you knew everything but actually knew sod all – about anything. So this was Eddie's brightest moment since he started here, and he entered the CID office feeling high and proud.

He looked around and the only person he saw with any direct connection to the Shaw case was Khan. And that was some shock in a crowded office like this one, there must have been sixty people in here. No wonder they needed the room, he thought, as he approached Khan. "Where's Benson?"

Khan looked up, "Squeezing one out. Should be back in an hour."

"Tell him I want him."

Khan raised his eyebrows.

"Please."

"That's better."

Eddie tutted and walked towards the corridor leading to his own office when he saw Benson enter the main office, Mars bar dangling from his mouth. "You can give up looking now, they found the last Golden Ticket."

"Huh?" Benson frowned.

Eddie stepped in close, "I need you to get me into the archive store."

"They gave you stripes, Eddie; you can get yourself in there."

"I'd need clearance from God."

"Then get it," Benson put the Mars bar back in his mouth and began walking away.

"Benson. I need an exhibit. From the McGowan scene."

"Fuck!" And then quieter, "I can't do that."

"Come on, just get me in there. You said yourself if I found anything—"

"I meant I'd help with stuff I was allowed to help with, Collins. Forget it." He turned away again.

Eddie stood his ground. "McGowan's your connection."

Benson stopped. He turned.

"You found her. It's important. It's the link between the past and the present."

Benson stood on the spot, the muscles in his cheeks throbbing as he thought it over. "Get me a reference number. And not a fucking word of this to Cooper."

Back in 1979, the Major Crime Unit was just wishful thinking in the mind of some empire-building top copper who foresaw the need for a dedicated, highly trained, highly motivated team of detectives and crime scene investigators armed with top-notch computer equipment and ground-breaking technological wizardry, all housed together in one purpose-built building.

Eventually, twenty-five years later, some of that shopping list came true, but not all of it. Back then, when DNA technology was in its infancy, when computers were run using valve technology, and when scenes of crime officers worked their own division alongside

CID who'd been extracted from the latest payroll robbery, paper was still the in-thing. And all the hundreds of thousands of police officers' pocket note books, all those tens of thousands of crime scene reports had to be kept somewhere until some bright spark came up with the notion of transferring them to electronic files that could be stored inside a matchbox.

Eddie stood in front of the sliding spike-topped gates around the back of Killingbeck Police Station once again. This place was like dog shit stuck under his shoe; couldn't shake it off.

The gates creaked open and he walked inside listening to the ghosts of long-dead arguments and tantrums, and within five minutes he was in a large section of an underground cell area that was no longer fit for purpose as a cell area – but was ideal for storing paper in.

The only good thing about this place, from Eddie's point of view, was that there were no mice or rats, and it was reasonably well lit. Oh, he thought, there was another good point – there were no people around. He had absolute solitude.

As he walked along the ends of the shelf units, scanning the year codes that reached back to 1966, he wondered if he'd ever find Duffy's scene book and the reference number for the bandana. 1979 crept up slowly after what seemed like an hour's walk, and he paused at the label: SOCO1979LEEDS. The shelves were further split not by divisional identifiers, because they had no consistency, each senior command team stamping their own divisional boundaries within the force area, but by compass points, and then districts. Slowly, tracing a finger along the rows of high-stacked boxes, Eddie traced his way to North Leeds, Headingley and Hyde Park.

In total there were thirty-eight cardboard crates full of SOCO examination books.

"Fuck me," he whispered.

It took fifteen minutes to find Duffy's book. In box number twenty-two, he recognised Duffy's forward-slanting scrawl over the spines of a dozen books from 1979. In the eighth book, August to September, he found exactly what he was looking for.

He read all of the pertinent parts of Duffy's report, even had the chance to read the scene notes that he'd made at the time, before taking out his phone and photographing the pages in case he needed to refer to them later. It was comforting to see that Duffy's memory of the scene was spot on – his notes confirmed everything he'd said to Eddie that afternoon.

Chapter Twenty-eight

Overtly Covert

— One —

EIGHT-THIRTY, AND EDDIE DRAINED his fourth mug of coffee. He came out of his office buzzing, intending to make his fifth but his mind was drawn back to the Ros conundrum, sticking to it like shit to a blanket, and he was so absorbed that he had forgotten to bring his mug. His office door closed behind him just as Duffy walked in through the main office door. Both stopped and stared at each other.

"Thanks for coming in, Dufflebag," Eddie smiled.

That knocked the sharp edge off Duffy's cold, defensive demeanour, and he visibly relaxed, shoulders taking on that familiar rounded aspect. "I sent you a letter," he said. "You know, a resignation letter."

"A 'fuck you' letter?"

Duffy nodded, "Yeah, kind of."

"And?" Eddie folded his arms, enjoying seeing Duffy squirm a little. And then he began to smile, and pretty soon Duffy was smiling right back.

"Ignore it," Duffy said. "Just throw it in the bin."

"No chance," Eddie winked. "I'll keep it for the next time you piss me off."

"Feeling better, you old shit?" Duffy and Eddie turned to see Kenny grinning like a fool from the far end of the office.

"Fix yourself a brew, then go and take Sid through the monthly stats for me, eh?"

Duffy looked back at Eddie, a softer look in his eye now than at any time Eddie could ever remember. "Cheers, Eddie."

"And take it easy, okay?"

"I will."

Eddie clapped him on the shoulder and headed for the door. He turned and said, "But don't take the piss or I'll put you on sick leave myself with a broken nose, okay?"

"You're all heart!" Duffy yelled after him as the door closed behind Eddie.

The letter from Duffy hadn't materialised. Eddie wondered if the old guy had ever got around to posting it. Or even writing it.

The fresh mug of stolen coffee would have to wait, but it didn't matter now because Eddie was ready for the world. He felt good, especially after seeing Duffy back in town firing on all three cylinders. He chuckled to himself – it was working, trying to understand people, it really was working.

Mostly.

Three strides along the corridor and Sid came into view. Today he sported purple corduroy skin-tight trousers, winkle-pickers and a white shirt with lacy cuffs so long that he could trip over them. Sid was smiling. "Don't do that," Eddie said.

"What?"

"Smile."

"Why?"

"It makes me nervous. Like my flies are undone or something."

"They're fully done up, don't worry. It's the first thing I checked."

Eddie stared at him. "Then why are you grinning like a village idiot? Got new underwear on?"

"I don't use underwear."

Eddie covered his eyes with a hand, "I so did not want to visualise that."

"You asked." Sid pulled out a sheet of paper from the wad he was carrying. "Here. Results from the gum you gave me."

"Gum?"

"Chewing-gum, Eddie. The littering offence?"

"Oh yeah, that. Thanks." He snatched the paper.

"Want me to notify CID of the DNA hit?"

"Nope."

"Division?"

"Nope. Thanks." He rounded the corner into the CID office, and his eyes settled on Benson just as he was biting into a bacon sandwich. Brown sauce blobbed onto his shirt, and Eddie laughed again. "Benson, you've shat down your shirt." He took the seat next to him.

"Aw, bollocks, that was clean on as well!"

"I got the exhibit reference number for the—"

"Eddie, we need you for a house search. Benson will give you details…" Cooper stared at Benson and his slowly growing brown stain. He shook his head and walked away, "We really must get him a bib."

"What house search?"

Benson rubbed at the stain with a napkin. "DNA gave us a name for the woman in the car."

Eddie waited as Benson spat on the napkin and continued to rub. "I'm getting old, Benson."

"It's a woman called Samantha Price. She was a drunk, and a shoplifter. Her husband's name is James Price, known locally as Jim."

"Jim? Wow, you don't say?"

"Anyway, he's some small-time villain—"

"Small-time as in burglary?"

Benson nodded. "Not only that. He's a mechanic."

Eddie stared off into the distance. "He could be our…"

Benson was nodding, ready to take another bite.

"I got the exhibit reference—"

And then Cooper appeared from nowhere again. "This is going to be a discreet look at James Price's house. If we find nothing, we're out of there quick without him knowing we've ever been inside, alright?"

"Right, boss."

Eddie said, "You think he's holding Elizabeth Shaw, don't you?"

Cooper looked at his watch, "Be ready to go in ten minutes." And then he left as quickly as he'd arrived.

Eddie studied at the nominal sheet Sid had given him.

"What's that?" Benson asked.

Eddie folded the sheet and slid it into the back pocket of his jeans. "The exhibit reference number. Remember?" He thought about the woman in the car, about who she was and why she was there, firing scenarios around and hoping one would stick. Maybe Liz Shaw wanted to be free of her husband. But why? Maybe Liz Shaw and Jim were an item. Eddie's eyebrows rose. It was a possibility, and the best way to wrap up that little present was to get rid of the incumbent Mrs Price at the same time.

— Two —

They weren't exactly inconspicuous. At the end of the street were two plain cars, both Vauxhalls and both sporting registration plates that were almost identical. If anyone had got close enough they would have seen "police" on the tax discs too. Not that that was needed; the twitching curtains, the sideways glances from passers-by, even the jeering of some local youths on push bikes made it obvious to Eddie that everyone around here knew the law was messing about on their territory.

It would have been less suspicious, he thought, if they were all sitting in two marked vans; at least then the locals would just assume they were serving a warrant or handing out some grief to the local dealers again. No big deal. A regular occurrence.

It made Eddie nervous. "You know all this could blow us out of the water, don't you?"

Cooper was obviously aware of it too. "No point backing out now; what's done's done. Let's just finish—"

"What?" Eddie was sitting in the back, an empty space at his side. In front, Cooper and Benson kept an eye on the street. The other car had Khan and DC Lynne Butcher inside. Eddie leaned forward. "If we stop now, nothing's compromised. But if they see us go into Jim's house, he'll find out and the job's fucked."

Benson looked across at Cooper.

Cooper ground his teeth. "Let it go, Collins."

"But—"

"He's coming," Benson nodded in the direction of a man strolling up the street.

Eddie turned to see him; a man far too tidy to live around these parts. If the locals had a single brain cell between them, they'd realise that this guy waltzing up the shit-littered footpath in his shiny shoes and new Levis was a plain copper, and that little fact coupled with the plain police cars parked at the top of the street, meant that Billy Smart's Circus was in town. Simple as that. "Fuck me. Really, is that the best you can do, Cooper? He stands out like a dick at a lesbian wedding!"

"I said let it go."

Eddie turned to Benson. "Have you met him before?"

Benson shook his head.

"See? Even Benson clocked him. He might as well be in uniform!"

"His name's Jenkins and he comes highly recommended; can get through any mechanical door lock in less than a minute."

They watched Jenkins as he approached the dirty white UPVC front door. Jenkins tried the handle, and then, as quickly as a magician, brought out what appeared to be a single, no-nonsense, key. He slid it into the lock, pushed and shoved a little, and then the handle dropped and the door opened.

Eddie stared at him, thinking.

"Come on," Cooper got out of the car, then Benson. Lynne climbed from the car behind, leaving Khan alone to watch over the vehicles. Within moments there was a crowd of plain-clothed police officers slowly shuffling in through Jim Price's front door.

Eddie sighed, grabbed his camera, climbed out and went to see Khan who wound down his window, "If anyone asks, just say we're from 60-Minute Makeover." Eddie ambled towards the open door, waving at the people watching through their windows. This was about as covert as a Chapeltown Carnival.

Inside the terraced house it smelled of lone man. That smoky, sweaty smell that didn't quite match the neatness of its surroundings. The place was sparsely furnished, yet reasonably clean and tidy. There were no pictures on the walls, no ornaments to catch the dust, no pets, nothing of sentiment; just a place to exist. Definitely single male territory.

He entered the hallway and Cooper closed the door after him. "Right, Eddie, I want you to start at the top." Eddie shouldered people aside and walked through into the kitchen where he opened the cellar door. "Oi!" Cooper shouted. "Don't ignore me."

Everyone quietened. They heard Eddie's descent into the cellar, his boots grating on the cold stone steps.

"Prick," Cooper growled. He turned to Lynne. "Start at the top," and then to Benson, "Lounge." They both nodded and left without so much as a smile; Jenkins tucked himself away in a corner of the lounge where he could keep an eye on the street through the window. There was tension in the group and it was obvious even to an outsider like him, that when Cooper was riled, it was better to stand well back.

Cooper drew in a couple of deep breaths and with gloved hands began opening the kitchen drawers, checking under the sink, feeling across the top of wall units, peering inside boxes of cereal and moving aside the pots of Super Noodles whose only company in the cupboard was a tin of Smart Price beans.

In the lounge, Benson could see nothing incriminating either, nothing that gave away Jim Price as being a murderer – nothing even remotely suggesting he had a life. "Waste of time, boss." He searched the wall unit and found among Leeds City Council letters and red utility bills, an old Argos catalogue, and a single photograph of a woman. She looked happy, in the middle of a pub somewhere with a shot glass held near her lips and a smile in her not unattractive eyes. She was standing next to a man, Jim, with her arm around his waist. They looked good together.

He put the photograph back, then checked the wall unit's front panel to see if it moved, to see if anything was hidden behind it. It didn't, it was firmly affixed. He checked the sofa – a three-seater leather monstrosity that took up most of the floor space. He removed the cushions, felt down the backs of them, checked underneath, all with no gain.

He gave the coffee table only a cursory glance. It had an overflowing ashtray, an empty tobacco pouch and a few cups. He then moved on to the TV, which took all of three seconds. A flat-screen with a crack running through its middle. No wires connected to it. Benson searched for computer games in the drawers beneath – what did this man do to entertain himself? There were no bottles of booze around, there were no books or magazines, no porn, no dart board! With a sigh, Benson stood.

———

Even from up here, Lynne could hear the sounds of a search going on in the rooms below her. There was no banter though; that was missing, and it left an unfamiliar hole for her. On every search she'd been involved with there was joviality verging on a fucking stage show – pranks, laughs, and piss-takes aplenty. But it had to come from the top man; like a permission to laugh. But with the mood Cooper was in, no one dare utter a word.

They all searched in silence, and she did likewise. She found two wardrobes, a crusty double bed and a set of bedside drawers with socks and boxers inside. There were clothes, trainers, cigarette rolling equipment, and a baseball bat. That was it. The bathroom too yielded nothing of interest; mould and stains were the only décor, torn lino on the creaking floor, and a tap that dripped into a facecloth in the sink.

———

Eddie heard Cooper ranting as he descended into the darkness. He turned on the Maglite, conscious of the fact that Jim, despite his car not being out front, could still be lurking in the house somewhere – the cellar being a prime location. And secondly, if Jim wasn't here, maybe he was stupid enough to leave Mrs Shaw tied and gagged down here.

He rounded the corner at the foot of the stairs, feeling the chill nip at his arms. His torchlight flicked around the bare cellar walls, at the web-encrusted rafters inches above his head, the copper pipes running like a maze there too, with seemingly random electrical wires entwined with them.

And then he found a light switch. Eddie dropped his camera on the cleanest piece of floor he could find.

The bulb was barely big enough to cast a circular glow on the floor, but it was enough to show the detritus down here: the plastic garden furniture, the lengths of timber, bits of children's toys, a pair of old loudspeakers next to an equally old Technics twin deck record player. Beneath the bricked-up coal chute, Eddie saw the work bench, which was made of three planks of scaffolding board resting on a pair of woodworker's trestles.

He crunched over the solid concrete floor and shone his torch at the large screwdriver right in the centre of the bench. It was large enough indeed to have been used to force a uPVC casement – very much like the one in Terry Shaw's study and kitchen. A coil of solder sat next to a cheap electrical soldering iron and a few lengths of electrical wire.

There were two pairs of cheap headphones, and they looked relatively new. The ear padding was missing from them both. There was a new blister pack of two tiny luggage padlocks, the type you'd find on one of those rotary displays in bric-a-brac stores. The pack was new but the padlocks were missing.

Eddie stood back in the centre of the room, and shone the torch very slowly around him, getting the feeling there was more still to come. Cooper had Jim Price right in his sights as a prime candidate for the death of Sam Price, and he had some serious questions to answer about Liz Shaw too. All they needed were clues, stepping stones that would take the entire investigation towards its conclusion, yet there were still so many unanswered questions floating like dust motes around Eddie's mind.

Propped at a precarious angle against the damp outer wall, was an old display unit with smashed glass panes, warped shelves and chipboard doors that refused to close. Inside the drawers were mouse droppings; spider webs attached the unit to the floor and wall with a natural grace straight from a horror movie. Eddie shuddered and stood, ran the torch at the rearmost webs, and noticed how some had been torn away and lay like strands of filthy hair, clinging to the mouldy wood.

Eddie looked closer, then stopped. He could see a disturbance in the dust that coated the slanted side of the unit. And there on the floor, in more dust, was the unmistakable impression left behind by a Doc Marten shoe. A tingle swept Eddie's skin. "Another stepping stone." He grabbed a scale and a label, positioned them at the side of the footwear impression and photographed it, holding his flash unit between his ankles to give the best definition with oblique lighting. Once that was done, he peered behind the unit, and what he saw made him smile.

With gloved fingers, he removed a crumpled and damp sheaf of paper. It detailed the electrical circuits of a Bosch fuel injection system fitted to Mercedes vehicles. He fired off more photographs before replacing it.

"Come on, Collins."

He took a last glance around, then grabbed his camera, the scales, and headed for the stairs.

In the lounge, the team was standing in a circle looking pessimistic, pulling off nitrile gloves, shoving them inside out back into their pockets. "Anything?" Cooper asked.

Eddie shrugged. "Actually, yes."

"I don't mean to be rude," everyone turned to look at Jenkins who was still standing by the window, "but can this wait until we're outside again? He could come back any minute."

Cooper nodded, "Out," he said, "so he can lock up."

"Thanks," Jenkins mumbled. "If you need me again…"

Once outside, the team began walking uphill towards the cars. They could see Khan leaning against one, his arms folded, jaw working at some gum. Eddie heard Jim's front door close behind him, saw Jenkins working his key in the lock, his eyes on the street, keeping alert for Jim. "Be with you in a second," Eddie said to the group, and returned to the house, to Jenkins.

Jenkins looked up at Eddie, "You need to go back in?"

"Nah. I just need a word."

Benson drove steadily back towards the MCU, and Eddie relaxed on the back seat while Cooper ended a phone call. "What did you find, Eddie?"

"Same footwear marks down in the cellar. The same type that we found at Shaw's house, and that SOCO found at Liz Shaw's dentist."

"He's our man, then," Cooper smiled.

"That only gets him for burglary." Benson rubbed at the brown stain on his shirt, sharing his attention with the road every now and then.

"Worth pulling him in for. See if he'll cough to more in interview."

"He won't cough to more," Benson said. "If he thinks all we have on him is burglary, he'll roll over laughing and take it. Three months inside and he's as free as a bird."

Eddie cleared his throat. "And evidence that he could have tampered with Liz Shaw's car."

Cooper turned in his seat. "What evidence?"

"Papers. Wiring diagrams for Mercedes fuel injection systems; soldering iron, wires, that kind of stuff."

Cooper raised his eyebrows. "Nothing to suggest she could have been there?"

Eddie shook his head, watched the scenery go by.

"You put everything back?"

"Why don't you just bring this guy in? Ask him some awkward questions and let me get my hands on his house. I need to do a thorough job."

"When I want it forensicating, I'll give you a nod, alright?"

Eddie's mouth fell open: forensicating? What the hell was that?

"Benson's right, he'll say nothing. No, as soon as he comes back, we track him. He's going under obs from this afternoon." Cooper looked at Benson, "Jack that up for me." Benson nodded, parked the car in a restricted bay and climbed out without a word.

"And what if he doesn't come back?" Eddie got out and slammed the door.

"Why wouldn't he?"

"Because it's coming to a head. Whatever's going down with Liz Shaw can't go on for much longer. Her body has to surface sooner or later. Anyway, last I heard, Pot Noodles are fairly cheap and readily available—"

Benson opened the reception door, "He'll come back because that's where he works from. He doesn't know we've been inside."

"Yet!"

"Eddie—"

"Wait a minute, what about Terry Shaw, you going to stalk him as well?"

Cooper stopped in the reception, turned to look at Eddie.

Eddie peered over his shoulder at Moneypenny's weekend replacement, and then Cooper began talking.

"No. We're going to give him some good news for a change, help relieve some of his tension, and some of the tension he's putting on us for a quick end to all this." And then Cooper headed for the double doors, obviously thinking the conversation was over.

Eddie followed quickly, "Shaw's in on this, Cooper. If you talk to him now, it's going to fuck up an entire—"

"There's no connection between these two, Eddie."

Eddie kicked the doors, and shouted, "McGowan is the fucking connection!"

Cooper didn't even stop, "Christ's sake. His wife drew a few lines in a book."

"Cooper. Stop now!"

Cooper did just that. He took a long deep breath and slowly turned. Benson backed away; Moneypenny's stand-in hastily looked down.

Eddie stared at him. "And then she died in a rigged car accident before someone started playing swap-the-stiff."

"Do you really think we're going to open..." Cooper paused, seemed to realise he was shouting, and shouting about a potentially sensitive subject. He walked towards Eddie, pointing a finger. "You really think we're going to reopen a Ripper investigation based on what you've got? I've spoken to the chief about it, and he's in total agreement. We keep it quiet, under wraps until, or if, any further evidence comes to light."

"But—"

"Get real, Eddie. The only way we're going to find out what the hell's going on here is to talk to Shaw."

Eddie dropped the camera bag and got right into Cooper's face. Despite his heaving chest, his desire to shout at the stupid man, he kept calm, and he whispered, "Please. Just give me some time. Put obs on him for now, alright, but please... please don't tell him his wife wasn't in that car. I'll get you that evidence."

Cooper looked at Benson. Benson's face was expressionless, but Eddie thought he saw the most discreet of nods. Cooper sighed and then walked off.

Eddie looked to Benson, "Is that a yes or no?"

"You think I'm gonna ask him after you've put him in a mood?"

Eddie set off after Cooper, but Benson took hold of his arm. "Leave it," he said. "He's even more fucking stubborn than you are." Eddie tried to pull free, but Benson tightened his grip, "If you go after him, he'll say no just to piss you off."

"What?"

"Treat him like a big kid and you won't go far wrong."

Eddie relaxed, "Unbelievable."

Benson let go. "Anyway, I think there's another connection between Price and Shaw, besides McGowan."

"Like what?"

"I wonder if Price was a hanger-on that knocked about with Terry and Liz and a few others back at uni. I spoke to one of their friends and she mentioned a sleazebag but couldn't remember his name. I'm going to ring her, see if she recognises the name."

Chapter Twenty-nine

The Consequence

EDDIE TAPPED THE STEERING wheel. He was trying his best to be patient but was failing. He was on his third cigarette in less than forty minutes. The cup of coffee from the drive-thru was empty and his throat was dry, and not for the first time did he consider just forgetting the whole thing and going for a refill.

The lane he was parked on was dark and deserted. There were no properties around; it was a country road, a spur off the main drag through Swillington that ended up going nowhere, and consequently it had no street lights. It was however, popular with fly-tippers, noted Eddie, and probably would make a fairly decent dealing site too if it wasn't so close to the main road. Through the open window, Eddie could hear the incessant noise of traffic thundering past, and he flicked away his latest cigarette to join the others in the dust.

Around the corner, up ahead, a pair of headlights washed over the rubbish bags and the sandstone walls lining the road.

Within a few seconds, the lights went out and the car cruised up to Eddie's Discovery. A man got out and approached, fishing in his pocket for something.

"Jenkins," Eddie said. "I thought you weren't coming."

"I got busy, sorry." He handed it over to Eddie, and then without even looking back, returned to his car.

Eddie said thanks, but it was wasted. The car disappeared as quickly as it had arrived, and Eddie stared at the envelope.

He swallowed but his dry throat merely clacked. This was one of those times that could turn him from being a fairly decent law-abiding citizen into one of those people the police hunted. He held onto the envelope, and then he thought of his father's face, the sorrow and the pain that had twisted it, that had made him cry.

Some people thought that the law didn't apply to them. But these people, the ones that inflicted misery on complete strangers on a daily basis had decided that they were above the law, that whatever possessions their victims had, were undeserved by them, and should be liberated.

Why did people think they had a God-given right to other people's belongings?

And why did people think they had a God-given right to inflict misery without fear of consequence?

Eddie was that consequence.

Chapter Thirty

Influencing People

— One —

"WHERE ARE YOU GOING, SON?"

Eddie jumped at the sound of Charles's voice. "Still can't get used to you being here, scaring the shit out me in the middle of the night."

"It's not normal you creeping around at this hour."

"Really? It's like being haunted by your conscience. Except my conscience doesn't wear Y-fronts. And corduroy slippers."

"So where are you going?"

"Out. For a drive."

"At two o'clock on a Sunday morning?"

"It's when I think best. No one else around."

Charles paused. "Am I cramping your style?"

"Like father like son, Dad; I don't have any style." Eddie looked at Charles's pale, skinny chest, at all the ribs and all the veins running around in there. "That reminds me," he said, "I must get a new A-Z."

Charles stepped forward. "Want a coffee? Offload a bit."

Offload? That actually sounded good; get it out, purge his system; release the demons. "Nah, I'm okay."

"Lying little bastard."

"She left. Forget about it; it's no big deal."

"My arse. I've seen you drift off into thoughts that are deep. I've heard you tossing and turning for hours every night."

"Not so much turning, Dad," he winked.

"Give over! You act all tough on the outside, but inside you're as soft as freshly curled shit—"

"You are disgusting, you know that?"

"But true! You shouldn't burden yourself, you should let it out."

"There's nothing to bloody let out, now give it a rest."

"Tell me, son."

In frustration, Eddie growled. "Okay, okay, I'll tell you if it'll shut you up."

Charles breathed out and smiled as though there was no one alive could pull the wool over his eyes.

Eddie clicked his fingers, "Ah, I know why you're fretting so much. You're worried she's coming back, aren't you?"

"No, what rubbish."

"You are!" Eddie laughed, "You're frightened she's coming back and we'll turf you out."

Charles was silent.

"Dad?"

No response.

"Hey, I was only kidding. Dad?"

Charles eventually looked at him. "Is it true?"

"No. I told you she's gone. She isn't coming back. And even if she were, which she isn't, but even if she were, I wouldn't kick you out."

"No, but you'd make my life hell until I had no choice but to leave." There was venom in Charles's eyes, and he knew it, so he looked away, and he swallowed, and it was easy to see the regret there.

Eddie shuffled across to him. "I'm not playing games, Dad. If two women moved in here, I would still want you to stay. This is your home now. You're safe here; I'm not going to kick you out, okay?"

"Hmph."

"Look at me."

Reluctantly, Charles swivelled his head somewhere in Eddie's general direction.

"I said, okay?"

"Okay."

"I don't know how many times or in what different ways I have to keep saying it to you, but it's true, right."

"You going to tell me exactly why she left now?"

Eddie looked at the ceiling, "You're a nosey git. She was up-to-date with her hep jabs, but she wasn't up-to-date with her canine jabs."

"Eh, I don't know—"

"Canine, Dad. Pertaining to dog?"

"Oh. Go on."

"She was on a job in Alwoodley and was bitten by a rabid Dachshund." Eddie kept a straight a face.

Charles was beginning to squint. "Are you messing me about?"

"Do you want to know or not?"

"Okay, go on."

"Thank you. Turns out the dog was from Eastern Europe. It had been used as a terrier, to get down into the burrows of the fruit bat."

"I thought fruit bats lived in trees?"

"No, that's the pipistrelle."

"Oh right, didn't know that."

"Anyway, this dog was bitten by a Desdomonus."

"Desdomonus, right," Charles nodded.

"Which is why it was brought to the UK, where it bit Ros."

"And? What happened?"

Eddie whispered, "She developed facial hair. And her ears grew larger."

"You're having me on!"

"Have some respect!"

"Sorry. I didn't mean to... Go on."

"And then she developed a liking for black pudding and Winalot."

"Really?"

Eddie nodded, "Before long she was taking time off work to watch The Twilight Saga while hanging from the light-fitting."

Charles took a step back, rubbing his bare arms. "Kind of cold in here now, don't ya think?"

Eddie headed for the door, "That's the new syndrome they've just discovered: Gullibility Syndrome," and started laughing.

"You little bleeder! Here, you're not a sociopath, are you?"

"Do you know what a sociopath even is?" Eddie grabbed his coat.

"It's someone who can't adapt to certain social situations. That sounds to me like you're a sociopath. You should be on pills, or locked away."

"Cheeky old sod."

— Two —

Eddie turned out the headlights. He kept the motor running as he looked up and down the street trying to gauge its status – hostile or passive, normal or just dormant, waiting for the stupid man to get out of the car. That made him snort: normal? Around here?

Around here what passed as normal was high unkempt hedges, yards full of rubbish with discarded nappies blowing around the gutters and settling among the spent needles. Normality was the smashed windows of drugs deals gone bad, the barking dogs and street gangs, the teenage mothers who thought they knew what life was all about, and who thought that society should be providing for them and their little bastards as the absent father pissed his social cheque away and burgled for some more.

Eddie turned off the engine, let the clicking of the Discovery's exhaust finally cease, and then cracked the door, and slid out. He lit a cigarette, shielding the flame from the wind, and then locked the car. His eyes finally synced with the almost total absence of light and he marched up the street towards payback time.

He tapped the Maglite that dangled from a loop on his belt, and took quiet steps in steel-toed combat boots – hopefully he wouldn't be forced to use those, but he would if it came down to it.

For the last time he questioned his rationale. He worked for British justice – envied around the world for being corruption-free, on the grand scale of things. And here he was, taking justice into his own hands. Again. But there were some things that needed a more personal approach, a more detailed intervention than a magistrate could offer. And there were some things that British justice just never addressed at all: the victim being one, and revenge being another.

Tonight, Eddie hoped to address both those issues.

Number 16 came up on his left side, and Eddie took another good look around, flicked away the cigarette and slid a pair of smooth black leather gloves on. He listened too, but the high hedges moving in the wind obliterated everything. He grabbed the master key from his jeans pocket and, deftly avoiding the detritus on the path, made it to the door.

The building looked like a regular semi-detached house, but the council could squeeze even more lowlife into these places if they split the building into four flats, each with its own entrance door; two in the middle of the frontage for the upstairs tenants, one at each side for the ground floor.

Number 16 was ground floor, right hand side. He knew the layout of them too, having seen the insides of these places at the hundreds of burglary scenes and the scores of serious assault scenes, and the handful of murders he'd examined over the years. In the hall the bathroom would be to the left, kitchen to the right, lounge at the end. In the lounge would be a door to the right, and that's where he'd find the robbing little bastard, bare arse sticking in the air, leg curled around someone else's teenage mother.

Eddie lifted the letterbox flap and listened. He heard nothing, not even the groans or snores associated with the obligatory pitbull or wild-bred staffy. So now he checked around the back, being careful again of the shit that littered the so-called garden. He thought of Englishmen and castles – and how these Englishmen had no self-respect and probably couldn't even spell castle. There were no lights on either in the flat, or in the entire building, no windows open.

Back at the door, Eddie eased the key that Jenkins had kindly given him into the lock. First success was that it fitted nicely, and after a bit of persuasion, the key turned silently – success number two. He pocketed the key again. The handle squeaked as he depressed it, and Eddie grimaced. The hallway was devoid of any furniture or carpet and so the squeak was amplified, was even accompanied by its own echo, but the third success was the door swinging almost silently open. Eddie kept the handle down, slipped into the hallway, and closed the door behind him before slowly releasing the handle again.

He stood still, breathing the stench of stale body odour and last night's curry left-overs. He thought there was a hint of urine in among the collaboration of smells too, but couldn't be sure. In here darkness ruled completely and he was never going to see anything, no matter how long he allowed his eyes to grow accustomed to it. He reached down and blipped the Maglite switch. The light was on and off again in milliseconds, but it left enough of a ghost on Eddie's retinas to register the hall as safe, no obstacles to clamber over, and no sleeping dogs.

Once at the lounge door, he listened again, surprised by how much noise even the rustling of his clothing made. He was looking forward to this, but part of him, the sane part, was nervous as hell.

The door was ajar, and through the gap he could see a meek orange glow, a flickering kind of light that might have been candle light, but the humble hiss he could hear told him that the gas fire had been left on – and why not, these arseholes never paid their bills anyway. With the tips of his fingers, he gently pushed the door open and stepped inside. The bedroom door, full of fist holes and slits where it had been attacked with a knife, was wide open.

Eddie breathed silently through his open mouth.

The flickering orange light was brighter, and it was indeed the gas fire. It lit up the room well. He could see bottles and cans strewn around the floor, could see the pile of dirty clothing on the scratched leather sofa, could even see the X-Box and the massive TV over in the corner by the curtained window, and the plates of congealed curry scattered around as though this prick had had a party and just crashed afterward, hoping the council would come and clean up after him.

On the small, stained coffee table were two empty bottles of Stella and an ashtray. There were roll-up cigarette ends and chewed gum in and around the ashtray, and more scattered around the floor. On the walls were pictures of a New York skyline, of builders with their legs dangling hundreds of feet above the earth, enjoying a packed lunch on an exposed steel girder. And next to it, another all-time classic: the female tennis player scratching her bare arse. And they said taste was dead.

Eddie took from his pocket a small clear plastic bag and opened it, trying to keep its rustling to a minimum. From the bedroom, he heard snoring, and for a second he paused, and stiffened, eyes wide, slight tremble in his hands. He took the ashtray and emptied it into the bag, sealed it and put it in his coat pocket, dropped the ashtray onto a leather chair.

Now it was time for Eddie to find the rings.

He knew most burglars off-loaded their stolen gear within a day of taking it, but sometimes jewellery took longer, especially the more unusual items. You took something like his Mum's engagement ring to a pawn shop or a shady jewellers and they'd ask too many questions, or just offer you a shit price so you'd sling your hook and try somewhere else.

A lot of these fence-type places were regularly visited by the police, and they always demanded to see paperwork relating to the more exotic or expensive items they had for sale. Of course, there were ways to circumvent this process, and if Craig Shipton was half the thief Eddie thought he was, then he would have used those ways, would have off-loaded Steph's jewellery long ago, and he'd never see it again.

But that was only part of the purpose he was here. He hoped to get the jewellery back, of course, but if he didn't, he still had the second reason for this visit: revenge.

Eddie crept into the dark bedroom.

He could see a lone figure sprawled under a tangled duvet, a hand hanging over the edge of the bed, a shaven head, almost buried under a pillow confirmed that Craig was here. Eddie slid the heavy Maglite from its loop and he gripped it, held it high and was about to smash it into this kid's exposed shin when he stopped. He blinked, swallowed, and lowered the torch again.

Silently, he sighed, and mouthed "bastard" to himself. Now was not the right time to have a guilty conscience!

Part of him said the kid deserved it, that he should go ahead and crack a few bones and then have some fun with him before leaving. And part of him said that beating was too good for this lowlife scum, that he was responsible for his father's nervous disposition, that he'd almost given the old man a fucking heart attack; that he had him just where he wanted him, a role reversal of what happened to his dad.

Yes, that part of him said beating was too good for the little twat, and he should kill him – he knew how to do it, he knew how to do it and walk away a free man, and remain free. Because sometimes, he told himself, scum like this never learned, even from a beating in the name of justice, and he'd be back out there again in a week frightening more old people and stealing their memories from them.

Eddie raised the torch again, felt the weight in his hand and knew one quick blow would snap a tibia. Two would smash a cranium. Easy as that. Do it, walk out the door and know you'd done society a favour. He gripped the torch tighter.

And then the light came on.

The girl stood there without moving. Her hand was still by the light switch and in it she held an evil-looking knife with serrations all down the back of the blade like a prehistoric stickleback, and a glint on the sharp side that meant business. She held a stained off-white quilt to her bare chest with the other hand; she was the pile of dirty clothing Eddie had seen in the lounge. Her dirty feet had black-painted toenails, and they set her smeared black lipstick off nicely. But even the neo-Goth face make-up couldn't hide the black eye or the split lip. Her ears were pierced from the lobe to the helix, except that her left ear was full of crusty blood where the last three rings had been pulled out.

She stared at him, her eyes black, squinting, as were Eddie's, against the naked lightbulb dangling from the ceiling. She was cool, she was calm, no screaming, no hyperventilating.

Eddie knew he was in trouble.

"Craig," she said.

The body beneath the quilt on the bed groaned, and stirred.

"Craig."

"Fuck off."

This was no time for pleasantries, Eddie knew, this was no time to try and reason with an armed woman who didn't recoil at the sight of a stranger in her home; this was a time for action that told her he meant business. This was a time to break a leg.

His attention was split between the armed girl by the door, and the slowly stirring arsehole in the bed. She could see what was about to happen and she dropped the quilt and made a lunge toward Eddie. Eddie swung the torch at Craig's lower leg and the sound of steel cracking bone made the advancing girl cringe, but it didn't make her retreat. She bared her teeth and suddenly the room was a cacophony of screams, and Eddie was trapped in its centre.

Knowing that Craig was now occupied with dealing with a broken leg, Eddie swung the torch out to his side, where it contacted the naked girl's chin. He hit her much harder than he'd intended – he meant her no harm, his gripe was with Craig there, and his blow to her face was supposed to be defensive. But momentum had given it power enough to break teeth. She hit the deck; her scream of anger now muffled by closed swelling lips, and became a sorrowful yelp of pain. Tears made new tracks down her smeared mascara. She held her hands over her mouth – eyes screwed shut for only a second.

This was bad, Eddie told himself. He was about to bend and help the girl, to say sorry, that he hadn't meant to... On her left hand, noted Eddie, was a pair of rings. Steph's rings. Eddie stood again, mouth open. To his left, Craig held his shin, writhed amid the filthy quilt, screaming in agony. To his right was a naked girl who'd been dragged through a hedge backwards, who was still armed, and who had rapidly got her pain under control. She stared at Eddie, and took away her hands. Blood dripped into her lap, and Eddie felt bad all over again.

"Give me the rings," he said.

The girl stood.

"I said give me the fucking rings."

"They're mine."

She pointed the knife again and Eddie took a breath. "Drop it before I break his other leg."

She paused, stared at Craig performing some strange horizontal dance, girders standing out on his neck, teeth bared, and screams and profanities spewing from his mouth.

She advanced a step and Eddie raised the torch again.

"Give 'em," Craig yelled.

"What!"

"Give them to him."

Eddie looked at her.

"They're mine. You said we were engaged now!"

Eddie was stunned. "You fucking scum." He began the second blow and the kid raised his arms in protection, eyes squinting against the impact.

"I'll get you some more!"

Eddie stopped and faced the girl, and through gritted teeth said, "Give me them now or I'll cave his fucking head in." He stared at her, soaking up her uncertainty. "You know I will, and then I'll cut your fucking fingers off if I have to."

"Give them up!"

The girl threw the knife across the room and petulantly pulled the rings off. She held them out to Eddie, "Who are you?" She stared at him, and Eddie could see that Craig's yelping and screaming was disturbing her thoughts, and she yelled, "Shut the fuck up, Craig!"

Eddie put the rings into his back pocket, and closed in on her, close enough to smell the alcohol on her breath. He looked down at her and snarled, "If I hear he's burgled an elderly person again, I'll be back. And next time I'll finish him off."

The girl looked at Craig.

"Get me an ambulance!"

"Did you hear me?"

She nodded and then spat blood in his face.

Eddie opened his eyes and he saw her smiling at him. Sick little whore, he thought. He pushed her onto Craig, who screamed again, and then he left the bedroom, turning on the lounge and hall lights as he went. He found a coat hanging on a nail in the kitchen doorframe and wiped her blood off with that. Even now, when things were scrambled in his mind, he was thinking forensically by not wiping her blood onto his own coat, even though the need to get it off quickly was instinctive. As he wiped the blood on to the coat, he saw something black and woolly poking out of the pocket. Eddie grinned as he pulled out a balaclava.

Chapter Thirty-one

There is Such a Thing as Fate

— One —

EDDIE YAWNED. LAST NIGHT had been a long one. He looked at his watch as if trying to calculate the amount of sleep he actually had. He reckoned somewhere between two and three hours. And already fatigue was nipping at his mind like a constant companion that kept whispering, "Sleep, sleep, sleep".

"You got authority?"

"It's for Superintendent Cooper."

"I need it in writing. Inspector rank or above." The storeman stared at Benson, unfeeling, uncaring. Rules is rules.

Benson stared right back and drew an envelope from his jacket pocket. He handed it over. "I'm an inspector."

He took it, slid out the sheet of paper and read it. He looked at Benson and nodded. "I'll be in my office if you need me." He walked away, glancing back when neither Benson nor Eddie spoke. It must have appeared very suspicious.

Eddie scanned the racking, followed the labels, crabbing to his left, searching.

"I could get disciplined for this," Benson whispered.

"Stop moaning. All the best coppers are mavericks. Don't you watch television?"

"I don't want to be a fucking maverick. I just want to keep my job and my pension."

Eddie stopped searching and said, "You know this is the only way, don't you? Cooper is ready for blowing the whole thing wide open. Soon as Shaw gets to find out what's happened, him and Jim will be on their toes, and we'll never see them again."

Benson looked at his watch, "Get on with it."

Eddie checked a slip of paper. "It's here." He reached for the box labelled: 1979. CA/79/17638 – P79-4675 ARCHIVE Q2. McGOWAN.

He lowered the box to the floor, removed the lid and he and Benson bent to see what was inside; a jumble of paper and plastic bags, yellow evidence tags sticking up all over the place like markers. Benson went to stand by the corridor, as though fearful the storeman would make a reappearance, and Eddie snapped on two pairs of gloves and DNA mask. Gently, as though handling rare museum pieces, he brought out thirty-five-year-old paper-wrapped exhibits one after the other until he found exhibit CKD25 – the bandana.

"Got it," Eddie said through the mask.

Benson tapped his watch, "Whenever you're ready, Quincy, no rush."

Eddie cut through the seal and carefully withdrew the bandana. He unfolded it onto a clean sheet of brown paper. Benson, arms still folded, shuffled over as Eddie began to photograph it. He brought the camera in close on the love heart – red, as it turned out. "Does that look personal to you? I mean, it's like someone made it for someone else; not mass produced."

"What's it matter, we're—"

"Liz Shaw drew an arrow pointing directly to this heart. She recognised it, Benson. This whole thing revolves around what she found in those books. That's what matters, and it's what Cooper can't get his head around."

Benson swallowed, "We're fucked when this comes out. There are protocols to follow for this kind of thing, and Cooper's very touchy about protocols, especially where The Ripper is—"

"We don't have time to cut through the red tape and lick all the right arseholes!"

"Alright, alright!" Benson pinched the bridge of his nose, "If that was stuffed in her mouth, how the hell are you going to get user DNA from it?"

"If I avoid the blood, concentrate on the scrunched up section in the middle, I might be lucky enough to miss McGowan's saliva—"

"And hit the sweat spot?" Benson smiled for the first time today.

"Horatio Caine, is that you?"

Benson chuckled, then nodded, "Come on, faster, you tit."

Eddie took a fresh swab from a batch poking out of his camera bag, dampened it from an ampule of sterile water, and began slowly caressing the tip of the swab over the material. "All I need are just a few cells of his."

"Wait a minute, you're going to want me to submit this, aren't you?"

Eddie carried on swabbing, saying nothing.

"I can't do that! This isn't a regular MCU case, Eddie. I can't authorise Low Copy swabs at two grand a pop from a Ripper case, it has to come from—"

"Five grand, actually. I want it on four-hour turnaround, and it's Sunday don't forget. Don't worry about authorisation, I'll sort that at my end."

Benson squatted down a few feet from Eddie, and let his head rest against the racking. "You know that even if the DNA from that swab matches the DNA taken from Terry's toothbrush, it'll be inadmissible in court?"

"If we get the result I think we will, we can come back and do it all again legally." Even through the mask it was clear Eddie was smiling. He sheathed the swab, pulled the mask off and grinned even wider, "I love the word 'we'. It's got such an in-the-shit-together sound about it."

— Two —

Eddie flicked the cigarette out of the window and, with the phone clamped between his ear and shoulder, sat and slurped coffee. On the desk before him was a tube with Terry Shaw's blue toothbrush inside, and next to it a clear evidence bag containing the swab from the bandana. "Hello? Yes, four hours please. Yes. Authority is Jeffery Walker. Thank you. Yes, they'll be with you in about an hour. Can you ring my office with the results? Cheers, yes, Eddie Collins, major crime."

Eddie put down the phone, sat back in his chair and jumped as Benson entered with Khan.

"Ready?" Benson asked.

Eddie picked up a pen and drew the form towards him. At the top it said Home Office Laboratory, and at the foot of the page was a box with 'Authorised by'. Eddie signed it Jeffery Walker, handed it and the exhibits over to Khan. "Don't lose these, don't stop for an all-day breakfast at Little Chef, and don't end up in a fucking ditch somewhere."

Khan snatched the exhibits, and then the paperwork, glanced at the signature, and looked back at Eddie. He was about to speak, when Eddie said, "Is there a problem?"

Khan opened his mouth but Eddie cut him dead.

"I said is there a problem?"

Khan sighed, "No."

"Good. Now fly, little robin, fly."

Khan made no secret of his dismay; the window in Eddie's office rattled long after he'd slammed the door. He looked at Benson, "You know there was a kid at the scene, don't you? In a push chair."

Benson only nodded. Eddie continued to stare at him as if inviting some input. All Benson said was, "I do my research, Collins."

"Sick bastard."

The windows had only just stopped rattling when Cooper entered. Benson and Eddie both jumped as though they'd just been caught kissing.

"What are you doing in here?"

"Erm—"

"We both have feelings for each other," Eddie said. "I know I said you were the only one, but you've lost so much weight over the years that I don't recognise you anymore."

Cooper shook his head at Eddie, then said to Benson, "Out." Benson laughed as he went. Cooper turned to Eddie, "I agree we watch Shaw for now, but if we get nothing I'm bringing them both in."

"You found Jim Price, yet?"

"Nope." Cooper closed the door after him.

"Now there's a surprise."

— Three —

Clouds crept in from the west, and the sunlight skulked away taking the warmth of the spring day with it. A thin orange stripe lingered at the horizon. Shadows disappeared and a diffused greyness took their place, saturating the air with a monotone murkiness. In the new greyness two burnt-out vehicles, sitting forlorn on the concrete apron of a disused garage like abandoned fire brigade training exercises, took on a sinister look. The part burnt, part soot-stained sign above the two huge roller shutter doors proclaimed 'Brooklands Garage – Repairs and MoT Work'. The paint had faded, was flaking off piece by piece with each new gust of wind. Melted plastic guttering hung from the roof like it had been designed and installed by Salvador Dali.

Brooklands Garage was bang in the centre of an equally abandoned light industrial estate that had failed twenty years ago because of substantial rate increases, because of consistent burglaries that had pushed insurance premiums too high to manage, and an E. coli water infection that was, it was rumoured, caused by terrorists. There never was an E. coli water infection; it was just a rumour that the whole estate had latched onto, but it had served to hasten many of the tenants' departures to a new estate less than five miles away with better motorway access.

The estate was home now to families of foxes and families of travellers who stayed for a week before moving on to a newer estate they'd heard about only five miles away with much better pickings. Nature was slowly reclaiming it.

Jim drove around the estate first, looking left and right as he closed in on Brooklands and the two burn-outs parked out front. To the side was a rock-strewn weed-encrusted track that disappeared around the rear of the building and along the far side to emerge at the concrete apron round the front again. He drove around the track, the little Escort's suspension creaking and banging on the potholes and rocks.

On his second circuit, he parked behind the building, next to his old breakdown truck, shut off the engine, climbed out and listened for a good five minutes before walking to the right side of the building. It was large for a car garage, built entirely out of blackened red brick that in places was crumbling, succumbing to erosion and persistent weeds that could grow out of the tiniest of cracks, flourishing in abandonment. A nest of breeze-block add-ons for oil storage complemented coils of barbed wire that sagged like dying slinkies between rusting supports atop the perimeter wall.

He looked around incessantly, trying not to look like he was looking around, until he reached a large Vent-Axia fan set into the brickwork four feet off the ground. He flexed his fingers like a safe-cracker and then silently pulled the fan on well-oiled hinges, opening it from the wall like you would a cupboard door. He peered inside and then, seemingly satisfied that no one was lying in wait for him, he closed the fan, returned to the car and took a rucksack and propane bottle from the boot.

Again Jim paused, resting against the car, and smoked a roll-up, taking his time, feeling the gentle flutter of nerves while listening to the estate and the hum of traffic half a mile away punctuated by the scream of sirens. As if scared by them, he froze, eyes wide, until the sound retreated and faded into the traffic hum again.

He knew that complacency was the easiest way to end up behind bars, and Jim had no intention of relaxing his well-practised routine. He flicked away the roll-up, hoisted the rucksack over his shoulder, and picked up the propane bottle. He walked the hundred or so yards to the front of the building, where again he paused to make sure no one was watching.

The padlock snapped open, and although he'd expected it to, he still grimaced at the noise as it clattered against the steel door. He gritted his teeth and then let himself in, bringing the padlock in too so no one could lock him in. He set down the bottle with a boom while he dropped a steel bar into two hooks behind the door. All this security was Jim's ritual for keeping safe, his carefully considered ritual against easy capture.

Familiarity guided Jim over the obstacles strewn around the floor, helped him avoid the two exposed mechanics' pits, one for each of the roller shutter doors, and led him to another steel door at the back of the garage. He paused, listened at the door, and then let himself in. It smelled of ammonia in here.

She was badly illuminated by four dirt-encrusted skylights. A woman sat shaking in a wooden chair. Her head flicked from side to side as she realised her captor had returned. Her breathing was fast and shallow.

"No need to fret," he kicked aside empty water bottles.

But she was fretting. Across the top of her head she wore a steel band that, at the ears, joined another band that ran right around the circumference of her head, simultaneously rendering her blind and mostly deaf at the same time. Held by tiny padlocks, the kind you'd find on an item of luggage, through loops in the ear bands, was a further band that anchored the whole contraption in place like a chin strap.

Between the metal bands and her eyes and ears, he'd taped furry black circles stolen from some cheap earphones he'd bought, there to further dampen her senses and minimise the discomfort. Comfort was severely lacking where the band crossed the bridge of her nose, evidenced by the open wound there. It leaked a small rivulet of blood that had run either side of her mouth. She looked like a grotesque clown.

Jim stared at her, "Sorry about the nose."

She held her breath and he could see the tendons in her neck stand out like a lattice of anticipated pain, saw her hands snap into fists. He felt simultaneously wicked for doing this to her, and powerful because he had done it to her. He dropped the bag on the table by her side and bent to check the bar and cuffs that bound her hands eighteen inches apart. Attached to the bar was a slim cable that connected with an eye-loop on the wall, affording her a yard or two of movement – certainly enough movement to get to the commode. It still looked in good order, though there was redness around the cuffs where she'd been pulling.

"Gotten a bit cold out." He tried to keep his tone friendly, like he was having a one-way conversation with an old relative who was hard of hearing. Cheery, but stern, he chose to think of himself.

It was the first time he'd spoken to her using sentences. Usually, he'd bark a command and expect her to obey. If she didn't, a slap convinced her to cooperate. "Soon have you warmed up." From the bag he took another half dozen bottles of water, cracked the lids off each and set them down near the edge of the table. He threw what empty bottles she had managed to place back on the table, over into the far corner.

The woman shuddered and pulled at her ties.

He took the propane bottle over to the small heater, swapped an empty bottle for the full one and relit the fire. "There," he said, "be toasty warm in no time."

He approached her, crouched nearby and said, "Brought you some warm food." He took out a small key, touched her shoulder and said, "Remember the deal. I'm taking off the chin strap now so you can eat, okay?"

She kept rigidly still and Jim stopped taking the food out of the bag and waited. "I said okay?"

This time she nodded, though the tendons in her neck and those in her wrists were still taut; she was frantic, and his hopes that she might settle down and relax once this became something of a familiar routine for her were proving hopelessly wrong. As soon as he released one padlock and let the strap fall to her chest, she began to scream. The wound on the bridge of her nose gaped again as the strap dug in, and fresh blood seeped into her mouth and coated her teeth. It dripped from her chin.

Jim ignored her and reached inside the holdall again. "Here," he said, "I'm going to put it in your lap, okay?" She still screamed. He shouted, "I said 'okay?'"

The screaming subsided, became a ragged and hurried panting. Eventually, fatigue robbed her of energy. "Okay."

"Cheeseburger, fries, and some coffee." He smiled at her. "Not much, but the best I could do."

The woman stopped sobbing, appeared to listen to Jim's voice as he passed behind her.

"Eat, alright, while I go and empty this." He lifted the potty out of the commode, held it arm's length, and walked around her again, craning his neck to keep his face away from the worst of the smell. "I brought you some moistened wipes for, you know…"

Jim took the potty out of the room, headed for the toilets and flushed it away. He returned to find her in exactly the same position. "You should eat that while it's still warm."

She remained silent and still.

He tutted. "I brought some Savlon and plasters for your nose." And then he looked at her hands, saw the broken nails and winced at the blood. "And for your fingers too." He busied himself opening a pouch on the bag. "I knew it'd rub, but I didn't have any padding…" She remained still, trembling, almost lifeless. "If you don't eat, I'll put the chin strap back on and go."

She began to sob again and began fumbling for the burger with her right hand, her left floating aimlessly in air eighteen inches away. She almost got the burger to her chin when she began screaming again. She stood, and Jim backed off a pace or two. She yelled and threw the food across the floor, hot coffee burning her legs. She screamed hysterically, pulling at the cuffs, trying to yank them off her wrists, to pull the cable from the wall, grabbing the steel band across her eyes, jagged nails digging into her forehead. Saliva flew from her mouth, more mixed with the blood from her injured nose and hung in long strings from her wet face.

Jim grabbed the cuffs with one hand then slapped her hard across the face, knocking her back into the chair, but she continued to thrash about as he pulled the chin strap back into position and locked the padlock through the loop.

Beaten and exhausted, she wept.

———

"I'll put the wipes there on the table. You've got plenty of water left and the heater should last you till… Look, I'll sort your nose out next time, when you're in a better mood. Or you could do it; stuff's on the table."

The woman continued to thrash about and for a moment or two Jim thought she could really do herself some damage. And then he realised it was his presence that was causing it; she'd calm down when he left, just like she did the last time, and the time before.

"Look," he said, "I'm sorry. I didn't want to do this. Not to you."

Though her jaws were clamped shut, she spoke like a bad ventriloquist, moving only her lips to form the words. She spoke with a voice full of pain and anger laced with fear, "You know me?"

Jim put his hands together whispered, "Oh I know you, alright. You're Liz Shaw."

Her head slumped forward but she remained quiet, perhaps contemplating her next move. "And what's your name?" she asked.

"Ah," he smiled, realising her next move was to befriend the monster, tumbling down the hill towards embracing the Stockholm Syndrome perhaps? "Jim."

"Jim what?"

"Just Jim."

She nodded, lifting her head up as though smelling the air. "I can help you," she whispered. "If you'll let me." She paused, waiting for Jim to make a reply, but he didn't; he folded his arms instead and listened to her. "I work for a charity that helps the homeless, the disadvantaged… I could help you."

He said nothing. The smile had gone now, though, and he thought perhaps it was time he did likewise.

"Is it money you need?"

Jim closed the rucksack. "Do you need me to bring anything the next time I come over?"

"I can get you money?"

"Lady things, I mean. You know."

"My husband, he can get you some money. Jim?"

"I'll take that as a no then."

"Are you holding him to ransom?"

"Goodbye, Liz."

"Jim? Please, let me talk to him, I can help with the negotiations."

Jim ground his teeth, tempted to tell her all about it, and he even leaned forward, ready to whisper in her ear. But something stopped him. Maybe it was some kind of loyalty to Terry, he didn't know. Maybe it was the chivalric side of him that believed a deal was a deal until it was broken. As far as he was concerned, it hadn't yet been broken. He shuffled towards the door.

"Jim?"

"Goodbye."

"Jim! Jim don't leave me again! Jim, I'll get you more money! Please, please, Jim!"

The scream went right through him, it seemed just the right frequency to puncture his eardrums, just the right frequency to make him lose his temper, just the way Sam had made him lose his temper. Everything she ever did was the just the right fucking frequency! Just the one that pushed his buttons! He dropped the rucksack. Was at Liz's side in a heartbeat. "Stop!" he yelled in her ear, hands inches from her throat.

She shrieked, jerked away from him, but she stopped, she did, she stopped dead. She was holding her breath.

Jim peered at her, panting like he had when Sam went still. "You think I'm cruel. You think I'm a lowlife fecking scum." He closed up until his lips were almost kissing the steel band over her ear. "Don't you!" She jerked away again, but said nothing, hands gripping the chair until a crescent of blood oozed from her broken nails. "Fate," he whispered. "Fate brought you and me together, Liz. Like old friends reunited." He found himself smiling at her, his hands now clasped before him like a sinner making confession. "I have to tell you something." He had her attention, perhaps even had her respect, and now he felt brave enough to sit on the edge of the table before her, and smile. Feck chivalry. "I saved your life."

Her head lifted slightly.

"Oh yes I did. Fate, you see. If it hadn't been for me, you'd be dead, Liz. Very very fecking dead."

She turned her head towards him and Jim felt a shudder scamper across his back. It was as though she could see him. She seemed to smile at him, a kind of knowing smile that made him nervous. Her lips moved, "What do you mean?"

"I never saw a future for you and Terry."

She swallowed at the mention of his name.

"I always thought you were too good for him. You two were totally incompatible. He was a creature of impulse, you see. Whereas you... well, you believed in research. You did your homework, Liz."

Her forehead creased up above the steel band. "Where do I know you from?"

"Uni."

"Jim," she whispered, more to herself than to him. It was as though she'd finally put the name, the voice, and memories of the seventies together, and struck gold. Her voice shook, "Jim?"

He laughed, "The one and only."

"What do you want?"

"Oh," he shrieked, "the sixty-four thousand dollar question!" He walked around her, musing, and she tracked him with her unseeing eyes. "I want a taster of what you two have had all these years. I want to relax. I want a big fecking steak! I want five-star luxury, Liz." He stopped smiling, "But d'ya know what I'd like most of all? I'd like to be free. And that's where you come in."

"I can get you money, I already said—"

"Shut the feck up!" He breathed in deeply, taking in the smell of a gas-heater and the curious stench of an empty piss bowl, relishing in the encroaching darkness, the feeling of power and claustrophobia. He cleared his throat, paid attention to Liz, and said, "This is Terry's doing. He wanted me to kill you, you see. He too wanted freedom.

From his past. Like me. Nothing can truly buy that though, can it? I know that; I'm not fooling myself."

Beneath the strap, Liz's chin was trembling and despite her obvious efforts to restrain them, tears dampened her lips and washed blood down her chin. Translucent rubies fell to her chest.

He brushed a hand across the back of her neck, "Fate," he said, "brought us together, and guilt will tear us apart."

Chapter Thirty-two

The Decision

— One —

EVERYONE HAD GONE, AND the light was disappearing from Eddie's office. He sat there with his chin on his fists, had mumbled goodbyes to Sid and the others more than an hour ago. The coffee cup was cold, and he was considering calling it a day, maybe stopping off at the chippy on the way home so he wouldn't have to suffer any more of his dad's cooking, when the phone rang and Eddie almost had a heart attack.

He leapt at it, "Eddie Collins."

After the call, he stared again at the wall, his breathing steady but his heart flicking all over the place, and he wondered if throwing away the tablets was such a wonderful idea. His palms were hot, throat dry.

That was the easy bit, he thought, now for the hard part.

Eddie stood at Cooper's door, unsure of how to proceed. He looked around, saw Benson and another couple of detectives huddled around a monitor across the office, giggling at some joke. Benson, for some reason, looked in Eddie's direction, the joke forgotten, concern now dominant. It was way beyond dusk outside now, and most of the lights in the unused areas of the office were automatically dimmed or switched off; mood lighting for coppers.

Eddie cracked his knuckles and was about to knock and enter, when it opened and Cooper jumped. "Collins. Scared the shit out of me."

"Got a minute?"

"Can't it wait?"

Eddie said nothing.

Cooper understood that whatever it was, it most certainly could not wait. How often did Eddie call round for a natter with the big boss? He sighed and turned around. "Out with it," he walked to his desk, dumped his briefcase and sat, folding his arms.

"Any joy with Jim Price's obs?"

"What?" Cooper squinted.

"Just wondered if he'd showed—"

"He hasn't returned home. Okay?"

"Right. Good."

"Good?" Cooper stared, then got up, "I haven't got the time for you to tell me what you really want, Collins. I have the tatters of a life to sew back together."

Eddie cleared his throat, "Terrence Shaw was at Shaney McGowan's murder scene."

It took a while, maybe fifteen seconds, before Cooper showed any sign of a reaction. He was old, thought Eddie, tired from a long day shouting at people; bound to take its toll. Cooper flopped back into his seat, rubbed the white whiskers that dared peek out from his chin, and whispered, "Tell me you've not done something stupid."

Eddie laughed nervously. "You remember how we took both toothbrushes from Liz Shaw's bathroom?"

Cooper nodded.

"The bandana that Shaney McGowan had stuffed in her mouth…"

Cooper sat up straight. "You matched DNA between Shaw's toothbrush and that bandana, didn't you?"

Not that tired, obviously, Eddie thought. "It was his bandana. Liz made a heart—"

"Didn't think to run it by me first?"

Eddie was about to answer when Cooper carried on.

"And why was that? I'll tell you why you didn't mention it. You didn't mention it because you'd have had to seek my authority to do so. And I would have declined."

"But—"

"Who gave you the authority, Collins, to examine murder exhibits from the archive store? And who gave authority for the lab, notwithstanding the enormous premiums they charge for LCN work?"

"I was doing it to—"

"Who!"

Eddie noticed how quiet it had become out there in the main office. Everyone loved a dust-up; it broke the monotony, gave the day a sparkle.

"Putting aside the astronomical cost of that exam, you have exceeded all authority up to and including chief inspector rank. Did you ask Jeffery?"

Eddie looked at the carpet.

Cooper shook his head. "You have single-handedly damaged any future legal proceedings that might bring McGowan's murderer to justice—"

"Not single-handedly, boss." Benson stood in the doorway, shoulders drooped.

"You! You were in on this madness?"

Eddie said, "I forced him—"

"Oh shut the fuck up, forced him." Cooper stood, hitched up his slacks. "You know, if this goes to court, which it probably won't once CPS finds out you circumvented all known police protocols as well as the Police and Criminal Evidence Act 1984—"

"I believe Thou Shalt Not Kill precedes that," Eddie said.

Cooper pointed, mouth in a snarl, "Do not get flippant with me, Collins, or I'll throw you through that fucking window!"

Silence.

Cooper growled in frustration, "The evidence you found was obtained illegally; it can't be used—"

"So we ask him for a legitimate sample for comparison—"

"And why would you do that, Benson, unless you already knew he was guilty?"

Eddie coughed, "Say we do get a legitimate sample and it goes to court, how are we going to look if we win? Incompetent for letting a murderer toss it off for thirty years, or would it make us look like heroes for never giving up?"

Cooper slapped his desk, "You don't get it! We're talking about a Yorkshire Ripper investigation here. There aren't any fucking heroes! They're not going to shake anyone's hand, they're going to ask why we got it wrong."

"And why did we?" Eddie stood firm.

"Because we didn't have the technology back then."

"But we do now, that's what I'm trying to say!"

Benson and Eddie stood together in the doorway. Cooper breathed deeply, trying to calm himself down. "The approach with the courts and the public is so far above your level of thinking that you'd die of asphyxiation."

"And you're—"

Benson elbowed Eddie, "Shut it."

"It has nothing, nothing, to do with you," Cooper pointed at Eddie. "You're there to get the evidence if and when told to do so." And then he turned to look at Benson, "And you… you could be suspended for this. You know that, don't you?"

Benson nodded, gritted his teeth.

"No chance of a Queen's Police Medal, then?"

Cooper snapped a look at Eddie and his narrowed eyes told him to be quiet. He returned his attention to Benson, "Don't come in tomorrow, Tom."

"What?"

"Stay at home, please." And then he looked at Eddie, "You too. I'll be contacting Jeffery first thing in the morning."

— Two —

Eddie sat opposite Benson at a scratched wooden table in the arsehole of a local pub, and drank a Coke that was more expensive than a shot of Glenfiddich, and from a glass that had lipstick on the rim. The place was noisy, it was smelly, and the music was awful, something by Boy George on an eighties compilation CD. Why couldn't they ever play any decent rock from that era, Eddie thought. And why had he even agreed to come to a pub in the first place? If he'd wanted to drown his sorrows, as the saying went, then he could do it at home cheaper and get a far greater buzz from it. "I hate these places."

Benson looked up, the hand slowly stroking his pint glass pausing, "You surprise me."

"Pubs. You ever think what wankers would do if pubs didn't exist?"

"Strangely, no."

Eddie smiled, "Well you'd be fucked for a start."

"Why do you have to insult everyone?"

"All facts about you are insults." Eddie smiled inside; that line was just too good to use only once.

"Yeah, you keep telling jokes, mate. Meanwhile I'm in the shit, big time." He took another gulp of beer. "Twenty-five years I've been doing this crap. Four years," he said. "Four years from being able to piss off."

Eddie's smile perished. "They're not going to bin you."

"You have no fucking idea. You really think being good at your job matters? Not anymore. It's all stats now, and they can manipulate those to suit whatever their agenda dictates." He sighed, "No room for old school coppers no more."

Eddie stared at him, then through him, lost in his own thoughts, "I can just picture Jeffrey's face when he finds out I forged his signature."

Benson cracked a smile at Eddie's predicament; not much of a smile, but it was there.

"Ha, and my dad's going to kill me when he finds out that we'll both be living off his pension…" He trailed off, thinking.

Benson noticed, and asked, "What?"

"Some old guy, a garage owner not far from McGowan's scene had information for the police the day after she was killed."

"So? Wait, wait. I'm really not interested. I should go home and lick my wounds and fall asleep with the job paper."

"He fell down his own inspection pit and died before the police could get to him."

"Who?"

"The old guy. At the garage?"

"Oh."

"He was found by a worker there. A mechanic."

Benson sighed, "Collins, you're starting to piss me off. What the hell are you getting at?"

"James Price is a mechanic, remember? This whole thing revolves around James Price. He rigged that car, broke into Shaw's house, swapped her toothbrush."

"I rang Claire Holden, by the way. She confirmed the Jim she knew from uni was James Price."

"There you go, another brick in the wall." And then, "That's what music they should be playing."

"What?"

"Never mind."

"Anyway. Look, we're out of this. It's nothing to do with us now. Let them find James bleeding Price."

"That's the point." Eddie sat up. "He's still missing."

"Yes, I know he's still missing. So?"

"You're such a pessimist. How many garages are there round here? Ones that were here thirty years ago?"

Benson shrugged. "What's it matter; it'll be a fucking Tesco's by now."

"It doesn't matter?"

"We're out. Sooner you get that through your thick head, the better we'll be."

"You can sit here crying into your pint with your thumb up your arse, or you can try and—"

"Don't say 'do the right thing'. I've been trying to do the right thing all my life and it's led to here, to tonight, where I'm suspended, where all the right things have amounted to exactly fuck all." Benson glared at Eddie, and then downed his pint.

"Find the bastard."

Benson nodded at the Coke, "Another?"

"I wasn't going to say do the right thing. I was going to say let's find the bastard ourselves because that's what people like Cooper won't expect. They'll expect you to sit in some shite pub licking your wounds all night. They have the power to make you feel like shit, but only you have the power to make yourself feel on top of the world, Benson."

"You sound like a BT advert."

"True though, isn't it? Now are you going to show Cooper how old school coppers operate or what?"

"Not very good at pep talks, are you?"

"I don't have to be; this thing sells itself."

Benson's cheeks throbbed. He stared at the empty glass. Then he took out his phone, hit speed-dial and listened. "Chris, are you night cover? Good, do me a favour will you, open Exodus and go to my saved searches." He stared at the glass, and licked his lips. "Password's nipple5, lower case." He looked up at Eddie's surprised face and shrugged. "Yep, that's it, Jim Price. Has his employment history been added yet? Yes please." Benson patted his jacket, searching for a pen. "Around 1979, summer or autumn." He pulled a pen from his inside pocket and Eddie slid a peeled beer mat in front of him. "Cheers," Benson said into the phone, "you got an address for that?" He scribbled on the mat, then said, "Great, cheers for that. Have a good one," and pressed 'end'.

"Well?"

Benson clicked the pen, slid it back into his pocket. "Brooklands Garage. About a mile from here."

"Was that the only one, the only employment?"

"Only one for the entire year. There was no change of employment until March '81."

Eddie stared at Benson, wondering if he had the balls to see this through, or whether he'd get up and go fill that glass. "So? You old school copper or trainee pisshead?"

Benson didn't reply, instead he stared right at that glass.

Eddie was growing nervous. He wasn't exactly best friends with Benson, had had plenty of run-ins with him in the past, verbal and physical, but he wanted his company tonight – if he was going to go searching, he wanted Benson along for the ride. But, he'd do it by himself if necessary, however reluctantly. "Just come and have a look."

"I'm in enough shit as it is without digging myself—"

"Exactly! If we find Jim Price there, or even evidence that's where he's been, we're one step closer to…" and that's where he paused. Which was the carrot that would appeal to Benson the most? Finding Price, or perhaps finding Elizabeth Shaw? Eddie raised his eyebrows: that little thought had only just crossed his own mind. But he chose to play it safe. "We'd be one step closer to getting off the hook, mate. You'll be a hero, Cooper will have your cock out quicker than you could peel a Mars bar."

Benson slipped into quiet mode, eyes drawn again to the empty glass.

Eddie's enthusiasm also slipped, back towards apathy – a place he detested more than the pub he was parked in. His eager smile remained, though, and he still stared at Benson, urging him, but it was hollow, and he knew he'd have to go it alone.

"There'll be no one there. Or it'll be a pile of bricks now. Or a fucking car park."

Eddie stood. "Fine. You stay here and lube your thumb up, waiting for your bollocking. I'm going."

Chapter Thirty-three

The Visitor Bearing Painful Memories

THROUGH THE DARKNESS, AN old red Ford Escort drove slowly along the estate roads. At the wheel, Jim Price watched carefully; he was all nerves now he knew the police suspected Terry of some involvement with Liz's apparent death. Despite the coolness of the evening, his pits were wet with sweat, and beads of it clung to his upper lip.

He wondered, since the police were involved, if they knew more than Terry had let on. If he wasn't careful, it could end up being very serious for him – he didn't give a shit about Terry, but Jim liked to look after himself, and he'd do anything – anything – to make sure he did. And that was part of the reason he was cruising around this neighbourhood this evening, itching for the meeting he had planned.

After his second circuit of the estate, Jim pulled the car over a hundred yards beyond Terry's house and sat quite still for a moment as he gathered his thoughts and summoned some bravery. He took a last look around then climbed out. The interior light didn't come on, since he'd removed the bulb from it weeks ago.

Casually, like a resident out for a late-night stroll, he walked toward Terry's house, turned up the drive and knocked on the front door, nonchalantly glancing around as any caller who was awaiting a response would.

For the second time they both watched as the Escort crawled by, and through the bushes of the house they'd parked outside, could see its brake lights illuminate. Khan looked at Butcher, said nothing, and resumed his observation.

Within a minute, a small lone figure with a big nose walked into view, ambled down Shaw's driveway and knocked on the door.

"Did you see that?" Khan said.

"As stupid questions go, that's a top ten hit."

"I'm only making conversation."

"Why? I'm perfectly happy with an uncomfortable silence. It goes well with the smell coming off your feet."

Khan tutted.

"See," she said, "it's not so hard, is it."

He tutted again.

"Should I start calling you Skippy?"

Khan sat upright, "He's gone inside!"

"Calm down." Butcher took out her radio, selected a hotkey, and spoke directly to Cooper on his mobile phone, "He's just gone inside, boss."

"Stay where you are." Cooper sounded tired and distracted. "Let me know the minute either of them leaves."

Khan snatched the radio, "You don't want us to grab him?"

Butcher shook her head and rested her chin on her fist.

"We don't know where Elizabeth Shaw is yet. No."

"Gimme that!" Butcher took the radio back and glared at Khan, "Righto, boss."

Jim tried to relax, wiped his sweating hands down his jeans as the hall light came on and Terry opened the door.

"I should kill you—"

"But you won't. So cut the shit and let me in."

Once inside, Terry raised a glass of Bacardi to his lips and it was easy to see that his hand was shaking. "Why are you doing this? We were both responsible. This was supposed to fix the problem."

"I was supposed to fix the problem."

"Yes you were," Terry shouted. He topped up the glass, seemed to calm a little as he faced Jim again. "This was never about money. This was about saving our lives."

"Our lives. Our lives? You've got the bollocks to stand here in this little mansion of yours and tell me it was about our lives? You offered me money to murder your wife, so don't give me none of this 'not about money' bullshit."

"I offered you enough."

"Did you? You got any idea how I live my life?" Jim closed up on Terry, his Doc Martens squeaking. "Have you any idea how anyone outside this circle of yours lives their life, Terry? I've had to steal car radios and alloy wheels to get a loaf of fecking Warburtons." Jim's nostrils flared and he tried to contain the anger that was building inside. "People like you are ghosts. You walk through the walls that people like me spend our lives trying to break through. And you thought fifty was enough?"

"You think I've had it easy?" He waved his arm around the lounge, "This is just a veil, an advertisement for everyone else. Look at what I am." The animation subsided, and Terry's voice turned to a whisper, "You try to convince yourself you're a different man. But it's still there." He looked at Jim. "I can still see it: you hitting her with that thing. Blow by blow until you killed all three of us."

Jim almost laughed. "Oh come on, what's it feckin' matter. Thirty years and not one ounce of suspicion. And all because of your idea. Your idea." Jim sank into the sofa, draped an arm casually across the backrest. "You really think it matters to them if they haven't got the full picture? All they need is pieces. Little pieces."

Terry shouted, "I helped you!"

"Your DNA's inside her, Terry. Yours." Jim's face almost cracked an ironic smile. "Little pieces." He took his arm from the sofa, leaned forward, elbows on his knees, fingers twitching, teeth grinding. "We weren't taking her for a picnic; we were going up there to feck her." He stared at Terry.

"We were going up there to fuck her? We? There was only one person doing that though, wasn't there?"

"I couldn't... Not when her kid was there too, Jesus!"

"You were a joke to her, a pathetic joke!"

Jim stood, fists by his side, "Shut your mouth!"

Terry closed his eyes, and then began to weep. "Why did you have to do that to her? She wasn't laughing at you, you prick. She was laughing at us." By now, he was out of breath, and he looked at the glass on the drinks cabinet, surprised it was empty. "You left that kiddie without a mother, Jim." He reached for whisky this time, topped up the glass and took a gulp, and leaned heavily against the drinks cabinet.

He let his breathing slow and tried to calm down. "I thought I saw her, you know. Shaney McGowan. I was having a panic attack at a wedding. Louise Walker waltzed into the reception and I... well, I had an episode. And when it was over, I thought I saw Shaney. She was by the doorframe leading into the hall." His eyes squinted as though trying to see through a fog, "Could have sworn it was her."

He pointed a finger at Jim, "Who was it? Who did you put in Liz's car?"

Jim took a step back and smiled. And then almost as abruptly, he stopped smiling and his eyes lost their focus; they stared off into who knew what scene, perhaps reliving memories with Terry and Shaney, but more likely reliving memories of his wife.

"Samantha!"

Jim's eyes snapped back out of the dream and rested heavily on Terry. All humour, all the pleasant times they'd managed to share in that horror show they called a marriage, turned his demeanour sour and turned his mood hateful.

"You killed your own wife?"

"Don't sound surprised. It's all the rage these days. Yours was on the verge of dragging you down; mine had already done it."

"You're a lunatic."

"Yeah, I can see how you'd think that. But I'm not. Now where's my money?"

Terry's mouth fell open, "What? You expect me to pay you fifty thousand – for killing the wrong fucking woman?"

This time Jim did smile, "I suppose you could get me under the Trade Descriptions Act."

"And now you're continuing to be a pathetic joke."

"Really?" He edged closer, "You still think I'm a lunatic, too?"

Terry took a pace backwards.

"I can tell you where she is, or I can tell them. They can't tie you to her car, but one conversation with her, and they will tie you to that body, then all the little pieces fit snugly together. And then all this comes out into the open." Jim was grinning, and it was his turn to gesticulate, except he did it with a flourish, a caricature, like a panto dame.

That had been what worried him, but all it would take was one traffic violation, just a routine DNA swab down at the local police station, and that would be it: game over. For now, while ever Terry remained under the police radar by playing the part of a good citizen, he continued to breathe what passed as free air. Sometimes a person need not be locked behind bars in order to be in a prison. Terry drained his glass again. The bottle shook against the rim of the glass.

"Since you're offering, I'll have one of them."

Terry, stunned by how calm he felt, stunned by the conversation they were having – no, stunned by the civil way in which they were having this conversation, much more civil even than some he'd had with colleagues about work-related stuff, stuff that didn't matter at all when compared to... to murder. It was surreal, and a small part of him knew two things instantly: no, it was not a fucking dream from which he would awake at any moment; and he also knew the killing hadn't ended.

It was like the domino effect. And it would only end when there was but one player left. And, he considered, maybe not even then. God knows how hard it had been living with a secret like this for thirty years, and he wasn't sure if any sane person could live with that, and even more guilt, for a moment longer.

Terry walked through to the kitchen, suddenly desperate for one of the old cigars in the drawer. He lifted the packet: empty. He sighed.

"Want one of these?" Jim held out a tin of roll-ups.

Terry dropped the packet, closed he drawer, and turned. "No. I shouldn't."

"Bad for your health?"

"Something like that."

Jim nodded at the window. "They made a nice job; it looks good."

Terry acknowledged the resumption of small talk with a nod, "There was no need to wreck the damned thing; I said you'd need a bit of force not a stick of dynamite." For now, he would act out his part, but when the time came, he'd take a risk on being the only player left standing. He could play the mild and the meek all evening if need be; but eventually there would come a time when he wouldn't. And when that happened, poor old Jim would wish he'd never set eyes on a young tart called Shaney McGowan.

Unless Jim got to him first.

They returned to the lounge. Terry poured a whisky, handed the glass over. "We could both be getting our lives back straight if—"

"Yeah, only yours would be a hell of a lot straighter than mine."

"Why are you doing this? Fifty grand can change your life."

Jim sipped the whisky, keeping control of himself. He hated the stuff, "Yeah right. Give it a few years and it'll only just be enough to tax my car." Another sip. "One hundred."

Terry stared aghast, and something like a laugh fell out of his mouth but without a voice attached, like a fitful sigh. "I haven't got one hundred thousand. No way can I lay my hands—"

"Don't give me that shit! Fecking house must be worth a million."

"So take some fucking bricks then!"

Jim gulped the whisky.

"When we planned this, I siphoned cash from different sources, withdrew it in small easy to conceal amounts. I have that money here now." He swallowed, "I can't get any more, certainly not another fifty grand. I can't just pop into Lloyds and cash a cheque."

Jim threw the glass at Terry's head. Terry ducked so quickly that he fell to his knees. Jim stood over him, hands on hips, breathing hard, "You're lying."

"I'm telling you the truth." This is it, he thought.

Jim bent slightly and punched Terry full in the face. Terry fell flat on the floor, groaning and holding his face, reluctant to pull his hands away for fear of seeing blood on them.

Jim stood and lit a cigarette, and Terry scrambled backwards on his backside a few yards, just far enough away to stand without fear of being knocked down again. He left the room, and was back seconds later with a Nike rucksack. "As we agreed." He dropped it on the floor, stepped back, nodded at it, "That's all I've got." He rubbed his bleeding lip.

Jim drew on the cigarette and said calmly, "I know you've got the other fifty here because you're not stupid." He flicked ash on the carpet. "Right, listen; this is how it's going to work. I'm going to ask you really nicely for the other fifty grand." Terry was about to protest, but Jim stopped him with a pointed finger. "You're not going to say a word; you're just going to go and get it like you just got that one. Soon as I have it, I'll tell you exactly where she is and give you the keys to get in there.

"If you tell me once more that you haven't got it, I'm going to pick up this one bag and leave. In one hour, I'll be through the gates at Leeds Bradford Airport. In three hours I'll be in Europe. From a phone box there I'll make a call to West Yorkshire Police and tell them exactly where they can find her."

"And what's to stop me leaving? Right now?"

Jim grinned again. "Your passport is in the same room as your wife."

———

Khan was tapping his fingers on the steering wheel. "Come on, come on. Something happen."

"I could slap your face if you like?"

Khan resumed tapping, then caught sight of Butcher staring at him. He stopped, sighed. "Did you ever watch Through the Keyhole?"

"Good God."

"What do you think's going on in there?"

"How am I supposed to know? Just, just be quiet. Please. For ten minutes."

———

Terry wore a look of total despair on his face as he carried a second bulging Nike bag into the lounge. That's that, he told himself. He didn't have the guts to stop him, his old friend, Jim. Jim had been stronger; he'd held all the cards and even pulled out a few aces from up the sleeves of his oily T-shirt. Bastard. The worst of it was that it proved to Terry his own self-worth; it proved he was weak, incapable of taking control of a situation like this. If he could do it at work, why couldn't he do it now, when it really mattered? He felt shame, and he felt used as he looked at Jim's triumphant face. Bastard. He dropped the bag.

Jim opened it, rummaged through the cash inside, and then zipped it up. And the very fact that he wasn't arrogant about it, proved how absolutely arrogant he was.

"Where is she?"

"Brooklands. Remember, where I used to work?"

Terry nodded.

"You'll need a torch. Oh, and I've left you a little something on the table. Can't miss it." He held out a bunch of small keys and when Terry took it, he bent to retrieve his money.

And that's when Terry surprised himself. He brought his knee up into Jim's face hard enough to knock him backwards, losing his balance and landing hard on the tiled hallway floor. Terry continued to act without his mind being in charge of his fists, and he leapt on him, throwing punch after punch into the slowly reddening mass that was once Jim Price's face.

At first Jim protested. He tried to roll away, then tried to cover his face with his arms. But Terry was like something possessed and he beat Jim in a frenzy that was wild and hate-filled. And detached.

Eventually, Jim's efforts at repelling his attacker grew weak, and his arms fell to his sides.

Terry stood. His throat burned from dragging air in, it made wheezing sounds and it took him almost five minutes of propping himself against a kitchen chair before he was confident of not passing out or vomiting.

His legs trembled, arms shook. And then he picked up that chair and brought it down on Jim's already beaten face. After the third blow, the chair shattered, but Terry kept on and on until he held in his hands just a splintered backrest that was splashed with blood. It slipped from his grip. He fell to the floor, leaning against a cupboard, raking in breath, praying he wouldn't black out.

When finally he had his breathing under control, he looked across at what was left of Jim and burst into tears.

Terry stared at himself in the small mirror above the basin in the guest WC. He washed his face and tried to get all the blood out from the creases in between his fingers. His hands were red raw from the scrubbing, but he could still see it, great splashes of redness that were as stubborn to remove as fence dye. Water swirled red as it ran down the plughole. His lip throbbed.

He dried his hands and face, and became perplexed by the sight he witnessed in the mirror. It was like repeating a word so often that it loses meaning and becomes nothing more than a sound with waves and edges. His face didn't belong to him, and he wondered if he had actually gone insane. He blinked, and some of the recognition returned, along with some of the confusion.

Where had all that violence come from? All that raw, instinctive hatred? It had all happened so very quickly that even now, just a short time afterwards, he would be unable to recount events with any degree of accuracy. Things just happened, and he'd gone along with them, like his body had moved all by itself, the autopilot had become brave and pushed Terry aside as it completed the job he wished he'd had the guts to do himself. So maybe he should feel proud. That thought stuck for a while, maybe ten or fifteen seconds, until Shaney McGowan's face filled the mirror over his shoulder. And suddenly he didn't feel brave anymore, suddenly he felt very frightened.

And it was that fear that turned his face resolute.

———

Butcher had become weary of listening to Khan, and had plugged her phone's earpieces in. The sounds of Pink flooded through her and now all she worried about was the battery running out before her shift finished for the night.

At her side Khan yawned, and the sandwich he was chewing fell out of his mouth and into his lap. He had one of those 'uh oh' moments, and of course it was the same time that Butcher chose to look around. She saw what was in his lap and almost threw up.

She took out the earphones and said, "You really are disgusting," and got out of the car.

Khan punched the ceiling.

Butcher walked down the road, pulling the plug on the phone. She crossed the road and hurried along Shaw's driveway.

"What the fuck are you doing, woman?" Khan uttered. And then he saw Shaw's garage door swing open. He watched in horror as Butcher sprinted around the corner of the house and flattened herself into the brick wall. Khan grabbed the half-chewed sandwich and threw it, along with its uneaten brethren, out of the window.

He saw Terry Shaw walk towards his Jaguar, carrying a petrol can and two black sports bags. Behind him, the garage door closed again automatically. Shaw climbed into the Jaguar. Khan started his engine, heart pummelling, adrenaline finally kicking in as his eyes widened and Shaw drove out of his driveway.

Without turning on the lights, Khan drove quickly towards Butcher, who by now had made it to the mouth of Shaw's driveway. She opened the door and leaned in, "Price is still in there. I'm staying. You follow him, and get another car to me asap."

"What if Price drives off, you're not going to be able—"

"Just go before you lose him!" Butcher slammed his door.

Khan turned on the lights then drove away shouting, "Bollocks, bollocks, bollocks."

Butcher ran towards the lounge window and peered inside. She couldn't see much if anything out of place, only what looked like a smashed drinking glass by the far wall. She crept stealthily around the side of the house into the brightness of the illuminated back garden wondering what Price would be doing in there alone. Maybe he'd already left via a back door.

Feeling exposed, she edged along the wall until she reached a kitchen window. She snatched a glance, and recoiled. Then she took another, longer, look. "Shit."

―――――――

Terry drove, as he had fought, on autopilot. He was probably two or three times over the legal limit, but that thought hadn't crossed his mind, and the long-held fear of giving a DNA sample should the police stop him went unconsidered. He felt sober. The violence, the excursion, and the high emotion eradicated the alcohol – obliterated it.

There were tears in his eyes and a strange feeling of victory in his heart. That victory though, was not without its misgivings. What was it they said about winning the battle but losing the war?

The built-in satnav told him to turn right at the end of the road.

It also showed an estimated arrival time of eighteen minutes. Eighteen short minutes to finish what he'd begun all those months ago. His mind saw Shaney's laughing face and the sunlight blazing through her blonde hair. His heart sank a little and some of that victorious feeling melted. And then he saw Louise at the wedding reception; the woman who had begun the most recent heartbreak of his life, how the sight of her had catapulted him back thirty years to see Shaney's face and hear her high-pitched laughter – a face he'd worked hard to blur and a sound he'd worked hard to tune out. All brought back to stunning life in wonderful Technicolor and superb Dolby. High definition, he thought it was called today.

Also, it was true what they said: what goes around comes around. He'd made a mistake, a very bad mistake, but he'd tried hard to be a good person since then, to make up for it, to counterbalance it. And he thought he'd done a pretty decent job where that was concerned. And then Louise happened, and Liz got curious. The counterbalance had started to crack and his life had fractured.

He turned right, looked at the sat nav. Seventeen minutes to the end of a long nightmare.

Chapter Thirty-four

The Rebel and the Scapegoat

"Bet you're glad you came along now, eh?"

Benson was sitting in the passenger seat, grimacing.

The van bounced over potholes. "Where the fuck is this place?"

"This is ridiculous. Turn back."

"Check the A-Z."

"Why? They started mapping backstreet shitholes, now?"

Eddie brought it to a halt a hundred yards from a dead end. The headlamps picked out damaged fencing, rotting signs, and old car tyres alongside faded gas cylinders and twisted shopping trolleys.

"There," Benson pointed to the right. There stood a single-storey building, its front embedded deep inside the shadows of a cold night, a dead streetlamp right out front. The side of the building disappeared into more shadows and melded almost elegantly with the blackness of the night.

"Eyes like a shit-house rat." Eddie turned out the van lights, and as his own eyes adjusted to the darkness, the sign over the huge roller shutter door slowly revealed itself: Brooklands Garage, Repairs and MoT Work. "Told you it was here."

"Park over there," Benson this time pointed left to a two-storey office block with smashed windows and a car park that nature was reclaiming; massive weeds filled the space where once the directors' cars would sit all day.

Eddie parked and pulled the Maglite from its charging cradle, and locked the van. He and Benson crossed the dead road and headed towards two almost indiscernible hulks of burnt-out cars parked at the front of the garage. Above them, drooping gutters swayed and creaked in a thin breeze.

"Look at the place. There's nothing here."

Eddie whispered, "You know, someone once told me a piece of music was shit. So I listened to it. It turned out to be the best thing I'd ever heard."

"What?"

"I don't listen to people anymore."

"I'll have that scribbled on your grave stone."

Eddie turned on the torch and they walked up the side of the building, along the muddy lane strewn with rocks, bricks, and emblazoned with old broken vehicle glass that every now and then reflected the light a strange green colour, making it look like an emerald walkway.

The earth was still heavily stained by oil, and where there was moisture, the oil shone through like a flat rainbow. Weeds had sprouted from every conceivable crack, taking root even in the crumbling brickwork, slowly pushing man aside. Stacks of old tyres littered the alley, broken pallets too, long ago discarded shelving units that hosted moss; decaying pieces of car added a strange almost graveyard-like ambience, enhanced by more weeds and twisted brambles.

They arrived at the back of the building and Eddie turned out the torch.

"What the fuck are you doing?"

"Ssssh. I'm being careful."

"I nearly broke a bastard ankle then, turn it back on!"

Eddie did, then turned to Benson, "Keep it down, Foghorn Leghorn." He peered around the corner along the back of the old building and there, parked up in the corner of the alley, almost concealed by a breeze-block outbuilding, was a breakdown truck. It wasn't covered in moss. And even though they were a good fifty yards from it, they could see it was recently parked there – the screen was clear, the tyres inflated, the paintwork shiny.

Like a couple of burglars, they crept up to the truck and peered inside the cab. It was empty of people, but the newspaper on the dashboard, among the litter of fast-food cups, was dated a week ago.

Eddie moved to the side where metal storage boxes contained rope, shackles, straps, jacks... and jacking bars. "Come here, look at this."

Benson crouched down, "What?"

"Jacking bar." He pointed to the furthest end of it. "Does that look like—"

"Blood," Benson said. "Yeah, it does."

"And hair too. Flaky red paint, rusted bar." He looked at Benson. "This is what killed Michael Tailor."

Benson stood, and whispered, "It's a job for later, come on."

They completed their journey along the back of the building, and Eddie again switched off his torch before peering into the blackness down the far side of the building. Nothing obvious struck him about the creeping blackness that greeted his eyes, slowly dissolving the green circle that floated in his vision. "Okay," he whispered, "come on."

"Why are we whispering? He's not here, there's no car."

"How do you know he hasn't parked it somewhere else and walked?"

Benson tutted from a yard or two behind, and turned on his own much weaker torch.

After only fifteen yards, Eddie came to a stop at the side of an old fan unit that seemed to cling to the outside of the brick wall like a rectangular limpet. He shone the torch at the fingers of weeds sprouting from gaps in the rubble at its base, and then let the light wander up the wall to the fan itself. The weeds, some of them, had been trampled, and the hinges of the fan were black with dusty oil.

"Sssshh," Benson breathed.

When Eddie turned to look at him, he had his finger pressed to his lips. Eddie smiled, "What?"

"I thought I heard something."

"What?"

"If I knew that I wouldn't call it 'something' would I?"

Eddie stumbled over the rubble and back onto the less treacherous lane that led to the front of the building.

Benson followed, his little torch illuminating areas of ground not much larger than the next footstep he was about to take, "What are we looking for exactly?"

"Exactly?"

"What?"

Eddie shone his torch at the lane and at the walls. "Don't know. There's something strange about this place. I mean, parking a recovery truck here?"

"It's a garage."

"It *was* a garage. Now it's a piece of shit in an estate of shit. So why leave a truck here?"

"Because this shithole estate is abandoned. It's obvious; no one comes here. So this is where he stays these days, in the truck. That's why obs on his house have been blank." Benson kept pace with Eddie as the corner of the building edged up on their left. Once at the corner, they paused, and Eddie peered around, could see the burnt-out cars on the concrete apron, could just about make out the road twenty yards away, and the silhouette of buildings across that road, but not much else.

Benson whispered, "What if he's in there? What if he's armed?"

"Scared?"

"He's a fucking murderer, what do you think?"

Once around the corner and onto the apron, they passed the dead cars on the right and the seized-up roller shutter doors to the left. At the base of the doors silt had collected and been colonised by weeds. Rain striking the mud had spattered heavy dust almost two feet up the rusty shutters. And then Eddie stopped at the entrance door. "Look."

The same silt had gathered at the foot of the door, but in it were a thousand arcs scratched into the dirt as the door had been swung open; it looked like a quadrant of Saturn's rings. He brought the torch higher, over the paint that was flaking away in sheets, to the padlock that gleamed brightly in the light. "Strange."

"What is?"

"Door's been opened."

Benson hesitated, "I don't like this." The drooping gutters tapped against the wall over their heads.

"Oh come on, you never wanted to be Bruce Willis?"

"If I was Bruce Willis, I wouldn't be worried about my fucking mortgage, would I?"

"Pussy," Eddie retreated to the corner of the garage, intending to go back up the side, searching for something, some way in.

Benson was out of breath when he caught up. "And you have, I suppose?"

"Have, what?"

"Wanted to be Bruce Willis?"

"Tom Cruise is more my style."

"What I mean is why don't you take things more seriously? You're always dicking about like a kid. This is serious."

"I'm Peter Pan all the way to my grave, mate." Eddie faced him, "What's brought this on?"

"You have." Benson stared him up and down, and his finger ended up pointing right at Eddie's face, "It all began with you hunting down that archived exhibit. It always begins with you being a fucking rebel, Collins, and it always ends with people like me being your scapegoat." He walked off up the side of the building, his tiny torch leading a way that was punctuated by mumbles and curses.

Eddie stared into the darkness. "Yeah, but apart from that."

His hands curled around the steering wheel as though it were a rope and he was dangling from a precipice with it around his neck. His knuckles were white, arms rigid, and his eyes stared straight ahead, unblinking. His mind had engaged autopilot and the Jaguar sped along the near-empty roads more or less by itself. Terry was busy thinking, and he was wondering what he'd find at the garage; he was hoping that all was not lost, that he'd be able to pick this thing up where Jim had left it, and secure his future. It wasn't over yet, there was still time.

And then he began thinking about her, about Liz. What condition she'd be in and whether he could do what Jim had failed to do. Could he actually... He swallowed, eyes blinked at last, and he forced himself to imagine standing at her side, his wife of twenty-eight years, forced himself to imagine the choice he had: her death or his freedom. He couldn't have the latter without the former. But could he kill her?

The satnav smoothly instructed him to take the next left, and Terry's autopilot did just that. The time to destination on the screen said a little over four minutes.

His heart kicked up another notch.

Two police officers, hoping to keep a low profile, while appearing busy by watching the rowdy behaviour of drunken students up by The Library in Hyde Park saw a black Jaguar drive by at speed.

"Hey, was that… was that the Jag?"

"That was it, yep."

They looked at each other, collectively sighed. The driver engaged gear, hit the buttons controlling the roofbar lights and the siren, while the other put down his coffee and radioed the news through to the divisional control room, "Charlie-Alpha Six Three."

Before they'd even turned a wheel, they'd lost him, and could only report a general direction of travel.

———————

The door slammed behind him and Cooper turned to see the hall light go out. He continued talking into the phone as he pulled his overcoat back on, "How the hell did they lose him? They only had to watch his bastard house!"

"He got in the Jag, boss, drove away at some speed."

"Where's he heading, do we know?"

"Negative, sir. Division sighted him up at Hyde Park; that's the last—"

"Get the helicopter up, and keep in constant touch with ANPR. Soon as that car flags a hit, I want ARVs to his location and on him. Taser authority granted."

"Yes, boss."

"I'll be Gold Commander soon as I get to the office."

———————

Eddie hurried to Benson's side, his Maglite obliterating Benson's candlelight effort. "Wait, wait, wait," he said. "Think about it, if I hadn't gone after that bandana, where would the investigation be right now, right this very minute?"

"Trundling along at an orderly and legal pace."

"Bollocks. It'd be sinking in the mud because everyone's afraid to think radically. Soon as something a bit risky comes along, people like you shy away from it and go hide behind the words 'investigation' and 'enquiries', when what you really mean is no one's given you the fucking answer yet!"

Benson glared at him.

"Well I'm giving you the answer."

Eddie walked off and Benson this time hurried after him, "So who was it got The Ripper name in the first place?"

"Exactly! So why would you be content to sit this one out? It was your legwork that got this whole thing going. Don't let people like Cooper frighten you. Don't let him stop the old school copper in you from following your instinct."

"I'm not frightened of him. I'm frightened of the sack. And if what we're doing here tonight is at all fucking illegal, that'll be his next move on me."

Eddie stopped walking. He faced Benson, "Listen carefully, if Cooper had got his way, Terry would have got a body back and had it buried by now. No one would have been any the wiser that it wasn't his wife's body, would they? No one would have known about Jim Price or poor Sam Price, no one would have known about what's inside this shithole garage."

Benson thought about it. "If anything."

Eddie shrugged, "Yeah," he said, "if anything. Now are you going to help me find out, or would you rather go and sit in the van?"

Benson puffed out a sigh that was part tension, part resignation. He nodded, "What you got in mind?"

"Over here," Eddie led the way to the old Vent-Axia fan. "The weeds and the hinges gave it away, and now we know someone's been coming and going through the front door, I wonder..." He stood before the fan and pulled the edge of it. It opened like a giant flap, silently.

Behind it was a black hole.

"What if he's in there? Waiting for us?"

Chapter Thirty-five

The Final Meeting

YOU HAVE REACHED YOUR destination.

Terry didn't realise he was holding his breath as he reversed onto the concrete forecourt of the old garage. Through his rear-view mirror, he looked at the shutter door and the personnel door next to it, bathed in red from his brake lights. He breathed again, his mouth dry, his lungs seemingly on fire, and finally managed to prise his hands from the steering wheel.

He switched off the engine and lights, and everything sank so suddenly into an eerie silence and brain-crunching blackness that for a moment he thought he'd died. A small residual fear accompanied him through the coolness of the night to the boot. He wondered if he'd ever see another, and he also wondered if this whole thing was a trap. What if she was already dead? What if she'd never been here, and inside were half the damned police force with Benson leading the charge!

Terry tried to swallow but couldn't. He gave up.

He took a moment to compose himself. He had to get his thoughts in order, had to supress the doubt and the guilt, and had to be positive if this was to work. And it had to work. If it didn't, he'd never be free again.

And that was a sobering admission. A cruel choice, he knew, but a necessary one.

As if in answer to a question, Terry nodded and opened the steel door of the garage. He shone the torch inside but the beam died long before it hit the far wall, such was the size of this place. Where the beam did fall, on the floor and on the side wall to his right, it showed him nothing to be alarmed at. "Where are you," he whispered.

He picked out the petrol can from the boot and then began a slow walk along the length of the garage, avoiding the rubble, the junk, and the two large inspection pits sunk into the concrete floor. From here they looked like black holes. Echoes walked with him.

To his right there were doors and a smashed office window, crazed, and splitting the light like a web of diamonds. It smelled of old oil and musty dampness, and the only sounds were his crunching footfalls echoing from naked brick, and the sloshing of petrol in the can. His torch skimmed past doors marked "Gents" and "Fanny", skirting others that were once store rooms, and still others that had no markings at all. They hadn't been opened in many years; webs clung to their dull surfaces.

Only a minute passed before he saw the door he wanted. The dust on the floor directly in front of it was disturbed, the handle was shiny with use. And there was a padlock too.

He put down the can, looked at the lock and tried several keys before it opened. He stood there, frozen to the spot, and this time swallowed a mouthful of neat adrenaline. A nervous sweat glistened on his forehead. This would be the first time he'd seen her since she drove away that night, with him in her wake pleading for her to stay.

Is that how he still felt now?

Knowing she was the one who could sink him, she had to go. But… no buts, he said to himself, no buts. Do the job, do it once, do it right. And then walk away.

Eddie shone the Maglite at the roughly cut hole through two layers of brick behind the fan.

"What you doing?"

"I'm going in."

"You what? You're going inside? There? What if something happens to you? I'll be fucked!"

"Sssshhh," Eddie turned out the light. "You hear something?"

"Very funny, Collins."

"This is getting worrying. My arse feels like it's chewing a squash ball."

"Look," Benson almost pleaded, "this is ridiculous. We wait for daylight, and come back then, eh?"

"He could be gone by tomorrow."

Eddie turned the torch on again and this time let its light fall through the hole. Then his head and shoulders disappeared from view. And then he promptly froze. "Fuck me."

Benson took notice, "What?"

Eddie pulled himself free. "Get some people here, now."

"You found something?"

"Not really, just a woman tied to a chair."

"For once I wish you'd be serious."

Eddie aimed the beam into the hole again and pushed Benson's head in there as well.

"Jesus wept," Benson scrambled backwards, almost falling in his haste to be out of there. He reached for his phone, juggling to keep a hold of the torch. The torch fell, went out. "Bollocks!" He grabbed it and shook it and the meagre beam awoke from its slumber.

Eddie pushed himself into the hole, writhing, walking his shoulders through into the chamber beyond, and managing to keep the torch alight.

Benson struggled even more now that Eddie's torch had gone. His own seemed woefully inadequate, but he fumbled for the phone's keypad, and dialled three nines. It rang twice and the operator asked him which service he required, "Police," he said.

Brick dust and loose chunks of mortar hit cold concrete on the far side of the hole, moments before Eddie's hands touched down. He clawed his way through, feeling his shins peeling skin as he dragged them over the sharp edge of the bricks. He landed in an undignified heap in the thirty-year-old filth and felt grit between his teeth, and more grit congregating in the corners of his eyes. It stank of faeces in here, of urine too. Cloying odours of old oil, grease, and eye-smarting propane. It also stank of mouldy rat shit, and he wouldn't be surprised to learn that's what coated his hands and knees right now. Better not look, he told himself.

So he didn't. Instead he trained the beam on the woman who was obviously aware of something happening because now she was struggling against some kind of tie on her wrists.

He'd been right. The Ripper books, then Duffy, then the bandana, the DNA swabs, and finally the fear of being kicked out of the force, had driven him to this. The conclusion of the investigation was less than fifteen yards away, safe and well. They'd done it!

And then he heard something metallic. He listened carefully, forehead creased, eyes squinting as if to hear better, wondering what the noise was. Keys in a lock. He turned the torch off and the door went bang.

Benson's small torch blinked every now and then, usually, he noticed, each time he came to an obstacle where a little light would be handy! It was as though the fall had concussed it and it wanted to go back to sleep. He'd managed to summon the cavalry and asked the operator to make sure an ambulance was en route too. He'd only glimpsed her for a moment, but… well, it paid not to take chances.

He rounded the corner and noticed that the metal door was now open. He stopped, and immediately felt vulnerable. Only then did he notice the Jaguar parked a few yards away. If he was expecting anyone here, he was expecting the crazy murdering bastard Jim Price. Not Terrence Shaw.

"Shit!" He squatted, shielded the beam with his hand and then scurried over to the car. "Feeling like Bruce fucking Willis now," he whispered. The car was empty. From it, he looked to the open garage door and wondered just how brave he was. Now would be a good time to take Eddie up on his offer and go sit in the van.

It was an option, but Benson really wasn't like that. He was no SAS soldier, he knew, but there were certain things one never did – and one of those things was never leaving a colleague in the shit, which was pretty much where Eddie was right now. He would also never let a guilty man walk free.

Fleetingly he considered retracing his steps back to the hole in the wall and warning Eddie. But something told him that option had expired about five minutes ago. There was only one thing left to do. Benson stood and entered the darkness of the garage.

His torch burst into tears at the enormity of the blackness before it. He took small steps, listening intently to every sound. Before long, he could make out a faint flicker of what could only be torchlight behind a part-open door way off in the far left corner. He brought his head up, and a new determination took control; the rational part of his head was on standby, and he took large steps to where Eddie, Terry Shaw, and probably Liz Shaw were.

Despite Eddie being a tosser, Benson was determined not to let him down.

Five paces later, he tripped on rubble, twisted his ankle and smacked his head on a cold and sharp lump of concrete. His torch rolled out of his hand and over the edge of the inspection pit. It clattered when it hit the bottom, and it finally died.

Blood from Benson's head also rolled into the pit.

Eddie could see her in the faint light cast by the portable gas fire. It was a mellow golden glow, which would have been wonderful on just about any another occasion; but here in this makeshift prison it was like taking a glimpse into an ante chamber of hell. Her hands were bound by a bar of some description, and the bar was fastened to the wall by a cable.

On her head appeared to be a metal contraption not unlike a hanging basket stolen from a pub somewhere. It covered her eyes and ears, and prevented her mouth opening. "Fuck," he whispered. It looked like a piece of medieval torture equipment.

The door swung open and Eddie held his breath. He could see the woman stiffen. Terry Shaw stepped into the room and Eddie nearly squealed. What the hell was he doing here? Had he bought Jim Price off, or had he been an accomplice? Eddie saw Shaw's face. It was full of resolve, it refused to acknowledge her distress, and it seemingly refused to yield to any emotion. It was as though he were looking at a caged dog instead of his wife. And that stoic look convinced Eddie that he'd been an accomplice, and had fooled the investigation all along.

Then there was a clatter from beyond the door that startled Terry enough to have him shine his torch back into the garage.

Eddie scurried forward, praying not to trip and fall. He stood near the woman but hidden from view behind a tall, wide filing cabinet a few yards away from her left shoulder. He was close enough to hear her breathing, close enough to see how she shook. There was a buckle or a loop on the contraption around her that rattled in time with her shaking; it sounded like metal teeth chattering.

Terry's light flooded back into the room, and Eddie saw her breathing increase; short sharp little breaths, shoulders hunched, tethers rattling, and the light shone through her grey hair, and illuminated the tears on her cheeks. Terry held the beam almost steady as he slowly approached his wife, kicking aside empty water bottles, grit crunching under his leather shoes. Her breathing quickened still further.

Eddie saw a table in front of her by the wall. It had on it several bottles of water, what appeared to be a passport and... He moved slightly to get a better view. It was a hammer. A prickle of tension ran the length of Eddie's body, and he wondered where the hell Benson was. He had no time to wonder further, as he saw Terry's hand reach out for the hammer. He clearly saw Terry's wedding band glinting in the torchlight, and couldn't believe what he was witnessing.

The hammer scraped against the table top, and Liz flinched. She began to weep, bubbles appeared at her nostrils, and her shoulders jerked as though she were sobbing, but trying to keep it quiet.

Eddie gritted his teeth and readied himself.

Terry's face crumpled. He began to cry as he gripped the hammer tightly. "Why did you have to look back, Liz?" His voice cracked, was shaky, unstable. He cleared his throat and scraped an arm across his face, erasing the tears, trying to purge the creeping weakness and reinstate the strength that he needed now more than ever before.

Liz's sob turned to a howl, and though the metal band restricted most of it, it sounded defeated, and it sounded more than anything else Eddie had ever heard, sad, forlorn, like a dying animal. He watched, mesmerised, as Terry's resolve cracked, as the hammer dropped to the table and the sobbing began. Eddie's heart tripped again and for a moment he became light-headed, thought he was going to pass out.

Terry reached into his pocket for the keys and Liz struggled in her chair. "I can't believe that I almost... Liz, I..." Terry unlocked the small padlocks to the sides of her head, and the chin strap fell away.

She took a huge gulp of air, and blood from her damaged nose seeped over her lips and onto her teeth. The rest of the contraption fell away and clattered to the ground. And Liz blinked in the torchlight as Terry leaned over to embrace her, his own face a twist of grief that made Eddie even more angry – he had no right.

Eddie shifted his weight and watched as Terry fed another key into the handcuffs. They too clattered to the ground, "Oh, baby," Terry whispered, "I'm sorry, I'm sorry, so sorry."

Liz rubbed her wrists, let him embrace her.

"We can go away," he said quickly, almost in excitement, "both of us, alright? Just the two of us, anywhere you like," Terry was smiling through the fresh tears, crying through the happiness of a new realisation, and he brought her steadily to her feet. "Well," he said, "what do you think? We can start over, get out of England altogether. Switzerland," he grinned, "you've always wanted to go to Switzerland."

Liz looked up at him, holding his arms to steady herself, and though most of her face was obscured, Eddie could see her nod, and he could see how Terry's eyes shone at the prospect.

"Come on," Terry said, and guided Liz towards the door.

Now what? Eddie thought. Hopefully Benson had called for the police, and they'd soon be here, but in the meantime, he was going to have to break up this wonderful reunion and hold onto Terry Shaw; no way was that bastard walking out of here. Eddie took a single step out into the open and froze.

"I know that you and your twisted little friend killed Shaney McGowan." Her voice was creaking, struggling to stay even and level, almost as though she were striving to be as devoid of emotion as he had been when he picked up the hammer. "When I get out of here, Terry, I'm going straight to the police."

Quick as a coin flipping through the air, Terry's eyes lost the shine of expectancy. His face lost the excited smile and became a wall of stone. And the coin flipped again and Terry turned vile and fierce. He pushed Liz aside roughly, lunged for the hammer and almost made contact with the back of her head as she fell to the floor.

The blow missed by inches and in shock Eddie dropped the Maglite. Terry paused at the sudden noise long enough for Eddie to wake up to what was happening. He threw himself over the commode, aiming for Terry, having no particular plan in mind, other than somehow to allow her enough to time to run.

His aim was fairly accurate and the two men collided, banging heads, hitting the floor in unison, dazed. The hammer fell from Terry's grasp, and his torch clattered against the concrete floor and rolled to the wall where its beam shrank into a golden hotspot, and the light it offered the room dimmed considerably. Beneath a veil of concussion, Eddie's instinct was to reach out and grab Terry Shaw, to prevent him causing any further harm to Liz.

It seemed as though Terry had come off better than Eddie. Already he was pushing himself up onto all fours, his eyes tearing into Eddie's as he lumbered forward, ready to engage in a fight.

Eddie shook his head, and made a grab for Terry just as Liz smashed the hammer into the back of Terry's head. She screamed like a banshee and swung the hammer again, missing this time, and the next time too. But in the soft glow from the torch, she finally made contact again as he cowered, cradling a maladjusted skull. The noise was like a nail being driven into a piece of stout timber, and Eddie cringed. "Liz!" he screamed.

Liz continued, her anger still in full swing, and it was of such ferocity, propelled by such a powerful hatred that it seemed she would never stop. The blows, instead of sounding like stout wood, sounded like soggy fruit hitting a wall.

Eddie yelled for her to stop, feeling splashes of warm blood speckle his face as he made it to his feet. He grabbed her by the arms and the hammer fell. He felt almost mesmerised by her feral eyes, by her bloody lips drawn back over her bloodied teeth, and mesmerised especially by the sight of the tears glistening on her cheeks. "It's okay," he said. "It's over."

She stared at him, panting, and then her eyes slid closed. Liz buried her face into her hands and cried. Eddie cradled her.

Eddie leaned against the Jag smoking a cigarette. Fifty yards away was an armed response vehicle, blue strobes flashing in the darkness. Nearer, were three police cars, two ambulances and an unmarked car with Cooper climbing from it, phone glued to his ear.

Benson shuffled through the doorway holding a bandage to his head. "They're insisting I go get checked out. So I'll see you later, yeah?"

Benson began walking towards an ambulance when Eddie called, "Hey."

Benson turned.

"Fancy another beer, when you're fit?"

Benson smiled, "Yeah, whenever you want."

"Benson, I'm kidding."

"Arsehole," Benson shook his head and walked off, leaving Eddie smiling.

Chapter Thirty-six

The Circus and the Letter

EDDIE BREATHED OUT SMOKE, pressed the phone closer to his ear. "Roger? Yes, it's me Eddie."

"What's up? I'm at a scene, Eddie."

"Did you go to 11 All Saints Grove last week? Burgled and then flooded."

"Rings a bell. Why?"

"It's my old fella's house."

"Sorry to hear that. It's just fate, Eddie."

"No such thing as fate." Eddie paused, wondering where he'd heard that before. "Yeah. Anyway, I went up to look over it and I've found a balaclava and some roll-up cigs on a dresser in the master bedroom."

Roger paused in his work, and he recalled the exam well enough, boiler taken from the loft, not much else amiss so far as he could tell. There was plenty of water damage, some smashed figurines in the lounge.

"Roger?"

"I never saw them."

"Obviously. Anyway, I've left them for you to collect when you re-attend, keys with the neighbour at 9."

Roger finally answered, "Right."

"No problem is there?"

"No," he said at last. "No problem, Eddie."

From the reception desk, Miss Moneypenny smiled, "Hi Eddie. Whatcha got there?"

Eddie glared at Moneypenny's chest, and headed for the double doors, "Lovely buns," he said. She might have replied "thank you", but it could just as easily have been Eddie's imagination.

He took the stairs two at a time, barged into the main office and then turned right, heading towards G34. As he neared, he could hear them inside.

In the office, next to his socks and boots, Kenny had his bare feet on the desk, a newspaper opened up across his lap, and the remains of a sandwich and its associated crumbs littered the floor and the parts of his desk that were still visible. With constant criticism, he watched Loose Women on a wall-mounted TV that was so loud that James and Sid were forced to shout their conversation. The ringing phones, all three of them, went unanswered.

Sitting at his desk, still in his winter overcoat, Duffy was dunking chips into a Pot Noodle, and forking them into his mouth, juice dripping from his bristly chin. Open on the desk before him was a wrinkled copy of Mayfair. He looked at that moment like one of the Most Wanted posters come to life.

James was perched on the edge of Sid's desk. Between them was a mug of black coffee, and a delicate china cup filled with aromatic tea sitting perfectly on a matching saucer. "It's very rewarding," Sid said. "But it hurts at first, makes your legs ache." He sipped his tea. "You should try it, it really gets your heart rate up, and there's all these people watching you perform, checking your technique."

James nodded, his eyes far away, dreaming of performing to a crowd.

"I once got my legs so far apart that I farted a bit. I lost marks for that."

"Can you teach me?" James asked.

"If you want to learn how to fart, Collins is your man," shouted Duffy. He picked up a ringing phone and dropped it again. "Fucking racket."

"Course I can teach you. You should limber up a bit first, you know, just to loosen the tight bits, but we can skip that and get down to the physical parts if you like."

The phone began to ring again.

James stood up, legs together, back rod straight. "Is my posture right?"

"Perfect, I'll just drape myself across your chest and you follow my lead, okay?"

Kenny shoved rubbish across his desk, searching. "Where's the remote? If I wanted to listen to women talking shite, I'd ring the wife." Another phone began to ring, and Sid turned the stereo on, the sounds of La Bamba filling the void missed by the TV and the ringing phones.

Eddie kicked his way through the doors and stopped dead. He heard the cacophony, saw the chaos, and at once his heart sank and his anger rose. For a moment, he contemplated shouting and screaming, but then another thought, seclusion, took hold and dragged him into his own office where he quietly shut the door.

Seclusion, though, was hopelessly optimistic. The sounds of the phones and TV and the music, and now, noted Eddie, of Sid singing, didn't so much drift under the door as smash it down in a burst of mortar fire. Eddie put down the boxes and sat in his chair. It had acquired a new squeak.

He folded his arms, satisfied that life was roughly back on track again. The books, The Ripper books, stared at him. He pulled one across; *The Ripper Years*. He turned to the Shaney McGowan chapter and idly flicked through until he came to its end, where there were several more photographs, some of them in colour. One that sprang out and slapped his face was one of the woman herself, of Shaney McGowan. She was smiling for the camera, and it was a genuine smile, not one of those forced 'cheese' ones. It was genuine because in her arms she held a baby daughter.

Eddie couldn't stop staring at her, at Shaney. There was something strong there, pulling at his attention. Maybe it was the eyes, how familiar they looked.

Eddie dropped the book. He pulled from the back pocket of his jeans the letter from Ros that had been there since yesterday. He took hold of it, gulped, and then opened it.

He stared at it, not wanting to actually read it, not wanting to know how he'd let her down and how she was back with her wife-beating ex-husband, Brian; or that she'd run off to pursue a life of lesbianism thanks to his piss-poor performances in bed.

He propped the letter up, took off his boots and then laced his hands behind his head, and reclined. He tried to read it from several feet away and failed; decided that was just fine, but the noise from the office interrupted his 'fine' and he leaned closer. But it seemed the closer he leaned, the louder they got.

He grew hot, his chest heaved, he sweated, and then he lunged for the door handle. Eddie burst into the riot that was the main CSI office and screamed, "Will you shut the fuck up!"

They all looked up.

Kenny silenced the TV, Sid stopped the music, and James answered one of the ringing phones with a courteous whisper.

Eddie was mightily impressed that just a few choice words spoken in the right tone, and using the correct volume could silence the most rowdy of offices instantly. And then he noticed Jeffery standing behind him. A lone phone still rang. "Would you mind answering that, please, Sid?" Eddie smiled.

"Certainly."

"Thank you so much." Eddie turned to Jeffery. "Tea?"

Eddie closed the door and tried to avoid the daggers that Jeffery was staring at him.

"What kind of boss would you think I was if I just ignored the circus I saw out there?"

Eddie tried to read Ros's letter now, but then realised that Jeffery had a better chance of reading than he did. He wondered if he should grab it and move it, but that would arouse suspicion. "I'd think you were great," he smiled. And then he stopped smiling, "Okay, it looked a little rowdy—"

"A little rowdy?"

"Let them blow off some steam once in a while, everyone's happy. Don't worry, they know where the line is, they don't cross it."

"Your line is a lot further along than my own."

There was a knock at the door.

"Oh good," Eddie's shoulders slumped, "that'll be the trapeze artist."

Sid poked his head into the office and shuffled in carrying two cups of coffee. He asked Jeffery, "Would you like sugar? We have Demerara—"

"That's fine, thank you."

"How about a nice biscuit? We have digestives, chocolate digestives – they're my personal favourite. Or we have fig rolls—"

"Sid."

Sid looked at Eddie. Then at Jeffery. "Right. Sorry." He closed the door behind him.

Eddie sighed, "You're bringing Peter McCain in, aren't you?" He slouched on the edge of the desk, stared at the floor and tried to reach the letter with his fingertips. He just knew Jeffery had been looking for this moment since he took over the job. One final fuck up and he'd be out of the door. And this was that fuck up. And really, it was nothing to do with him! He was busy and they'd just taken the piss once too often and got caught out.

Jeffery put the cup onto Eddie's desk and sat back in the chair, hands in his lap.

What's the use? he thought. He'd blamed them, James, Sid, Kenny, and Duffy, those arseholes out there in the main office. He'd blamed them for acting like schoolkids and running rampant while the teacher was taking a shit. But it wasn't their fault. Not really. He'd been an arse; had admitted as much, but he'd been so busy, not had a chance to—

"You were kind enough to take over when I put you on the spot. I know you didn't want this job. I knew you didn't have any management experience. But I still took you on. I wanted you, remember me saying that?"

"Yup. I do."

"I put my faith in you."

"I usually come to your office for my bollocking. At least there I can sit down in comfort."

"So today I decided to come to you. Glad I did."

"I bet."

"Despite the circus out there, I have to say that I'm impressed with how you've turned the office around."

Eddie nearly fell off the desk. Turned it around? From being a well-disciplined evidence-gathering machine, into a kindergarten? "But?"

"Their morale is much better now you're in charge. If they're happy, then they're working hard."

"And how's The Grey-haired God?"

"Cooper is delighted the Shaw thing is wrapped up. He won't admit it of course, but I know he is. But please, stay out of his way for the next few days," Jeffery smiled, then growled, "Don't ever forge my signature again. You fool, you could have signed it with your own," Jeffery raised his eyebrows.

"Really?"

"I told you that at your interview."

"So you did," Eddie nodded. "By the way, what's happened to Benson?"

Jeffery stood, "He's back."

Eddie nodded his approval; that's just as it should have been, but like Cooper, he wouldn't admit it.

"Anyway, I don't see the point of bringing in someone else."

"Really?"

Jeffery smiled, "You want to keep this seat. It's yours."

"Does this mean I get a Staples chitty?"

He held out a hand, "Congratulations."

From outside the office door, there came a loud cheer and applause. Eddie couldn't help but grin, "See what I have to put up with?" He reached down and took hold of the box, flipping open the lid. "I like to treat them once in a while. You staying for a doughnut?"

Jeffery opened the door and everyone who had congregated there, applauded and tried to squeeze into Eddie's office, reaching for the doughnuts. All that is, except Duffy. Duffy held out his hand and shook Eddie's. "What's doing, boss?"

Chapter Thirty-seven

The Letter - Revisited

"SERIOUSLY," CHARLES WHISPERED, "ARE you going to be okay?"

Eddie climbed off the bed. "It makes it easier knowing why she left," he handed Charles the crumpled up letter. "I suppose I'll never know if I'll be okay or not. But who does, right? So long as she finds peace, that's all that matters."

Charles untangled the paper and began to read as Eddie took a step towards the door.

"Oh, one more thing."

Charles looked up.

"There's no such thing as fate." Eddie put his clenched hand into Charles's outstretched palm. He unfolded it and then walked away, closing the door gently behind him.

Charles looked down and the sight of two rings, one a wedding ring, one an engagement ring, and both over thirty years old, looked back at him. Tears prickled his smiling eyes. He was thankful to have them and their memories back, and as he curled his own hand over them, he croaked, "Thanks, Eddie."

After a moment, he put the rings in an old tobacco tin lined with black velvet that lived in his sock drawer by his own bed. He felt safe again now.

He opened the letter, turned on the bedside lamp and read:

I love you, and I can see what being in a relationship is doing to you. I knew just breaking up with you wouldn't be enough – we couldn't work together, so it was better all round that I just quit and left.

And saying nice things to your face in McDonald's would have made it tougher. Much better to be nasty because it makes the split much easier, like kicking a beloved dog so neither of you will feel so bad about sending it to a new owner. To make it easier, I tried to offer an alternative – that my mother was ill, but I think you saw through it anyway, which is why I told you it was a lie at the train station.

She's been dead thirty years this year. I miss her so very much, each day I think of her, and I wish I could have done something at the time to stop her death. Instead, I just stared on. They thought I was asleep. Both of them. They both looked in my pushchair when they left the park.

Some things are scarier than dead bodies.

I recognised one of them at a wedding I was at in April. Funny how features never change. I was going to ask him if he knew my mother, Shaney McGowan, but before I could take a step I collapsed. That's when I decided I had to get away, Eddie. Nothing really to do with you at all, just a violent upsurge of bad memories and inescapable nightmares. That's why I left, and this time it's the truth. And why didn't I just tell you? Because I didn't want the sympathy. I didn't need the understanding. I just needed to be free.

I hope you'll understand, and I'm sorry for the pain I caused you.

I'll love you forever.

Ros.

Acknowledgments

There's a long list of people to thank for helping to pull this book, and all of my books, into something that reads like it was written by someone who knew what they were doing. Among them is my amazing wife, Sarah, who makes sure I get the time to write in the first place.

To <u>Kath Middleton</u>, Alison Birch from <u>re:Written,</u> a huge thank you for making sure the first draft wasn't the final draft – you will always be the first to read my books, and consequently always the first to point and laugh at my errors. It's because of you that this book has turned out so well, and it's because of me that you had so much work to do to get it there.

Thanks also to my Facebook friends in the UK Crime Book Club - really great support from everyone there, followers of my **Andrew Barrett Page,** and members of the **Andrew Barrett Book Group** for their encouragement, insight and constant giggles throughout the last year - all very welcome.

Thanks to all those people who are subscribed to my **newsletter** – that you participate, comment, and email me is not only very kind but very much appreciated.

A special thanks to Graeme Bottomley with whom I co-wrote the original script that this novel is based upon, not only for his permission and his blessing, but most of all for his wonderful insight.

Lastly, if you're one of those readers who care enough about the story, the character, and the time devoted to knitting them all together, to leave an honest review so that new readers might share your enjoyment, then I bow sincerely at your feet - you

keep the book world turning, and you keep me and my author friends tapping the keys.

About the Author

Andrew Barrett has enjoyed variety in his professional life, from engine-builder to farmer, from oilfield service technician in Kuwait, to his current role of senior CSI in Yorkshire. He's been a CSI since 1996, and has worked on all scene types from terrorism to murder, suicide to rape, drugs manufacture to bomb scenes. One way or another, Andrew's life revolves around crime.

In 1997 he finished his first crime thriller, *A Long Time Dead*, and it's still a readers' favourite today, some 200,000 copies later, topping the Amazon charts several times. Two more books featuring SOCO Roger Conniston completed the trilogy.

Today, Andrew is still producing high-quality, authentic crime thrillers with a forensic flavour that attract attention from readers worldwide. He's also attracted attention from the Yorkshire media, having been featured in the *Yorkshire Post*, and twice interviewed on BBC Radio Leeds.

He's best known for his lead character, CSI Eddie Collins, and the acerbic way in which he roots out criminals and administers justice. Eddie's series is six books and four novellas in length, and there's still more to come.

Andrew is a proud Yorkshireman and sets all of his novels there, using his home city of Leeds as another major, and complementary, character in each of the stories.

You can find out more about him and his writing at - **www.andrewbarrett.co.uk,** where you can sign up for his Reader's Club, and claim your free starter library. He'd be delighted to hear your comments on Facebook (and so would

Eddie Collins) and Twitter. Email him and say hello at - **andrew@andrewbarrett.co.uk**

Also by Andrew Barrett

The CSI Eddie Collins series:
The Pain of Strangers
Black by Rose
Sword of Damocles
Ledston Luck
The Death of Jessica Ripley
This Side of Death

Did you enjoy *Sword of Damocles*? I hope you did. You'll need the next in the CSI Eddie Collins series; it's *Ledston Luck*, and it's available from Amazon, Kobo, Apple, and Google Play.

Try a CSI Eddie Collins short story or a novella. Read them from behind the couch!

Have you tried the SOCO Roger Conniston trilogy?

Sword of Damocles is dedicated to

Sarah Jowitt

Reader's Club

Sign up and Read

As a thank you for joining the Reader's Club, I want you to enjoy a couple of free books, a starter library - I call this **Sign up and Read**.

I'll make sure you get a brilliant thriller and a stunning CSI Eddie Collins novella written in first person.

The Reader's Club features a monthly newsletter with details of new releases, special offers, and other goodies, together with news and snippets of interesting items. How do you join the thousands of other crime-thriller fans there? Simply click this link to my website (or type it into your browser), **www.andrewbarrett.co.uk**, and sign up today.

CPSIA information can be obtained
at www.ICGtesting.com
Printed in the USA
LVHW082040060522
718035LV00012B/277

9 781739 659325